Praise for *The Dog Year*

"Reminiscent of the best of Gail Parent and Alison Lurie, *The Dog Year* is the story of a woman who had everything, lost everything, and now wants to shoplift the rest, including the hope of life after the death of her heart, lost when her husband and child died in a dreadful accident. Ann Garvin's writing sneaks up on you: It is hilarious, until it's poignant, until it's heartbreaking. She leaves no heartstring untugged, no funny bone untapped, and every word she sets down is honest."

—Jacquelyn Mitchard, #1 *New York Times* bestselling author of
The Deep End of the Ocean

"With sharp wit and penetrating insight, Ann Garvin offers a tender look at love, loss, friendship, and that curious human epidemic, denial. As touching as it is funny, *The Dog Year* will take up residence in readers' (and dog-lovers') hearts. This is a completely winning novel."

—Sally Koslow, author of *The Widow Waltz* and
The Late, Lamented Molly Marx

"I know of few authors who are funnier or more sympathetic than Ann Garvin, and I know of few heroines more in need of comic relief and sympathy than Dr. Lucy Peterman. This novel will make your stomach hurt with laughter and your heart ache with sadness. *The Dog Year* is a kind, gentle, honest look at a woman whose life has come apart and a survivor who puts it all back together."

—Wiley Cash, *New York Times* bestselling author of
A Land More Kind Than Home and *This Dark Road to Mercy*

continued . . .

"Ann Garvin has written another hilarious, insightful, and heartbreaking book. Lucy Peterman is one of Garvin's signature characters: deeply flawed, nakedly honest, and a whip-smart sarcastic modern woman who finds herself adrift in a world that seems intent on leaving her behind. But Lucy does not give up easily. *The Dog Year* is a deeply intimate story of tragedy and recovery that readers and book clubs will treasure."

—Matt Bondurant, author of *The Night Swimmer* and *The Wettest County in the World*

"Ann Garvin's funny, heartfelt tale of one woman's loss, and the grief and staggering around that follows, is proof that if there's one thing better than a good book and a dog, it's a good book with a dog. Pure delight."

—Karen Karbo, award-winning author of *The Stuff of Life* and the Kick Ass Women series

Praise for *On Maggie's Watch*

"Compelling . . . A perfect fit for suburban reading groups."

—*Booklist*

"*On Maggie's Watch* shows how we thrive, how we go on, in a life that's neither perfect nor fair. [Garvin] writes with humor and compassion so well; just when I'd feel [I was] about to cry, the scene would twist and I'd laugh out loud. She has such a deep understanding for her flawed and trying-to-get-better characters; she obviously loves them, and so do we."

—Luanne Rice, *New York Times* bestselling author of *Little Night*

Books by Ann Garvin

THE DOG YEAR
ON MAGGIE'S WATCH

The
Dog Year

Ann Garvin

BERKLEY BOOKS, NEW YORK

THE BERKLEY PUBLISHING GROUP
Published by the Penguin Group
Penguin Group (USA) LLC
375 Hudson Street, New York, New York 10014

USA • Canada • UK • Ireland • Australia • New Zealand • India • South Africa • China

penguin.com

A Penguin Random House Company

This book is an original publication of The Berkley Publishing Group.

Library of Congress Cataloging-in-Publication Data

Garvin, Ann Wertz.
The dog year / Ann Wertz Garvin.—First Edition, Berkley trade paperback edition.
p.   cm.
ISBN 978-0-425-26925-1 (pbk.)
1. Women surgeons—Fiction.   2. Grief—Fiction.   3. Drug addiction—Fiction.
4. Dogs—Diseases—Treatment—Fiction.   5. Psychological fiction.   I. Title.
PS3607.A78289D64   2014
813'.6—dc23
2013044169

PUBLISHING HISTORY
Berkley trade paperback edition / June 2014

PRINTED IN THE UNITED STATES OF AMERICA

10 9 8 7 6 5 4 3 2 1

Cover photo by Cusp/SuperStock.
Cover design by Lesley Worrell.
Interior text design by Tiffany Estreicher.

To my family, in all the ways
that family can be defined.

ACKNOWLEDGMENTS

I'm a reader of acknowledgments. I like to peek into authors' lives. I like discovering that even the writers who make it look easy needed a hand. I love a good "thank-you," even if it's not about me.

The people who help an author to publication deserve more than a thank-you card with a sprig of lavender printed on the front. They deserve a visit from Oprah, a new car, an organ donation.

Since nobody really wants my liver, pretty though it is, these acknowledgments will have to suffice. Berkley, my publisher, and Jackie Cantor, my editor, get the kind of tearful thank-you that would embarrass all of us if done in person. To be able to publish with this company and this talented editor is truly this girl's childhood dream come true. Jill Marr at The Sandra Dijkstra Agency is the most positive, energetic, and lovely woman I've never met in person; I thank her every day for taking me on and believing in my writing.

People who know me know that my head is full of characters but not the rules of grammar. For help I needed Wanda Dye, Amy Reichert, and Tamara Scerpella, three friends who punctuated without judgment or a single eye roll.

Thank you to my wildly successful writing group (you know who you are), and to anyone who listened to me go on obsessively about whether my main character would do something or not: Linda Wick, Terri Osgood, Carolyn Bach, Elyse Tebon, and so many others. I should probably thank anyone I made eye contact with over the last three years.

My children are responsible for turning me from a self-absorbed woman to an empathetic human being. Julie and Meghan, I love you and thank you for understanding. My parents, and my brothers, Raymond and Jonathan, deserve every other nod: They modeled love for me every day so that I could write it down on these pages. To Millie and Peanut, my dogs: How did I live before your devotion?

And finally, to Brian Osgood: I wrote you into these pages and you appeared. Thank goodness. What are the odds?

1

It's Not About the Breast

In the hospital parking ramp, Lucy snuck a glance at a new mother placing her infant into an elaborate car seat. Her husband stood hovering at her shoulder, his hand gently touching her hip. The woman lingered, gazing at the tiny, beet-faced infant, love fairly oozing from her pores. Lucy waited until the new family drove away, watching the taillights recede all the way out of sight. That particular tableau of the American Dream could have been hers, should have been hers. It *would* have been hers, she knew, if she'd only stayed conscious and had the right supplies when needed.

Today she just had to get through the workday. "Get a grip, Peterman," she said to herself. She shoved open her car door and moved to get out. Instead she dropped her head to the steering wheel. She tried to pull the tough-girl mask over her sorrow and get on with her life. Instead she cried like adults learn to cry: silently and alone.

Grabbing the rearview mirror after her allotted ten-minute cry, she checked for tattletale mascara under her eyes, wiped her nose with the fast-food napkins she stashed in the glove compartment for this very reason, and got out of her car.

On the fifth floor of Med One Hospital and Clinics in downtown Elmwood, Lucy brushed a piece of lint from her shoulder and tried to anchor a springy curl behind her ear. With almost religious reverence, she placed her palms on the smooth counter and breathed in the disinfected, white, no-question-can't-be-answered aroma. For Lucy, there were no gray areas here. Sorrow, maybe; loss, certainly. But always in black and white. The doctor is IN. She widened her eyes and said, "God, I love Mondays."

Melissa, a brown-haired, plump, hyper-organized nurse who had worked with Lucy since the beginning of her tenure here, pulled her head back.

"I've warned you to keep that kind of thing to yourself around here, Dr. Peterman. Nobody likes Mondays. People like Fridays, Saturdays, but never Mondays."

"I love 'em. I get to see you, talk to people in pain, drug them, and cut out their problems. It's the next best thing to working in a candy store."

Melissa frowned and said, "You don't fool me, Dr. Peterman." She squinted at her. "You look pale. Are you sleeping?"

Lucy didn't answer her. "Where's my other lab coat? I hate the pockets in this one."

"I think you should talk to Menken." Stanley Menken was a fellow surgeon, a friend, and the clinic director. He was not, however, the kind of guy who understood weakness. Stanley and she were the same in that respect, and Lucy was not about to request a leave of absence. This was a man's world. Have a baby, take six weeks, and get back to work. Lose your family, go to the funeral, get back on track by heading to the office. Or in her case, the hospital.

Melissa continued. "Take one day a week off. You came back too early."

"Oh," Lucy went on, "I brought some good coffee and put it in the break room. I cannot drink that crap the med students bring in."

Melissa stared at her and put her hand on Lucy's closed fist. "Dr. Peterman."

"If I'm working, I can pretend that nothing happened. This is what I do. I work."

Melissa withdrew her hand and watched Lucy slip her lab coat, like armor, onto her shoulders, effectively changing the subject. She nodded in the direction of the patient rooms. "Your student got a head start this morning."

Lucy glanced over and saw Blake, her medical student, standing at the foot of a bed with his hands in his pockets and the door wide open. The woman before him clutched the neck of her gown, her legs exposed, her bare white knees pressed together.

As Lucy approached, she heard the student say, "It looks like you only have a thin layer of skin and subcutaneous tissue available to work with. That's unfortunate." He shook his head disapprovingly. "This predisposes to the formation of a capsular contracture." With a tone of voice that made it sound like he was translating for a child, he went on to explain, "This can produce an unnaturally round breast." Then as if to lighten the moment he said, "Better than baggy boobs though, right?" Then he winked at his patient.

Lucy moved into the room fueled by three things: memories of her own failings in the sensitivity department, powerlessness in the face of bad news, and furious anger. She yanked the privacy curtain closed, and as the ball bearings hissed into place, closing out the world, Lucy lost her righteous indignation at the situation and replaced it with empathy for the woman on the bed. She was able only to muster a scowl at the med student. To the woman in the backless, undignified gown, she said, "Hello, Mrs. Hallorman. How are you today?"

Mrs. Hallorman was a slim brunette with pore-free skin and eyes like large chocolate discs. She dropped her head into her hands, and as her shoulders shook, silent tears soaked her palms. Lucy put her hand on the woman's shoulder and handed her a tissue, but neither shushed her nor muttered that "things" would be fine. In Lucy's recent, and very bitter, experience, "things" were not always fine. Only eight months ago, she had lost her husband and her unborn baby in a single afternoon.

Lucy allowed a moment of silence for the woman's loss and another for her own. She pursed her lips and breathed through the memory of her husband's face on their wedding day and then, horribly, right after the car accident that killed him. Lucy caught her student's eyes over the distraught woman's head. He looked away and glanced at his watch.

After forty-five minutes of reassurance and education in that small, curtained cubicle, Lucy and the student stepped into the hall. "You are not to get started without supervision. Do you understand me?"

"I'm a fourth-year student," he said. "I've done surgery. I came from orthopedics."

He and Lucy looked at each other. She saw in his expression an unconcealed overestimation of his experience and an underestimation of hers. When he scratched his forehead, the shine of a manicured fingernail glittered in the fluorescent light. She motioned for him to follow her as she pushed her way into a small vacant office near the main desk. The door *shush*ed shut.

"Here's a news flash, pal: Reconstructing a woman's breast after surgery for cancer takes a little sensitivity. We're not doing celebrity makeovers here. It's not about swimsuit fittings or new breasts as high school graduation gifts. These women have cancer. Cancer in a very intimate place. A place that helped them to feel beautiful for the proms, sexy on their honeymoons, and more than a little ready for infants. A woman would rather die of heart disease than get breast cancer, because getting breast cancer is like being stabbed in the heart. The very least we can do is use language they comprehend."

"I understand," he said as he glanced over Lucy's shoulder into the mirror on the opposite wall and fixed a lock of his hair.

She eyed his lavender shirt and fancy shoes. "Tomorrow," she said, "you can quit with the fashion show. Women in this clinic just want good medicine, not medicine doled out by someone so concerned with his appearance that he can't even walk into a cancer unit without using an entire tube of hair gel."

He stood at attention as if realizing, like most men, that he'd miscategorized the tall, red-haired woman standing before him.

Lucy wasn't finished. "If you're going on this ride-along with me, listen up. When we meet with the patient, I'll make the introductions; you put away your smug-ass smile and listen. Afterward, I'll ask you what you heard."

She straightened the collar of her lab coat. The med student tried to look interested.

"Here are a few things to remember. If I let you speak, never label a woman's breasts as *anything*, let alone pendulous, baggy, sloppy, saggy, or slouchy. These are terms for old furniture, not biologic tissue."

The medical student stared and shook his head as if saying, *Of course not, never again.*

Lucy waved him off. "Medical students think terminology has no emotional meaning. I don't care who you are, nobody wants a baggy anything, let alone baggy boobs." The student began to look alert.

Lucy exhaled. "Listen, patients will use slang. Boobs, knockers, hooters, cans, whatever. Usually not tits though. Tits are crude and smack of strippers." He swallowed and looked around the room. There was a poster on manual breast examination on his right. He glanced away.

Lucy squinted at him. "Orthopedics, huh? I've told Stanley to rotate you people through proctology first. After you do sphincter work, a few knockers are nothing." Lucy moved to the door and touched the handle.

He frowned and said, "Excuse me, but don't we do a psychology consult for some of that stuff?"

"Oh my God, seriously?" Lucy dropped her hand and turned, blocking the med student's way. "That woman in there knows that she no longer needs to accommodate her breasts when hugging friends, carrying groceries, or feeding a child. Her scars and the sympathetic look in her husband's eyes will only cement those facts. Some of us know what it's like to lose their entire world in an afternoon. In this rotation, I decide your future. Do you need a lesson in loss?"

For probably the first time in his life, the medical student standing there was without experience or answers. Lucy took a deep breath and softened her voice. "Here's the thing, Blake. Breast reconstruction is all about remembering three things. Number one, nobody wants a belly that sticks out farther than their breasts. Two, women don't entirely equate breasts with sex but they know men do.

And three, given the choice between having a man or having breasts, in most cases the man might not make out so well in that competition. Women reconstruct for *themselves*."

She stared at the medical student until he dropped his eyes. "Wow," he said.

Lucy closed her eyes and said, "Yeah, *Dr. Phil.* Wow. Now go do your write-up."

Back at the nurse's station, Melissa pulled her head up from her notes.

"Did you set him straight?"

Lucy shook her head. "For one glorious minute maybe, but not for life."

"He'll get better. Most of them do after this rotation."

"I guess. It's exhausting work, training a person to be human."

"Maybe he should try being a human for Halloween. It'd be a stretch. Nobody would be able to guess his costume."

Melissa offered Lucy a piece of candy from a plastic jack-o'-lantern sitting on the desk and said, "You're coming, right?"

Lucy looked away. "Yes. Well, maybe. But I have another party I have to make an appearance at."

"Dr. Peterman. You're lying and you know it."

Lucy pursed her lips and tried a feeble, "I'm not. My brother . . ."

"Your brother called and said all was clear for you to go. Look, I know it's hard, with Richard gone."

Lucy raised her head at the mention of her husband's

name. Her Richard. He'd been the kind of guy that women overlooked—not because he was unattractive, but because he was just a brown-haired guy with a kind face. When Lucy described him to people, she'd say, "He's one part Matt Damon and three parts that plain guy you don't mind sitting next to on an airplane because you know he'll help you with your luggage and otherwise leave you alone." The Matt Damon part was on the inside but was the only part Lucy could see. Richard was everything to her. He was the social one. He carried her through parties, dinners, and balls like a Ford pickup hauls a pop-up camper on Memorial Day. He made sure she had no lipstick on her teeth, whispered reminders of spouse's names in her ear, and carried on a breezy running commentary at any party they attended together. It was the small talk that wore her down. She just couldn't do it. Didn't have it in her. Like any good surgeon, she either went right to the center of a person or deflected him with humor. There was no in between. That's just who she was. "I can get to work," she said to Melissa. "That's what I can do. I don't want to go to a Halloween party. I don't want to smile like I'm happy, make conversation about the weather, or meet new people."

Melissa put her hand on Lucy's shoulder but Lucy pulled away gently.

"Look," she said, "it's not your job to take care of me. And my brother's job is to just shut up."

Melissa rolled her eyes. "It most certainly is my job to take care of you. We don't have to be friends. God forbid," she added dramatically. "But this place pays me to watch over you."

"Only during office hours."

Melissa stared unblinking across the nurse's station.

"All right already. I'll try to come to the party."

Triumphant, Melissa saluted Lucy and said, "It'll be fun. You'll see. Now carry on, Doctor. Your minions need a tune-up. I'll see you tonight."

The amber light of the fall day morphed to the purple black of late evening as Lucy shrugged on her wool coat. She glanced in the mirror on the back of her office door and touched her hair, trying to smooth the frizz that had escaped her careful blowout. Even with piles of product, her naturally curly hair regained its shrubbery appearance the second a drop of moisture met even one follicle. Opening her carefully folded, empty lunch bag, she filled it with the contents of her lab coat pockets: a handful of packaged needles, several gauze pads, three rolls of tape, two suture kits, and a small 250-cc IV bag.

In the hall, Lucy moved through the less-traveled avenues to the front entrance, avoiding the cafeteria, where workers had hung a banner—THE NIGHT OF THE SEVEN DEADLY SINS—printed in bleeding-red paint. Black and orange balloons and streamers decorated its edges.

Spotting a colleague *click-clack*ing down the hall toward her, Lucy veered into the restroom. As the door closed, the handle caught the lab coat she'd gathered in her arms and yanked it and her lunch bag to the floor.

Rushing to gather the dropped supplies, with footsteps echoing in her ears, she watched a roll of tape bounce behind the toilet bowl. Scrambling to retrieve it, she bumped her head on the ceramic sink just as the sound of the footsteps retreated.

Pressing her hand to her head, her eyes filled with tears. She allowed one fat tear to escape, feeling it slowly traverse from her lower lash to her cheekbone to her chin. Sniffling, she wiped her face with the crumpled white coat still in her arms and stuffed the hospital supplies back into the wrinkled brown paper bag. Then she yanked open the door and headed straight for the exit, counting in her head. *Five, four, three, two.* Just before the electronic doors opened, she pitched the filled bag into the garbage next to the entrance.

The security guard tipped his hat to her, "Two points, Dr. Peterman."

Lucy was startled to see law enforcement so close to her. "And the crowd goes wild," she deadpanned.

Finally, safely ensconced in her car, exhausted after a day of playing a saint, she drove home to turn herself into an original sin.

2

If You're Happy and You Know It

A spray of leaves—yellow, brown, and red—swirled on the sidewalk of Med One Hospital and Clinics like a litter of dogs chasing their tails. Lucy pulled her coat closer to her neck and looked at her brother, Charles.

"Don't make me go in there."

A laughing couple ran past the car in a flutter of black fabric. The woman had a witch's hat perched on her head. Two people swathed entirely in green—skin included—stopped to kiss under the hospital overhang, then dashed inside.

"*I'm* not making you do anything."

"I hate how they look at me." Lucy shook her head. "I should have driven."

"Exactly why I'm here. You'd weasel out."

A man with a toilet seat around his neck and a zombie mask looked in the front window and jogged on.

Charles said, "You gotta admit, this year's party is better than last year's. That 'Come as Your Favorite Dead Person' theme was the epitome of bad judgment for a trauma center."

Lucy smiled at the memory. "It was a fun party though. Richard as Marilyn Monroe. That wig." Lucy looked down at her hands.

"Look, make your costume work for you. Put on your Road Rage license plate and get moving. Stage an uprising. It's Saturday night!"

"Be serious. Come with me."

"I'll be back in two hours. Have a drink. Be nice to people. Make some friends."

Lucy looked outside and watched as the car's rising exhaust swirled and disappeared into the night. Charles's voice softened. "It might help to talk to someone about it, you know."

"No way, Charles."

He leaned across Lucy and opened the latch on the car door. "I love you. You're stalling. Now get going."

An October wind hit Lucy full in the face. She grabbed the mesh John Deere hat on her head and threw it into the backseat. "See, even the wind thinks this is a bad idea."

Charles retrieved the hat and jammed it back onto his sister's head. Then he pointed to the front door of the hospital. "Go."

Lucy dragged herself through the large revolving doors into the hospital's atrium, and a security guard appeared from behind his kiosk. "Hey, Joe," Lucy said, smiling.

"Dr. Peterman. Have a nice evening. And stay out of trouble, okay?"

"No promises," she said.

Richard used to shake hands with the guards every day. Where most people treated security as if they were somewhat invisible doormen Richard did not. He put everyone in the category of equal, and everyone got the same treatment. She thought of his handshake and his strong forearms, developed from years of surgery. Thoughts of her beloved husband dissipated when Melissa shimmied over, straightening her pillow hat and the blanket wrapped around her hips. "Well, look who decided to party with the sinners."

"Like I had a choice. Why is this happening a week before Halloween, anyway?"

"We get to party twice then."

"Ugh. Great. What sin are you?"

"Check out my quiver," Melissa said, pulling a toy bow-and-arrow set off her shoulder. Red construction paper hearts with LUST printed on each one were attached to all the suction-cup arrows.

"Nice." Lucy smiled and removed her coat to reveal a sleeveless flannel shirt and a faux tattoo on her upper arm that read, AN EYE FOR AN EYE.

"Wrath, huh? I bet your med student would agree."

The two women moved down the hall toward the thrumming music and chatter. "I'm not staying long," Lucy said.

"I know you're not a drinker, but let's get you some alcohol. Just this once."

Another partygoer dressed as Wrath and holding an I'M MAD sign, handed Lucy a large red plastic cup filled with something fruity and pulpy. Melissa waved to someone across the room and said, "I'll be back." Taking Lucy's coat with her, she disappeared into the crowd. Lucy finished the sweet tasting liquid in one long drink.

The cafeteria was in full bloom. Sinners of all shapes and sizes milled around casually, eating spider cookies and tombstone cupcakes. Orange and black balloons and streamers floated among the partiers. A man in an inflated sumo wrestler suit, with an ALL YOU CAN EAT sign under his arm and GLUTTONY stamped on his forehead, chatted with a woman wearing a sandwich board painted to look like a bankbook, with GREED written on each line. Fixing her Monopoly money headpiece, she nodded at Lucy. The heavy base of Michael Jackson's "Thriller" thumped the room.

"Dr. Peterman!"

Lucy froze. Charise Schaefer, the wife of the chief of cardiology, Buddy Schaefer, was dressed in a double-knit pants suit and carrying a bulging purse filled with medals, trophies, and ribbons, and sidled up to her. "Don't you look precious," she said. "I'm having the after-party at our house." She wedged an orange flyer into Lucy's hands, with the words *Halloween's-a-comin'* in Comic Sans printed next to a winking jack-o'-lantern holding a martini. "What do you think of my costume?" She twirled. "I'm Pride, aka Mary Lou Retton's mother." On top of the stack of party fliers she held was an eight-by-ten of Mary Lou glued to a Wheaties box. "You know," she burbled, "Mary Lou was always extremely flexible, even as a baby. They say she has my smile."

Overwhelmed, Lucy said, "I . . . great."

"That settles it. You'll come to our house after this." Charise widened her eyes. "I have someone for you to meet," she added. "He's totally delish. A doctor like you. He's around here somewhere, wearing the most fabulous sloth costume. Has one of those beer-can hats on." As she scanned the crowd for Lucy's Miller-Lite-Man-of-her-dreams she said, "I'm a widow, too, and when my first husband died I got right back on that horse—and now look at me. A newlywed at forty-five. Now where is that man?"

Lucy said, "I'm going to make a quick visit to the restroom. I'll catch up with you." She jogged in the opposite direction of the bathrooms, stopping to fill her cup from another sin-manned drink station.

"So, Wrath Peterman, what do you think?" Stanley Menken, the hospital's director, sidled up to Lucy and opened his coat like a flasher in a back alley. He wore long underwear, and the inside of his coat was lined with see-through plastic pockets containing condoms, money, pill bottles, candy, and bullets. Pinned to his lapel were several soccer- and hockey-team buttons. "Each of the seven sins is represented by a pocket. I'm all of the sins combined. Clever, right? For the guy in charge?"

Lucy lifted her Nerf gun and shot a foam bullet at his forehead.

"Hey. Are you dissin' my genius?"

"Genius is one word. I prefer 'narcissist.'"

Stanley ignored her. "Marion is here, too. She's in a French maid costume. Ooh la-la."

Lucy grimaced. "Gross, Stanley. Friends or boss, I don't want to think about you and your wife dressing up as anything other than doctors."

"Speaking of Marion, she wants to get our progressive dinner party schedule back on the calendar. She's got some new desserts she wants to try out."

Lucy looked away and drank a large gulp of her punch. The music filled the space between them. Stan closed his coat. "It's time, Lucy," he said more quietly.

"Who says?"

Stan took a step back and said, "Talk to Marion. She's got some great ideas." Another physician dressed as Gluttony stopped to chat. As he and Stan made conversation, Lucy rested her back against the wall and let their talk about work weave around the music, laughter, and noise of the party. She leaned to the side and filled her cup. Stan said, "Right, Luce?"

"What? Sorry?"

"Your husband, Richard, had the best technique of anyone. Even in med school. That SOB showed me up every damn time."

"Me, too," she said.

"No he did not. You two were a couple of perfectionist peas in a pod." Lucy took another sip and Stan said to Gluttony, "The two of them schooled the entire staff." She closed her eyes and stopped listening. When she opened them again, Stan and Gluttony were staring at her.

"What?"

"You better slow down with whatever you're guzzling there, Lucy. The night is still young."

Gluttony lifted his cup. "Nah, sin away, baby. Bottoms up!"

Lucy drank. When she'd finished, she said, "Nobody likes a sober sin, Stanley. I'm going to find Melissa." Dodging the crowd, she weaved around partygoers, looking for her friend, and her coat.

Elyse Dietrich, an X-ray technician and the daughter of one of Lucy's patients, touched Lucy on her shoulder. "Dr. Peterman. I'm so glad to see you. I've wanted to thank you in person for your careful work on my mother. So many people treat elderly women like they don't deserve breast reconstruction because of their uncertain future. She says she feels like a million bucks because of you."

"You're so welcome. Tell your mother hello from me," she said. "Tell her tube tops are the new housecoat for women of a certain age."

Elyse laughed. "I will."

"What sin are you?"

"None, really. I didn't want to scare my daughter." She pointed to a name tag pinned to her Jackie O–style suit that read HELLO, MY NAME IS MRS. GOD, with a small halo dotting the i. "Gosh, these support hose itch like mad." She scratched her leg and the Kleenex tucked up her sleeve fell to the floor along with a grocery list titled "God's favorite foods."

Lucy's face flushed as the alcohol hit her empty stomach and she noticed the wallet-sized photo of a small boy labeled JESUS IN 5TH GRADE fixed to Elyse's pillbox hat. She took another gulp from her cup.

"So do you have any children?" Elyse asked.

"Almost," she said quietly, tripping over her words. "No, I don't. Your husband, Mr. God, has decided there will be no children for Lucy Peterman. Maybe you could put in a good word with him. Tell him what a good job I did with your mother." Taking another large drink from her cup, she said, "I'm kidding. Just trying to stay in character. How'd I do? Wrathful enough?"

"Very convincing," Elyse said. She touched Lucy on the arm. "It'll happen. Just be patient. It took me a year to conceive."

Lucy closed her eyes, as her heart did a loop-de-loop fueled by alcohol and anxiety. When she opened them, Mrs. God was gone. It seemed as if once again, her prayers had been spoken aloud to invisible ears.

The spiked punch, scenery, and noise created a mosaic of confusion and activity. A woman in a seersucker toga, holding a baby and an old Polaroid camera, her sin not entirely clear, approached Lucy.

"Hi, Dr. Peterman." The woman lifted her mask. "It's Jeanie, from medical records. Could you hold my daughter?" Before Lucy could answer, the woman flopped a loose-limbed baby into her arms. "I couldn't get a sitter but I wanted to come and take pictures. Can you believe how great everybody looks?" While Jeanie snapped photo after photo, the baby studied Lucy's face. She rested her chubby hand on Lucy's shoulder and stroked Lucy's hair, winding her fingers into her curls. After a moment the baby sighed and rested her head on Lucy's collarbone. Lucy closed her eyes and with the flash of the camera snapped them open again. "What a great shot," said Jeanie. Bundling the baby out of Lucy's arms and trading the infant for the photo, she bustled off.

Lucy veered unsteadily into the supply closet behind the food table. The din of the party muted as she shut the door and plopped herself onto a large cardboard box. Gazing at the developing photo, like her dreams materializing in front of her on the tiny square, she saw herself holding the daughter that would not be hers.

She looked around the minty-green room. There were towers of wire-and-metal shelving, holding every kind of hospital supply imaginable. The fluorescent lighting blinked and hummed above her. She savored the way the supplies made her feel: clean, orderly, and calm. Here she had everything she needed in case of a medical emergency. She could stop bleeding, clear airways, hydrate, and keep shock at arm's length. Lucy slipped five rolls of bandage tape into her camouflage satchel. She ran a finger across a pile of suture kits and selected two, grabbed some IV tubing and a handful of syringes. Shoving the supplies into her bag, she stood on her tiptoes and eyed a package of specimen tubes.

"You hiding out, too?" asked a matronly woman dressed

in green from head to toe as she emerged from behind the tall aluminum shelving.

Startled, Lucy jumped. "Oh! I thought I was alone." She squinted at the woman and tried to discern if she had noticed her theft. "I had to get away from all those people, especially that one with the party fliers."

The green woman said, "I know. If she had it her way, all employees would have to begin their shifts with a group hug and a facial."

"No joke," slurred Lucy. "If she had T-shirts made, they would read IF YOU'RE HAPPY AND YOU KNOW IT, HUG AN INNO-CENT BYSTANDER AND MAKE THEM MISERABLE."

"You're funny. I want your hair."

"No you don't. Once Wisconsin humidity hits, it's all cartoon hair and mirror-avoidance techniques. Trying to tame my hair with any one product is like trying to save the ozone by reusing the occasional Ziploc baggie."

"Hey, don't misunderstand me. I do like your hair, but I'm Envy. You know. We're supposed to act the part."

"Oh. Of course; Envy." Lucy shoved the photo she was holding into her shirt pocket and took another ill-advised sip from her cup. "So, Envy, what're you doin' in the closet?"

"This is my place."

"Mine, too! I come here a lot."

Lucy rested her head on the wall trying to stop the unhinged feeling in her head.

"Can't have too many hospital supplies," said Envy without a smile.

Ann Garvin

Lucy looked at the woman and tried to decide what she had seen. What she knew. She lifted her drink in a mock toast. Some of the liquid sloshed onto the tails of her plaid shirt. "Nope, you can't," she agreed. Unconsciously, Lucy patted the photograph through her shirt pocket.

Envy stood and took a step toward Lucy. "I don't know who you are, but it's time to go." She took Lucy by the arm, helping her to stand. But Lucy resisted her. "I'm a doctor and I wanna stay," she insisted. Envy, short, large busted and strong, pulled Lucy to a standing position and handed her the Nerf rifle. "I doubt that. You gotta go."

"Whoa, you're a serious little Hobbit, aren't you? I'm in plastics," Lucy added. Envy frowned, opened the door, and guided Lucy out of the closet.

"Well, even if that's true, Doctor, you still need to go."

Standing amid the fray of the party again, Lucy said, "I don't feel very good. I haven't had a drink in, like, a year." But Envy had walked into a gaggle of partiers and didn't hear her.

Melissa bustled by doing her best Lust imitation. "Whoa, Dr. Peterman," she said, "you don't look so good."

"I was fine until Envy over there shoved me out of my hiding place."

Melissa glanced over her shoulder. "That's Phyllis Parmenter. She's in charge of inventory for the hospital. Takes her supplies seriously. She had that nurse fired last year because of poor needle documentation and unauthorized usage of a sharps container."

Lucy felt a blaze of heat start in her belly and ferociously climb upward. "I think I'm going to be sick."

She staggered outside with Melissa at her heels. Rummaging in her pocket, she pulled out her cell phone, preparing to call her brother.

"Dr. Peterman, how much punch did you drink?"

"Too much." The fall air hit Lucy with a comforting blast. She bent over and let Melissa put her hand between her shoulder blades. She imagined Phyllis Parmenter, minus her all-green outfit, speaking with matronly authority to the administration office in the morning.

"I'm so screwed," she said.

3

Luscious

The next morning, standing in her beautifully tiled bathroom, next to the antique pedestal sink and the tall-glassed shower stall, Lucy pulled a roll of tape out of her satchel from the night before with a fearful expression on her face. Despite the amount of alcohol she'd consumed the previous night, she remembered everything. Even the gibberish she'd managed to blubber to her brother amid drunken tears. "I can either quit now," she'd said to him. "Or wait for them to come and get me. Or I can deny everything. Or maybe pretend I was staying in Wrath character and just joking about all those suture kits I took." Then she threw up once and fell asleep.

At the sound of a car engine turning into the cul-de-sac, Lucy snapped her head upright and shifted her gaze to the window. There was little traffic on the street, mostly wrong turns except for her few neighbors.

Lucy peered through the blinds and sucked in her breath. A city patrol car pulled to the curb in front of her house just two feet from her mailbox, which was a matching model of her renovated Victorian. When a police officer stepped out, Lucy looked around frantically. Her first impulse was to call her lawyer, flush the stolen supplies, and hide and run. Then with the wild clarity of her doctor-self she thought, *Do all of the above, but in reverse order.*

"Simmer down," she said aloud. She repeated Richard's phrase that meant *Namaste* to him, even as he waited for Med Flight to bring the latest Fourth of July fireworks casualty. "Expect the worst, hope for the best."

Springing into action, she shoved the roll of tape into her pocket. With the comic coordination of Charlie Chaplin, she wrestled her arms out of the bathrobe she wore over the clothes she'd slept in, hitting herself in the face with her sleeve and knocking her glasses onto the floor. She forced herself to stroll to the front door, smoothing her T-shirt and jeans from the night before. The police officer reached the top of the steps just as Lucy pressed her face to the screen in the door.

Feigning composure, she said, "Can I help you, Officer?"

She saw him squint through the mesh, and if he was disappointed to have lost the element of surprise, he didn't show it.

"Ma'am, I wonder if you might step outside for a

moment." He held his identification up so that she could see his pixilated face through the metal of the screen door.

"I hope I'm not in trouble." She laughed an uncharacteristically girlish laugh, which made her loathe herself. Once uncool, forever uncool. Why couldn't she laugh like a sophisticated woman? She touched her fingers to the font of her neck, said a silent prayer, and pushed the screen door open. As it screeched a warning, she imagined what she always imagined when someone saw her for the first time. The flash assessment. The categorization.

Not pretty.

She'd seen it work the other way her whole life. Her friends, roommates, colleagues . . . the beauties around her had been a daily demonstration of "pretty discrimination."

"Do you drive a blue Subaru wagon?" the officer was saying. "Possibly a 2010 or 2011?"

She let the screen door slap behind her and rolled the tape in her pocket around and through her fingers. *Let's get this over with.* "Yes, as a matter of fact I do. Why?"

"A Subaru wagon was involved in a hit-and-run today. A child was injured. We're checking registered owners in the area."

Relief blew through her lips, and so did her chance to stand out, however notoriously, in this man's eyes.

"Oh thank God," she said.

He removed his dark glasses. Stock police officer accessories, direct from the prop room at central casting. "What?" he said.

"Oh, I . . . I mean, that's terrible."

She was standing next to him and had to step back to take in his full height. He was trim and serious and not to be messed with. He cleared his throat. "Can I see your car?"

"Of course. Yes!" she said, and hurried to the garage as he followed her. "I can't imagine leaving the scene of a crime. But then the biggest offense I've committed to date is being the owner of a cat-at-large. Mrs. Bobo is very open-minded sexually and likes to cruise the neighborhoods." Lucy widened her eyes to show him this was obviously a joke. When he didn't respond, she added, "I secretly envy her." Giving the officer a double thumbs-up, the universal encouragement sign for idiots, she said, "Go for it, Mrs. Bobo. Get some for both of us," and smirked, knowing how beyond pathetic it was to live vicariously through your cat and worse yet, to confess it.

She hit the garage door opener and pulled the roll of tape she still held in her hand into the bright sunlight. Teasing. The policeman did a slow stroll around her car, examining each bumper with care. When he was finished, he turned and focused on her face.

"You know, we graduated from high school together. It's Lucy, right?" He tilted his head, looking puzzled, then pulled a notepad from his pocket and riffled through it. "I thought I saw a different name registered to this house."

"No, that's right. Lucy Peterman. Seventeen Viceroy Lane."

"Wait, here I have it." He consulted his notes. "Luscious Peterman. You're Luscious?"

"Ironic, huh?"

The officer furrowed his brow. "Ironic?"

"Don't worry, I get it. Apparently I was 'Luscious' at birth," she said, using another mannerism she loathed, the air quotation marks. *What's gotten into me?* "My mother named me when her postpartum nurse said I was so luscious she could lick me. Apparently intoxicated with gratitude, my mom named me Luscious. So here I am, left never meeting expectations and forever answering the question: 'You're Luscious?'"

His expression remained blank. "Okay."

"You can call me Lucy, like in high school."

"Okay. Lucy. Looks like no crime has been committed here."

Lucy watched him as he made his way back to his patrol car. "Don't be too sure," she said.

"What?"

"Don't forget my cat."

"I'll make a note of it." He spoke over the roof of the patrol car as he opened the door. "What do you do? If I remember right, you were valedictorian."

"Wow, good memory."

"You gave the speech. Made fun of Roland Antilla, the history teacher who could never remember anything about the War of 1812 other than the date. It was funny."

"I work at the hospital." She twisted the tape off her fingers and pushed it back into her pocket. "What about you?"

He paused for a beat, putting his glasses back on,

allowing her a minute to register the obvious and said, "I look for criminals who drive blue Subarus."

Lucy watched the cruiser as it executed a smooth, 180-degree arc, leaving the neighborhood the way it entered, with purpose and high-minded goals: find the bad guys, make the world a better place, go on with the day. With her own ideas of right and wrong conflicting with her felonious impulses, Lucy moved back into the house and down the hall to the bedroom she'd shared with her husband. Reaching above the bedroom door to retrieve a hidden key, she unlocked the door's shiny brass deadbolt. The click of metal slid from its casing and the door creaked open. A waft of her old life reached her nostrils, carrying inevitable memories: the way her husband smiled, conservatively protecting a crooked incisor from display. The way he hugged her, every single time, like she hadn't seen him for a week. Like she was a life jacket. The way he said her name. Lucy fished the tape from her pocket, lobbed it through the opening along with the filled satchel from the night before, and slammed the door, slipping the lock into place.

She pushed her back against the door and caught her breath. "Valedictorian, my ass," she said. "More like 'Most likely to be *arrested*.'" Walking down the hall toward the kitchen, Lucy veered into the living room, wringing her hands. Turning, she paced back toward the kitchen. On impulse, she stomped down the basement stairs and upended a box of old medical school folders and textbooks. Grabbing an empty printer paper box, she hauled the two boxes to the main floor and down the hall. Outside her bedroom, she retrieved the key again. She took a deep breath as the key hovered above the lock, watching its silver teeth tremble in her hand. Then she pushed it into the lock and slowly slid the bolt back. Picking up a box, she began to turn the door-knob when a scuffling of footsteps moving toward the front door caught her attention again.

"Hello? Luce?"

She snatched the key out of the lock and slid it back into its hiding place, then walked, breathless, down the hall. Her tall and handsome younger brother pressed his nose against the screen door. She breathed a sigh of relief.

"Stop that. You're going to wreck the screen."

"Somebody's crabby. Did I just see a police car cruising your neighborhood?"

"Yeah. I guess they go door-to-door sometimes to find their man."

"Does this have something to do with all that crying last night about stealing and jail? You were making absolutely no sense."

"No," Lucy lied. "I don't remember a thing after you picked me up."

"You said that if Envy gets ahold of you, you'll be out of a job. Something about tape and IV bags. Seriously, Luce, it's a good thing you're not a drinker. So what did the police want?"

"They looked at my car; some kind of hit-and-run in town that involved a blue Subaru. They cleared my car. But it turns out I went to high school with the cop."

"Is that how you beat the rap? An old admirer?"

"Ha!" she said a little too loudly. "Yeah. 'Weren't you the prom queen? I was always in love with you.'" Lucy laughed again. "Yep, I get that all the time."

Nodding, her brother said, "Me, too."

"At least, in your case, they have the queen part right."

"You funny lady."

"You are *not* still using that Asian accent. You understand that that's been considered hate humor since the seventies."

"When you're part of the Ten Percent Society and have a Vietnamese love interest, you're exempt from politically correct lingo. Hell, I'm PC just by being me." He smiled winningly and said, "So who was the cop?"

Charles was Lucy's younger brother and the only person in the universe who rivaled her husband in the game she called "Fun Facts about Lucy." He knew that Lucy both hated and was vain about her hair, that she had become a surgeon only because she aced calculus, and that she'd been a virgin before she met Richard.

"He never said. I never asked."

"Typical Lucy."

"Whatever." She spun away from her brother and kicked the boxes into the would-be nursery, the room Lucy slept in each night. When Charles and Lucy talked, Phong, Charles's lover, always complained that he felt like he was in the middle of a Nora Ephron movie where all the jokes were private and there was no faked orgasm scene.

Charles strolled down the hall and turned the doorknob of her bedroom.

Lucy popped her head around the corner and snapped, "What are you doing?"

"Bedroom still padlocked?"

"I don't want to accidently wander in there. I'm not ready."

"I think we should move you back into your bedroom, Luce. Sleeping in the extra room is ridiculous. It's been almost a year."

"Eight months."

"Let me see, if you're anything like Mom . . ." Charles slid his hands across the molding of the door. "Yep. Here it is." He held the key aloft, wagging it with triumph.

"No!" Lucy leaped for it. "Give it here, Charles."

But he held the key above his head and said, "Come on, grab one of those boxes and let's clean out your spare room. Move everything back into your bedroom."

She reached again for the key and said, "Stop it. This isn't funny." Something in her tone made him drop his arm and she swiped the key from his hand.

"Jeez, sorry. I thought that's why the boxes were here. That maybe you were going to pack up some of Richard's stuff."

"That's never going to happen. I'm never getting rid of

Richard's stuff. The boxes are for junk I have to bring to the hospital. Just some stuff I borrowed. No big deal."

Charles gazed levelly at his sister. "You're doing that thing with your pinkie."

"What are you talking about?"

"When you lie, you hook your pinkie like you're a dainty tea drinker. I don't see it often because you don't lie to me much. So what gives, Luce? What are you not telling me?"

"I'm just on edge, Charlie. The party sucked. I had to hold a baby, they're trying to fix me up with some doctor, and I need to figure out what to do about some missing supplies."

"What's that got to do with you?"

Lucy grabbed her crooked pinkie finger and said, "Nothing. But I have to go back to work and dodge Mr. Mystery Date after having thrown up in the parking lot."

"Is that what this is all about? I'm pretty sure you weren't the only sinner sinning at the party. Just go back in there like nothing happened at all. You know how it is; what happens at the Monster Mash stays at the Monster Mash."

"Act like nothing happened?"

Charles shrugged. "Remember in high school when I grabbed Tom Pakonen the football star's tight end at the prom and I blamed it on my date Melanie Skoviack? I just denied everything."

Lucy looked at the silver key in her hand and said, "That's exactly what I'm going to do then. Deny everything."

4

Thou Shalt Not

Lucy moved through the clean walls and floors of the clinic: a five-story throat lozenge. When she felt rough, sore, anxious, she came here. It was filled with two kinds of people: doctors like herself who excelled in chemistry and calculus but were often clueless when dealing with actual humans. Their insensitivity and poor eye contact were instantly forgiven in the clinic, if the tradeoff was a reduction in pain or an excised tumor. The second kind of people were the nurses and patients who gave Lucy's life meaning. Feeling considerably calmer after rounding on her patients, she made her way back to the nurse's station and found Melissa at the desk, tapping at her computer. Without pausing, Melissa said, "We missed you at the after-party."

"Aw. I missed you, too, Melissa. How many cases are scheduled today?"

"How'd you feel yesterday after all that . . . punch?"

"I'm ignoring you. How many cases?"

"Two. Second-stage breast reconstruction and placement of tissue expanders."

Lucy frowned. "Only two?"

"The Menken wants to see you. He said to reserve the morning for a meeting, so I moved everything to the afternoon."

Lucy paled. "Now? He wants to see me now?"

"That's what he said." And she turned away to answer the phone.

Lucy swallowed, her throat immediately dry and her hands sweaty. Her heart pounded like a kettledrum as she marched to the elevator.

"Wait! Lucy!" Melissa jogged over to the elevator doors, holding the stethoscope around her neck in a chokehold and carrying a file folder in her other hand. "Menken wanted me to send this up with you, for your meeting."

"What is it?"

"A six-month inventory of our supplies."

The elevator doors closed, blocking Melissa's cheerful face and leaving Lucy instantly sick, looking at the file in her hands. It was a short ride to the sixth floor, and when the doors opened, she hesitated then darted across the hall to the restroom. Shaking, she emptied her pockets of anything hospital-related into the trash and covered the supplies with damp, wadded paper towels. She leaned on the counter and looked in the mirror. She was sweating, and her pale skin looked gray.

"Deny everything," she said to herself, and ran her hand across her forehead.

Stanley Menken spent most of his time in the hospital holed up in his office, a short, dead-man's walk down the carpeted hallway. Lucy clenched her teeth. Mercifully, Janice, his longtime assistant, was not at her desk. Lucy knocked once and pushed her way in.

Stan Menken stood with his back to the door, looking out one of the large office windows. Yellow, gold, and brown leaves fluttered past.

Lucy breathed in and said, "Stan?"

Dark-haired and youthful despite his fifty-plus years, Stan Menken turned to her, briefly closed his eyes, and said, "We have film of you taking supplies from the hospital." He put both hands up, as if he were being robbed, and said, "Don't deny it—because then I'll have to show you the video, and I don't want to watch it again. I don't want to think about it any more than I have to."

Lucy straightened as if a chiropractor had entered the room and cracked her back. She opened her mouth.

"Is it drugs?" Stan asked. "Is that it?"

Lucy said, "No. My God. No."

"Jesus Christ," he said, but it came out as four syllables: *Jee-zus Kee-ryst*. "Then what? Why? Phyllis Parmenter says

the counts have been off for months. IV bags, lactated ringers, saline, tubing. Other things, too: chux pads, bandages,
irrigation kits." He walked over to Lucy and snatched the
manila file from her hand. He started to open it but instead
pitched it across his desk like a Frisbee. "The tape shows
you carrying a box of supplies to your car. You walked right
under the surveillance camera at the exit." He looked to the
ceiling and stretched his neck. "You're selling them. Is that
it? On eBay or something? To Canada?"

"No, Stan. No. I'd never do that."

"What then, Lucy? Why is my top reconstructive surgeon siphoning supplies? You starting your own clinic?"

Stiff-backed, Lucy lowered herself into the chair nearest
the door. "I . . . I don't know why I take the stuff. I don't use
it." As if presenting a neat, tidy solution, she brightened and
said, "I have it all. I can give it all back. All of it. Today."

Too loudly, Stan said, "It's not about the stuff, Lucy. It's
not worth anything compared to what you do for us here.
What you do for our patients. It's about you *taking* the stuff."

She shook her head so hard that the reading glasses
perched there dropped into her lap. "It's all in my bedroom."

"Don't screw with me, Lucy. What are you doing with it?"
The intensity of his anger threw a wall up between them.

"I'm not doing anything with it." She tried tightening her
lips but they trembled despite her efforts, and her eyes
filled. *Don't you dare start crying. Not now. Not you.* She
managed to say, "I don't even know I'm taking it. I mean, I

know I'm taking it, but it's like I'm watching someone else and I can't get her to stop. I put things in my pocket and, before you know it, I have more than my pockets can hold."

Stiff but relieved, Stan said, "That's the right answer, Lucy."

"What?"

"If you were selling or stealing for someone I'd have to have you arrested. It's a felony. You'd lose your license to practice medicine. If it's for you, for whatever the reason, I don't have to fire you. You can keep your job, go to treatment."

Lucy stood, knocking her chair into the wall. "Treatment!"

Stan gave her an incredulous look. "What did you think?" he said, angry again. "It's a crime. You lose your license and go to jail, or go to treatment and keep your job."

Lucy approached Stan at his desk. "I'm not a drug addict." She stopped and tried to think like a surgeon. Cut to the heart of it. "I took some IV bags. You said yourself, it doesn't cost the hospital much. No one is hurt by it."

Stan raised his voice. "It's called kleptomania. You might have heard about it in medical school."

Lucy pulled her head back as if slapped. "I'm not a kleptomaniac. I don't case the aisles at Macy's and steal lipstick." She broke eye contact and glanced at the family photograph that sat on Menken's desk. "Don't do this, Stan."

His jaw was tight, his lips thin. "It's done, Lucy. You did it and we're done. You can sign a form that says you stole for mental health reasons or resign right now and try to find another job with this on your record."

"We've known each other for years, Stan."

"Apparently I didn't know you as well as I thought. And Richard? Yeah, what would he say about this?" Stan produced a piece of paper and a pen and set them on his desk, in front of Lucy. Then he stepped back as if her behavior might be contagious. "Once you sign this, you've committed yourself to getting treatment. We will hold your position for a year. That is our obligation."

"Obligation?"

"Yes, obligation. Frankly, I'd fire you. When you take from this hospital, you take from me."

Lucy narrowed her eyes and said, "So that's what this is about? You're angry. Someone took something you couldn't control. Well, join the club."

"What part of 'Thou Shalt Not Steal' don't you understand?"

She sneered. "Scripture? You're quoting scripture to me? That's a little out of your domain, don't you think?" Lucy's voice dripped with sarcasm.

"Well, you clearly don't have a handle on *hospital* policy." The autumn leaves outside the window slowed in their play. The room felt suddenly coated in frost.

Shaking, Lucy shouted, "You leave God out of this. God has nothing to do with me. But I'll say this in my defense, Holy Stanley Menken. Next time you lose your spouse and your child in one afternoon, you can let me know what miserable thing you do to cope. I hope it's as harmless as taking an armful of IV tubing and not an armful of sleeping pills."

5

Beauty Is in the Eye of the Moldy

In the hall, flanked by security guards who only knew her as the pleasant, unremarkable doctor who occasionally needed a nighttime escort through the parking ramp, Lucy fought to keep her emotions hidden. She tried to smile but felt her lips twitch involuntarily. The older of the two guards, having seen much suffering in his years there, touched Lucy's elbow, offering his gentle assistance.

Looking up into his face and blinking, she felt shame settle around her sternum and sink to take up residence in her lower back. "Thank you," she said, opening her car door.

He nodded and said, "I don't know what's going on, but you know that line from *Young Frankenstein*: 'Could be worse. Could be raining.'"

She grimaced. "I'll remember that." Then she waved the security guard off. The look of relief on his face made it clear that he'd rather deal with vandals or peace disturbers than a distraught woman. Lucy checked her appearance in the mirror. She rubbed her smudged mascara from under her eyes and saw that her Stay Put foundation had not broken its promise. She didn't actually look any worse than she did after a long day in surgery, which was good because she needed to make a stop. Pulling out of the parking lot, she touched the Halloween-candy coupons bunched in her pocket and lifted them out; smoothing them on the dash, she drove to the grocery store. She left a voice mail on Charles's phone. "I'm getting chocolate. I need you. Come over." She hung up, hoping he would get the message. *A binge was coming, get help.*

Inside the store, she blew past the small plastic shopping baskets not made for heavy lifting, and wheeled the full-sized grocery cart over to the holiday aisle. One of the wheels dragged like a conscience, pulling the cart halfheartedly in the direction of the fresh produce. The other wheels squealed in protest.

Lucy examined the bags of Halloween candy, selecting Jolly Ranchers for their longevity, Reese's Peanut Butter Cups for their obvious yin and yang charm, and Charleston Chews for pure nostalgia. Before long, there were several candy bags in her cart. While Lucy considered a bag of mini Snickers, her hand, seemingly of its own accord, palmed a foil-covered chocolate jack-o'-lantern the size of her fist. Leaning close to the shelves, she slid the treat neatly into her pocket: a tiny sleight of hand performed without a deck of cards and no trick bunny in sight.

"Dr. Peterman, hi there. Having a party?"

Lucy whirled around, feeling the rabbit that was her heart jump into her throat. "Oh!"

"Jeez, I'm sorry, Doc. Did I scare you? I sure didn't mean to sneak up on you."

Lucy wrenched her hand from her pocket and looked around. *Had he seen her? Did he know?*

He was Stewart from frozen foods. Stewart looked like every fifty-year-old man in America, like the avocado pit her mother was forever sprouting on the kitchen windowsill. Round and smooth as an egg, with toothpick legs and arms and no noticeable hair above the water line. She cringed as she realized he was eyeing her shopping cart, sizing her up, possibly estimating the inevitable "paper or plastic?" decision at the checkout.

"No," she said too quickly, "No party. Why do you ask?" He pointed to the orange and black bags of candy with a puzzled expression on his face. "Oh no," she said with a nervous laugh, smoothing the flap of her pocket, "I'm making a drop-off at the food pantry." As if losing her grip on a ledge, she added, "They need a treat, too, sometimes."

Stewart laughed and shook his head. "Dr. Peterman, you always crack me up." *Always* seemed a bit much, considering most of their conversations were about the location of a frozen entrée or why he'd moved the Cool Whip again.

Once Lucy had asked him for a particular brand of frozen pizza and gave him her phone number in case he located it. He searched every Piggly Wiggly grocery in the area until he found one without sausage. Later, after he called her at home, she had pretended to be thrilled even though she had already eaten an egg salad sandwich and gone on with her life.

"I aim to be pleasing," he'd said, sounding like someone with a marginal grasp on English. But he was from Michigan and this was just one of his little quirks. Stewart was always making a muddle of common phrases. "Don't worry, be snappy," he would say with a wave, or "Beauty is in the eye of the moldy," or her favorite, "Blue flies are coming!" like he was announcing a biblical plague.

"Please, call me Lucy. I'm uncomfortable with the 'doctor' part these days." She began to slowly move away with her cart, hoping to put some distance between her bulging pocket and the possibility of Stewart noticing her bulging pocket.

He flushed. "Lucy, then. We just got in a new brand of lasagna."

"I'll make sure to try it next time I'm in." She picked up speed.

"I haven't had the chance myself. It's made for two people, which really means there's enough for four." Stewart held up four fingers for emphasis as he moved to keep up.

"That's true," she said, totally unaware of what was about to happen. She had little experience with subtle hints and the setup for a date. If she were savvy, she might have zippered her purse and hustled her sweets out the door but, instead, she was like a deer, misunderstanding the rifle and the kindly-looking man in orange. He took aim.

"Maybe we could do a taste-test together sometime. I'm

not much for main courses, but I make a good salad. I use spinach. Sometimes I put in pine nuts." Since Lucy didn't speak right away, he added, "And cheese." It dawned on her finally that he was asking her over for dinner and now her cart was trapped in the checkout line.

"Um, sure," she said, her mouth moving without her brain's permission.

Overhead, an amplified voice ended their awkward exchange, beckoning Stewart to return to frozen foods for a price check.

As Lucy continued to stand in line, her body half hidden between a cooler of Pepsi products and the magazine stand, she jammed her hand in her pocket and returned the stolen chocolate jack-o'-lantern to lie on top of an almost empty box of Oh Henry! candy bars. Glancing around, she shoved her selected candy onto the conveyer belt and paid in cash with record speed, refusing to use her rewards card.

The phone was ringing as she entered her kitchen. She gently placed her sugary loot on the kitchen table and picked up the phone.

"Charles?"

"Lucy, hi, it's Stewart from frozen foods."

"Oh," she said in surprise. "Did I forget something?"

"No, I just thought that maybe if you weren't busy tonight we could try that lasagna. I suppose someone as pretty as you already has plans, though."

"Pretty? I'm not. No, I don't. I was just going to recover from the day."

"Will you come over then? I'll make my special salad, the one with the cheese. You could come now. I'm just getting home from work. I have a little house at Twenty-four Lazy Park Lane. We're not very motivated around here, so take your time." And he gave himself a courtesy laugh for his little neighborhood joke.

Without wanting to, she said, "Okay."

"Really? Wow, I've wanted to ask you over for quite a while. This is great. I'll turn the oven on right now." As if this was the deal clincher. Once that oven was turned on, there would be no going back. Then he signed off in his usual scattered, cliché way. "Over and under then," he said, and the phone went dead.

Lucy walked to the hall mirror and took a long look. She turned sideways and pulled in her stomach. She checked her teeth. She touched her hair and placed a bit behind her ear. Still in her wool coat with her purse on her shoulder, she reached in for her ChapStick and bit her lips before putting it on. She slowly walked back into the kitchen and sat heavily in her chair, pulling open a package of peanut butter cups. The smell came to her like the whisper of a best friend. She shrugged off her coat, slipped off each shoe, and took a bite. *Beauty is in the eye of the moldy.*

She never intended to *not* go. But she never intended to go, either. Instead, Lucy walked to her bedroom door and placed her hand on the door frame, her cheek on the solid oak panels that only come with a leaky, older house. She let the memory of the accident float free of its restraints, let it circle around her head, and descend around her shoulders.

She and Richard, they'd been talking—no, laughing—in the car. The trip was an insignificant one, to a nearby town to purchase a new mattress. After that she could only recall the deafening *whap, whap, whap* of the helicopter and her seizure-like shivering, frenetic activity all around.

She remembered nothing else until the moment she saw Charles at the hospital, who said, "You've been in a car accident, Lucy. Richard didn't make it." She tried to sit upright, her hand moving to her deflated abdomen, her lips dry with a crusty seam of blood. She licked them in slow motion, trying to form a sentence that made sense, saw Charles go paler still and shake his head.

Now she touched the doorknob and lay on the carpet.

Much later, Lucy woke to darkness and a phone buzzing at her hip. She lifted her head from her numb and sleeping arm. Without thinking she opened her phone and croaked a dry "Hello?"

"Hey, I'm coming over in a bit. Can I bring over Mom's old trunk? Phong and I are getting a new dresser and we don't have room for it."

"What?"

There was a pause on the line. "Luce? You sound terrible, like . . . I'm coming over now."

6

The Pretty, the Ugly, and the Nasty

Lucy blinked at the dead phone and creaked to an upright-seated position. The neighbor's husky whined and then barked a hello to the night. A car door slammed. She began to make the move to a standing position, but instead she rested her head against the wall and sighed.

She was still sitting in that position when Charlie found her, the reliable old wall holding her up, the oak door to her bedroom keeping her safely out of danger.

"Luce. What's going on?"

Lucy lifted her eyes. The concern on her brother's face confirmed the inappropriateness of taking a nap outside your hospital storage–room-slash-bedroom. Lucy tried for innocent. "What?" she said.

Bending down, he grasped her arm and hauled her to a standing position. "What happened?"

"I lost my job."

"No you didn't. Come on."

"Okay, not lost, exactly. Just . . . postponed."

Just then, Charlie's partner, Phong, walked in the front door and moved quickly to help. Lucy brushed them both off. "I'm fine, you two. Can't a woman be a little foggy after a nap?"

"Luce."

"I'm just having a little pity party before the cops come. Look, I have chocolate." She snorted an almost drunk-sounding laugh and held up an empty plastic bag.

"Look, I took some stuff from the hospital and they're all up in arms about it. They want me to go to a treatment center for behavioral medicine."

Phong said, "Behavioral medicine. What the heck is that?"

"Impulse control. They think I'm a klepto."

"That's ridiculous," Charles said. "Seriously, Lucy. That's ridiculous. Right?"

"As it turns out, not so ridiculous." She paused. "Can we just not do this now?"

Charles hugged her in response. "Luce, we love you. You can tell us anything."

She hesitated. "It looks bad, Charlie. I know it does." She touched the top of the door frame and the silver key blinked in the light of the hall. Positioning the key, she bit her lip, slid back the bolt to her bedroom door, and pressed her face into the opening. Charles and Phong peered inside. Scattered across the room were teetering piles of white and blue-green hospital supplies. Bloated IV bags and neatly sealed packages holding items made of plastic or stainless steel: syringes, tweezers, scissors, and sterile sutures. An unorganized collection, but a big one: all good soldiers awaiting orders.

"You took all of *that* from the hospital?"

Phong placed his hand on Charlie's arm.

Charles lowered his voice. "Lucy?"

"Yeah. I did. Looking at it like this, I can't believe myself how much stuff is in here."

"But why? Hospital supplies? What does it mean?"

The flush started at her collarbones and rapidly moved north. "If I'd stayed conscious that day, if I'd had the right equipment, I could have saved him, Charlie." She caught sight of one of Richard's tennis shoes turned on its side. The unmade bed from that morning, eight months ago; his running pants tossed and crumpled on the floor. The lump in her chest pushed her out of the room, and she pulled the door shut.

Charles took hold of his sister's seemingly boneless hand. When they were kids, he remembered, he used to walk on Lucy's right, a chubby, feminine, suspected gay boy, while a pretty neighbor girl took her left. Bullies would throw snowballs and shout out nicknames: the Pretty, the Ugly, and the Nasty.

"No, Lucy. You couldn't have saved anyone."

She lifted her eyes to her brother and spoke in the voice of a little girl who'd lost everything. "That's all I've got, Charlie. I can't explain it."

Charles hugged her again, resting his chin on her head, as he whispered to Phong, "You go get our toothbrushes, jammies, and a huge bag of bridge mix. The Brach's kind, not that low-grade generic crap that has nothing but creams. We're having a sleepover."

With a watery smile Lucy said, "Yeah, Phong, get your own candy. This stockpile is for the rest of my life in the slammer."

Charles and Lucy sat together on the couch while Phong reclined nearby, a quiet witness to sibling symbiosis. When Richard was alive, the four of them used to play games sitting across from each other, guessing each other's hints. Phong and Lucy were always paired as teammates, which reduced Lucy's otherwise unfair advantage of being either her husband's soul mate or her brother's DNA mate. Their favorite game was one they'd invented of misheard popular song lyrics, the goal being to correct the mistaken lyric and identify the artist who sang it, or wrote it. Stewart from frozen foods would have been either amazing at the game or hopeless; Lucy couldn't decide. Lucy's "Lost and Raving" was solved as "Constant Craving" by k.d. lang for six points. Richard's "I'll never leave your pizza burnin'" easily racked up points when decoded as The Rolling Stones' "I'll Never Be Your Beast of Burden." They'd laugh and search their memories for embarrassing lip-synching moments in their lives.

But this night would not play out with laughs and snorts. It would be the kind of evening no one could have predicted only a year ago, but had been predetermined the day Richard died.

Lucy worked a long piece of dental floss into her teeth. "Why'd you come tonight, Charlie?"

Charles said, "You always answer the phone 'Peterman,' like you're in the ER, ready for action. Today you just said 'Hello,' like you were eight years old. Plus when you called earlier you invoked the chocolate SOS."

Lucy sighed. "Now that the jig is up, I wonder how far I could go into a life of crime: drug trafficking, grand theft auto, aggravated assault." A brief smile skittered across her face, revealing a chunk of chocolate still stuck to her incisor. "Aggravation comes so easily to me. Assault is surely just around the corner at the Bitch and Battery Bar and Grill, where two-for-one specials are always available—because every night is ladies' night."

"You're not a bitch, Lucy," said Phong.

"Well, maybe not, but I stood up a perfectly nice man wanting only to serve me a double portion of lasagna. And I raged at my boss after getting caught stealing. Worse yet, the only gnawing in my chest about this whole thing is that I feel generally embarrassed and angry but not guilty."

"A man?" said her brother with interest.

"Don't get excited, Super Tramp, he might be a little special needs. But still, I should call him. I may be depressed, but I'm not usually unkind."

Phong said, "I give you permission to call him in the morning."

"Thanks, Phong." She heaved a frustrated sigh. "I'm so pissed at Stanley. I just want to do my own thing."

Charles shot Lucy an incredulous look. "Since when is stealing your thing? Are they pressing charges?"

"I don't mean *that* thing. I mean the other thing: surgery. And no, it's worse: in my opinion therapy is worse than jail time."

Charles said, "It's about time."

"What's that supposed to mean?"

"I've been trying to get you to see a grief counselor for months. Plus, you know this isn't the first time you stole something and got caught."

"What are you talking about?"

"You think I don't remember Maine?" Charles turned to Phong to fill him in. "It was years ago, when we were kids. Our folks rented this tiny cottage on a beach, and we had total freedom. We biked everywhere and must have captured the entire population of starfish while we were there. We'd bike to Wiersibicki's Five and Dime. You could get real penny candy there."

"Whatever, Charles." Lucy looked at Phong and said, "I stole a root beer barrel and a Pixy Stix."

"I hate Pixy Stix," said Phong.

"God, me, too. What was I thinking? The woman working behind the counter made me empty my Barney Rubble change purse right in front, at the cash register. Her nametag read, MY NAME IS GLADYS. I'M HERE TO HELP! She told me to get out of her store or she'd call the cops." Wistfully, Lucy said, "Someone finally did, Gladys."

"She never looked glad-anything," Charles said.

"After that, I never dared going back into that shop again."

To Phong, Charles said, "I had to buy her candy from then on." Then he turned back to his sister. "What set you off back then?"

"Who knows? Mean girls. My weird hair." Lucy picked some caramel out of her teeth. "When you were a kid," she asked Phong, "did you go on vacation?"

"I was on the boat then. Not much candy there, but lots of theft."

Lucy sat up. "Right, the boat. Coming over from Vietnam. Of course. God, Phong, you must think I'm really a spoiled brat."

Charles said, "Nothing like a straight shot of perspective, huh?"

Phong smiled. "A hard childhood doesn't outrank a tough adulthood. Chocolate would have been good on the boat, though."

Charles reached for Phong's hand and gave him a supportive squeeze. They had the kind of love that all the big blockbuster movies advertised. Across a crowded chicken barbecue on the Fourth of July three years ago, Charles had seen Phong request a double scoop of vanilla ice cream on his homemade apple pie. The grandmotherly woman serving up the ice cream said, "You're too thin." To the clerk next to her she said, "Margo, give this man a free scoop." Then eyeing Phong again, she said, "I suppose it's all that rice you eat. No nutrition. Like eating snow." Instead of impatience or insult, Phong smiled and said to the woman, "You have the loveliest blue eyes. Looks like you could use another volunteer in this chow line." Charles watched Phong finish his pie, put on an apron that read, DROP YOUR PANTS, I'M A NURSE, and for the next hour and a half proceed to sling pie between his new friends, who he'd learned were named Hazel and Margo, the suppliers of the free scoop. Next to a game of beer ball, in the shade of a makeshift dugout, Charles watched the three of them and fell in love with the diminutive Phong. After the pie ran out, Charles approached and asked the two older women if Phong was free to go and find some shade. As Hazel took the apron from Phong she said, "Your English is really good, kiddo." To Margo she whispered, "I wonder if he was one of those adopted kids."

Hazel shook her head knowingly. "No, they only get rid of the girls."

Now Charles glanced at Phong and said to Lucy, "It's possible that life is just about trading compulsions. Maybe the key to success is finding the one that doesn't kill you or land you in jail."

The three of them sat there in the quiet night, listening

privately to their own obsessive thoughts. Charles yawned and said, "Mom used to steal, too."

Lucy and Phong turned their heads in a move that would have been the envy of two high school girls in synchronized swim practice.

"Mom use to steal?" Lucy said, incredulous. "No kidding."

"I don't know how much or how often. Obviously nothing like this," he said, pointing his thumb over his shoulder to Lucy's bedroom. "But sometimes, I'd be shopping with her and she'd admire something. You know, like a Christmas pin or some lip gloss. Later I'd see her wearing it. And I knew we hadn't bought it. I always emptied the cart and bagged the stuff."

Their mother had never played by the rules, and for a gay boy who loved to write computer code and a girl who'd declared at the age of ten that she wanted to be a nun who interpreted for the deaf, that was a good thing. When Lucy waltzed around the house with a white turtleneck hanging from her head, signing the lyrics to "You've Got a Friend," her mother enrolled her in College for Kids and challenged her to sign what she learned. After signing *brain*, a finger to the temple, and *paralysis*, a move that looked like one of Michael Jackson's in the "Thriller" video, Lucy was hooked. Learning sign language and physiology was too slow for quick-thinking girl-Lucy so she cut loose from the signs, both for communication and communion, and went to medical school instead of church.

"You're lucky, Luscious," her mother would say. "You will always be more than your good looks." God bless her mother's blindness to her daughter's physical shortcomings. "Girls will compete on footing that you will always command—the level ground of the mind," she told Lucy. But Lucy was more interested in watching her mother paint a thin, perfect line on her eyelid, finishing with a flourish that floated up like a cat's tail. She watched her mother wrestle herself into a bra that cupped her breasts like the fluted foam packaging of the Asian pears in the grocery. She listened to her mother bemoan the ravages of aging, childbirth, and menopause. Her mother's behavior contradicted her words, and her father's gazes confirmed them. Beauty was important.

Sitting on the couch now with her brother, Lucy considered this new information, that her mother had engaged in petty theft, and said, "Well it's true then: The fruit doesn't fall far from the nut."

"I think that in our family, I'm the fruit and you're the nut. Mom was probably just bored."

"You think my propensity for stealing is genetic?"

"Well, if it is, then Mom's the link. You didn't get it from Dad. Remember when he got audited? The IRS ended up owing him."

Theodore Peterman, Lucy and Charles's father, lived every day of his life at the intersection of Atticus Finch from *To Kill a Mockingbird* and George Bailey from *It's a Wonderful Life*. He shoveled his neighbor's sidewalks in the winter, mowed beyond his lot line in the summer, and overtipped every harried waitress or bellboy he ever came in contact with. Where their mother worked the angles, their father operated as straight as an airport runway, and when the IRS cut him a check for $12.43, he framed it and mounted it on the family photo wall, next to school pictures and family portraits. Twelve dollars and forty-three cents, glorified in a glass-covered dime-store frame. "Benjamin Franklin would approve," he said, nailing it in place.

"Clearly you got Dad's genes, Charlie."

Phong turned to Lucy then. "All this nostalgia is nice," he said. "But more important, Lucy, what are you going to do?"

"I'm going to attend the minimal number of therapy sessions they've mandated, and then get back to work. I'm going to get over my anxiety and clean out this room. I'm going to . . ." She stopped and considered what would be next on the list. "Well, I don't know what else."

Charles said, "Try and meet new people. Work through the grief and loss from Richard's death. Move out of the guest room and back into the bedroom. Think about doing something other than just working all the time."

Lucy shoved a bag of unopened chocolate away and said, "You just don't understand, Charlie. I don't want any of those things. I want Richard. I want to have his baby. I want to talk about our jobs together and hold his hand. I don't want a new life. I want my old one." She put her head back on the couch and two tears raced each other to the tip of her chin.

Phong said, "It is going to get better, Lucy, but you know what they say: Sometimes it's gotta get worse before it gets better."

Lucy sighed. She thought about Stewart from frozen foods. "Blue flies are coming," she said.

7

Lose It and Live Again

In the U. S. of A., if you wake one morning and need confirmation that the lump in your breast, newly discovered in the shower, is only a non-cancerous fibroid and not cancer, or if you decide that you could leave your abusive husband if only you were able to talk to someone with letters after his name, you can call a clinic and wait, for what could be months, for an appointment. But if you are a plastic surgeon with sticky fingers, you are shoved, against your will, to the head of the line. Getting in to see a particular physician at a health-care clinic is like trying to train a cat to come: It will only come to you on its own time. In Lucy's unfortunate case, *its* own time was a week, and the clinic was housed in the very place Lucy wanted to avoid: the hospital she stole from.

With her head down, avoiding eye contact, she scuttled

through the parking structure, veering away from the broad front doors and over to a side entrance.

In the hallway, trying to look inconspicuous, she heard someone calling her name.

"Dr. Peterman?" Lucy turned to see the approaching Mrs. Hallorman, the last patient she'd seen before being discovered as a thief. "Your staff called. Said I have to have another doctor. That you aren't my doctor anymore." Becky Hallorman's normally luminous skin was now tinged with worry and fear.

"I'm on leave for a time, but I'll be back."

"How long? Will you be back for my surgery?"

"I don't know. I—"

"I don't want anyone else. I feel like you understand what I'm going through."

"I do. I do understand."

Becky Hallorman touched Lucy's hand. "Did you know you were leaving? Why didn't you tell me?"

There were many things Lucy hadn't considered when she repeatedly slipped a syringe or a hemostat into her pocket and walked out the front door of Med One Hospital and Clinics. She hadn't considered the word *theft*, for one thing. Nor did she really consider medical paraphernalia separate from herself or her position at the hospital. The hospital, her job, seemingly owned her. If she had to work hours well past a traditional workweek, giving most of her time to the hallways and patients who walked them, she never asked for extra dispensation. So, honestly, when she took a roll of tape without thinking, it seemed petty for the hospital to call it stealing. It had also never occurred to Lucy to consider the existence of security cameras, or the cost of replacing missing supplies. And it had *really* never occurred to her to consider the impact on her patients of being discovered a crook.

"I'm so afraid," Becky said with desperate eyes.

Lucy stopped. She gripped Mrs. Hallorman's arm. "Don't let that fear take root, Becky. Pry it loose. Cancer and fear feed off each other. Here." Lucy rummaged in her purse and found her business card. With a Sharpie, she penned her home phone number. "Call me any time, day or night."

Then, using her master key, she slipped inside the side door and started up the stairs to the tenth floor. On the fifth-floor landing she stopped. Breathing heavily, she unbuttoned her gray wool jacket just as the door to the pediatric floor swung wide. She jumped back, narrowly missing a collision with Charise Schaefer, Junior Leaguer, hospital volunteer, and self-appointed mascot.

"Look who it is!" Charise crowed. "What a surprise. I haven't seen hide nor hair of you since the Halloween party. Shame on you for missing my after-party and keeping my doctor friend waiting." She wagged her naughty finger at Lucy and gave her the look of a superior mommy.

"I went home pretty early. I ate something that didn't agree with me."

"Drank something, I heard. But no matter, I forgive you. Are you on your way up or down? I always take the stairs. That way, I can eat whatever I want and keep my girlish figure." Charise spoke with a definite nasal twang, a hold-over from her rural Minnesota roots, which she tried to hide by wearing clothes from DKNY and BCBG and keeping her tanning packages up to date.

"You go ahead. I'm catching my breath."

"Gotta keep moving if you're going to increase your fit-ness," Charise said, at which point she linked arms with Lucy. "So when can we get you to meet my guy? He's divorced. Married a real witch, if you know what I mean. No kids, which is ideal, don't you think?"

Lucy pulled her arm free. "Charise, I'm not dating yet. I only just lost my husband a few months ago."

"Oh, I know, sweetie. And I can see why you'd want to wait, but I've read that a date within the first year as a widow is directly associated with successful bereavement and subsequent marriage. I Googled it."

"Successful bereavement?" Grabbing the door handle, Lucy said, "This is my floor."

"Urology?"

Lucy read the plaque: SIXTH FLOOR. Urology. She nodded. "I haven't had a good pee since my husband died. Maybe I should clear this up before I meet your guy. They think polyps or a despondent bladder. Something to do with grief, I guess."

Charise pulled her arm free and said, "Polyps?"

"Yeah. Viral polyps."

Watching Charise evacuate the stairwell as if Lucy had threatened to wipe a bladder polyp on her immaculate silk shirt almost made the whole exchange palatable. Hoping the last four flights, which would take her to mental health, would be less like an obstacle course, Lucy slipped her coat off and counted the stairs. The offices on that floor weren't much different from the plastic surgery suites. Maybe a few more plants. Definitely a lot more brochures: OCD, anxiety disorder, depression; one-stop shopping. The bathroom Lucy visited in order to wipe her sweaty hands featured signs with contact numbers for abuse hotlines. DO YOU FEEL SAFE AT HOME? one read.

In the waiting room, she took a seat in the comfortable, calming, plum-and-gold upholstered chairs. A coffee machine perked in the corner next to several current magazines offering ways to get "Your Best Self." One article featured a kitchen renovation that would allegedly bring a family together, reunite loved ones, and heal all hurts. Another hawked the ten-pound solution to all troubles, including a slow economy: "Eat less—Spend less. Lose it and Live Again." Lucy considered the energy it would take to rifle through each magazine, find the right article, and read up on the various keys to happiness, and decided, quite possibly, that doing so was just too grueling. Besides, in her experience, once you lost it, it was hard to live again.

The door to the clinic's offices opened and a strikingly beautiful girl walked in. Lucy examined her with the unabashed scrutiny that was the province of women who don't think they are pretty. This girl's blond hair was thick and blown flat as a paint stirrer, her makeup flawlessly applied.

As Lucy stared, she realized the girl was actually a woman, considerably older than Lucy had first thought.

The woman took a seat. She had an almost perfectly symmetrical face with cheekbones that could part hair. The lip gloss and mascara she wore ran interference, distracting onlookers from her clearly sagging spirit. She was dressed in a soft, loose sweater and jeans that made her look like a casual starlet waiting for the paparazzi to snap her photo. Lucy caught sight of a wrist, more bone than flesh. Aware of Lucy's eyes on her, the woman tugged her sleeve down, inadvertently exposing a collarbone that jutted out like a fracture. She was a gorgeous bag of angles covered with luminous pale skin and fine, downy hair.

Lucy had certainly seen her kind before. Plastic surgeons, even the ones who dealt with reconstruction, as she did, saw their share of eating disorders. When starving, purging, and exercise didn't get rid of the inevitable consequences of life, whether due to aging or the birth of a baby, they would come to her, unwilling to live with any evidence of entropy, weakness, lack of control, or imperfection.

Lucy caught the woman's eye and smiled. A soft breath escaped from her lips. Then she leaned over and said, low-voiced, "I steal stuff I don't need."

Something sparked between the women. They were team captains of their respective pathologies. Without a smile the woman said, "I won't eat what I *do* need."

The assistant at the check-in desk signaled for Lucy to enter the counselor's office. Before doing so, she pulled a business card out of her purse and said to her waiting-room companion, sitting on what had to be incredibly uncomfortable pelvic bones, "If you want to come over some time and not eat . . ." She left the sentence unfinished. The woman's spider-like fingers unfolded and grasped the card. She nodded, offered a brittle smile, and said, "Okay, thanks. I'll bring something you don't need."

Lucy's therapist didn't look like anyone she'd met in her short-term experience with grief counselors. Historically, she found therapists to be overly personal people prone to making generalizations and wearing clogs. But this one, Dr. Tig Monohan, wore *normal* around her shoulders like a shawl. She didn't have the kind of eyebrows that Lucy associated with therapists, the ones that conveyed sympathy or disapproval with a twitch, but she did have glossy brown hair and she wore nice pants.

"So this is how it works, Dr. Peterman. We start here with an evaluation. I'll ask you some questions. Please answer as honestly as you can and then we'll decide what kind of therapy would be the best for you."

She sat with her hands in her lap. The little girl in the principal's office. The bad girl from the playground. She'd worn black pants and a cashmere turtleneck to show how seriously she took her situation.

"Here's the thing," she said as she glanced around. "How am I going to get here every week for therapy without running into everyone I know asking unanswerable questions? Yes, I stole a bunch of incontinence pads. No, I don't want to come to the Christmas party. No, those two things are not related."

"That's part of the deal. You have to own this. No more denial."

"I don't deny that I did it. That would be hard to do, given the video surveillance camera and amount of stuff in my bedroom."

"Denial comes in many forms. But we'll get to that." Dr. Monohan riffled through the papers on her desk.

"I don't know why I do it." Lucy's stomach did a flip. "I mean, I'm not so far gone that I don't know it's wrong. I'm actually a pretty good person. I just want to go back to work."

Tig stopped shuffling papers and trained her gaze on Lucy. "Your status as a good person isn't at issue here, Dr. Peterman."

"Stealing is bad."

A smile flashed across Tig's face and she nodded. "Stealing *is* bad," she said with measured humor and raised eyebrows. "The bible tells me so. Shame on you."

Lucy met Tig's eyes. Nonjudgmental acceptance. She felt her throat close with gratitude.

"May I call you Lucy?"

Lucy nodded.

"Look, Lucy, I've got people in here who can't live without multiple addictions to pain pills, alcohol, and weed. One of my doctor patients smells women's feet while they are under anesthesia. Yesterday, one of our higher-ups admitted to asking strange women to lick his balls. You're the light at the end of a long week."

"Seriously?"

"Serious as a breast lift. That's plastic surgery humor," she added. "I thought you'd appreciate it. Being a therapist is all about knowing your audience."

Lucy blinked. "So are you saying this is just a formality?"

"Ha! Don't you wish. No. You've got issues, Lucy. We're gonna check those issues out, hopefully get you to stop taking IV bags, and reinstate you into medicine where you belong. Make no mistake, though: You've got some work to do."

"Okay. But I think I can stop stealing anytime."

"Oh, I'm sure you do," Tig said kindly. "I've been an alcohol and other drugs therapist for ten years; I know intention is a great short-term fix, but I don't want you stealing tampons from a gas station in three months. We're going for a long view here. You're getting a tune-up that includes working on your impulse control and working through your grief. That's going to take some time."

"How long?"

"That's up to me. And, to some extent, you." She met Lucy's eyes. "You'll work in this office, and go to regular meetings of Alcoholics Anonymous."

"What? No . . . I."

"We're a small town. That's all there is for easily accessible group therapy that deals with addiction."

"Forget it. There is no way I'm going to AA."

"Then you'd better find a new job." Tig looked her straight in the eye. The women faced each other like two brick walls, one intact, the other crumbling. Lucy's glance faltered and Tig spoke again, this time more gently. "I'll be there. It's part of my clinic commitment. Since we send all kinds of people to the meetings, we find it's helpful to have a therapist there, at least some of the time. Now some questions, just to get the details out of the way, an assessment for the record. Have you ever stolen things that you really didn't need?"

The question worked like a stun gun on Lucy. She was a thief, a crook, and a robber. This last word made Lucy grimace. She thought of a masked face, a striped suit, a filled sack, the Hamburgler.

Tig answered her own question, consulting her notes. "Unless you're planning on opening a clinic, I'm assuming you didn't need the twenty-two suture kits and fifteen packages of latex gloves." She looked at Lucy over her reading glasses and Lucy nodded. Tig continued, "Did you feel a sense of pleasure or relief right after you stole these things?"

"No. Sometimes, I didn't even notice what I was doing. I'd come home with a pocket full of two-by-two pads and not remember taking them."

"So no sense of pleasure or relief? No feelings of anger?"

"Most days, I don't feel much of anything."

Tig put her pencil down. "When did that start?"

Lucy cleared her throat, remembered coming home after the accident. The silent house. Oatmeal on the counter congealed and uneaten, evidence of her morning sickness, a feeling she now regretted hating. She saw her husband's coffee cup. She shrugged.

"I've got a full schedule, Lucy. Lots of people in and out of here. The longer this takes, the less you get to be a surgeon."

"Jeez, what's the rush? I'm just clearing my throat here."

"I've found that addiction and denial need less kid-glove treatment and more tough love, Lucy. We don't have a ton of time if we're going to save your job. It doesn't do either of us any good to soft-sell it."

Lucy dropped her head. "I love denial. I don't know how I'd get through a day without it." She swallowed hard. "After my husband died—" She stopped, held her hand up to signal Tig to wait. She tried again. "Richard had a penchant for reading obituaries. He cut out the more memorable deaths or photographs and tacked them to the fridge." She shrugged. "Sometimes it was a story he liked. Other times, there was something about the face of the person who'd died. It sounds morbid, I know. He saw it as a reminder to stay in the present." Lucy stared at the swirl in the carpet, heard her husband's voice, *Life is what you do, Lucy, my sweet. And you do it until you die.*

"He liked to quote Zorba the Greek when he was being philosophical about life. The last obits he saved were photographs of two men, printed next to each other in the newspaper. Bob Grabben and Stanley Stolen died on the same day in August." She stopped, looked at Tig. "I remember wondering if Mr. Stolen or Mr. Grabben had ever shoplifted, self-fulfilling prophecy and all. I guess I started after that."

"You think your husband was giving you some kind of coping strategy?"

"A message from beyond? God no." Lucy paused and looked around the room. "That's all I got. I don't know. I had to do something."

"Are you going to keep taking stuff, Lucy? Do you think you can stop?"

Lucy's eyes drifted off and floated to a corner in the room. "Women like me, we aren't just given things. There's no one standing in line to help us hang a light fixture, change a tire."

"Women like you?"

"You wouldn't understand. You couldn't, not with your long neck and perfect eyebrows." Tig sat back. "Women like me," Lucy said, "we have to ask. Stand in line. Take."

"So that's what you tell yourself? That's your justification?"

Lucy scoffed. Closed her face like the door of a safe in an old western. Spun the lock shut. "I want to go back to work. When can I go back to work?"

Tig scribbled something on a piece of paper and handed it to Lucy. "This is a non-traditional AA meeting; I don't actually lead it, but I listen. The group is a wonderful mix of people—a microcosm, I believe, of what's really out there. Listen, Lucy, you do my job for a while and here's what you learn. No one is normal. Everybody struggles with something. Marital problems, depression, codependency, maybe a looming fascination with shoes or leather bags that keeps her working overtime shifts to pay off her debt. Whatever. Stop thinking everyone else has it together. It's not true. Precious few people have life figured out. 'Normal' just isn't normal anymore."

"Let me ask you this . . . the ball-licking guy? Does he get to keep working? Because I could have done something like that instead. I just need to know for the future."

"Twenty meetings, Lucy. Get started, and come back to see me in a week."

Lucy clenched her jaw and moved quickly out the front door of the clinic, arriving at her car breathless. Alcoholics Anonymous. No effin' way. Once out of the parking lot, she fastened her seat belt, and turned on the radio. Etta James's voice belted out, "At last, my love has come along." She snapped the radio off and instinctively made the turn that would take her home, but at the final possible second she yanked the wheel and bumped over the curb and into a parking lot, nearly skidding into a bicycle rack. Her large leather purse flew off the seat, revealing two suture kits, a stack of plastic medicine cups, and a 50-cc IV bag. Three rolls of bandage tape bounced onto the floor.

She rolled her eyes in disgust and spoke directly to the mess. "Really?" she said, as if the rolls of tape were triplets who refused to stay in their car seats.

She gathered the supplies, piled them onto the passenger seat, and covered them with her coat. Sitting back, she gazed at the yellow awning above the painted window of Lavish Lattes and Luxuries. It fluttered like a wife in a housedress, waving her inside. She thought of Etta James, belting out her signature song. At last . . .

The door chimed prettily as Lucy pushed into the store. It was a riot of hand-thrown pottery, jewelry, and the smell of rosemary and lavender. Here, she could anonymously escape her life, uninterrupted by memories or do-gooders on patrol. Only college girls on break from classes worked the register, and never could Lucy's appearance compete with the furious texting that was taking precedence at the counter. What the hell, she thought. No one would notice what she was about to do, and there would be no starting AA until . . . well, until she said so.

The store was stocked with ceramic containers filled with lotions and flowers growing in saltshakers. Papier-mâché suns hung in corners next to Christmas lights and paper ball lanterns. Gourmet chocolates sat on tables, tempting ceramic frogs that held notices of author readings and jazz on Saturday nights.

This place is truly Luscious, she thought picking up a ceramic bunny and putting it into her purse. *So unlike me.*

She'd never been able to come to terms with the name her mother had bestowed upon her. There was nothing luscious about her. One look made it clear. And everyone knew she knew it. She didn't have the swagger of the easily beautiful, the knowledge of her own visibility in the world. In fact, she was acutely aware of the contradiction between her name and her looks and walked with an, *I know, I know* in her posture. If she'd been a Tracy or a Susan, she wouldn't have gone through her early life with quite so many questioning looks. That's why these days she rarely called herself anything but Lucy. She glanced at the girl behind the counter, put a hanging fern between them, and selected a tulip candleholder, hesitated, and put it back on the antique kitchen set.

It could not be easily fixed, her lack of lusciousness. She was not a makeover waiting to happen. She'd been reinventing herself with marginal results since she'd become aware of her aesthetic failings, way back in third grade. It had been a harsh lesson doled out by the one hearing-impaired boy in her grade. Jeffery Wonager looked at her and signed "Ugly You." There were a few signs everyone in their class knew: stupid, fat, boring, *ugly*. Even then, considering the multiple possibilities, Lucy knew there were worse things than being ugly—but not many.

Her brother had been there, of course, defending her even then. He'd shouted, "Jeffery Want-a-girl, you big loser!" forgetting the insult fell on truly deaf ears.

People had gotten the message though: Mess with Lucy and you'll get Charles on your case. Charles, the only gay fourth grader in the history of Ulysses S. Grant Elementary School. It wasn't much of a threat, but in the homophobic town they'd grown up in, there was a collective, unspoken fear that gave Charles a lot of power: If he'd consider being gay in a small Wisconsin town, who knew what other impossible acts he might be capable of.

A small cache of silver rings sat in an accessible glass display case at the end of the counter where the college girl on duty stood gazing at herself in the reflection of a shiny watering can. Lucy touched the rings, glanced at their inexpensive price tags, slipped several onto her finger.

Lucy worked tirelessly on her appearance. She bought expensive clothes and spent a fortune on facials and beautiful haircuts to tame her freckles and kinky red hair. She'd had braces in high school, teeth whitening in medical school, and a mouth guard for preservation during residency. She bleached and plucked and waxed every last errant hair on her body; not that anyone since Richard ever saw what she had going on south of her chin. But she was a like a loyal marine in the beauty battle, even if it didn't exactly result in winning the beauty war.

The shop girl finally noticed Lucy, with one hand in the silver rings, the other holding a florid bouquet of mums, autumn roses, and amber daisies. As Lucy handed everything over to the girl to be rung up, she silently calculated the price. There was the sale price to be factored in, the 10 percent discount she would receive as a frequent shopper, and the additional buy-one-get-the-second-one-half-off discount. She quoted the total to the college girl at the register before the electronic wand was even lifted from the counter.

"Whoa," the girl said.

"If you think that was fast, you should see me at euchre. I crush 'em at the nursing home. We play for teeth." The young woman laughed. She may not have been a mathematics whiz, but at least she had a sense of humor.

In addition to being a skilled surgeon, Lucy knew a thing or two about people. She knew that they didn't notice Brillo Pad hair and close-set eyes if they were having a good time. The other thing they didn't notice was the act of slipping a smallish silver ring into the outside pocket of a purse while ostensibly rummaging for a Visa card. A moment of magic. Lucy knew she had the ultimate disguise: She was a smart, funny, well-dressed woman, not a common criminal. Everyone knew thieves were male and came with either a skateboard, a piercing, or a gun in tow. But her? No way.

Back at home, she unfolded her brochure to examine the meetings schedule for her town's chapter of Alcoholics Anonymous, and with a blank expression on her face, examined the ring on her finger.

"No way," she said to herself.

8

Everybody's Got a Job to Do

The interesting thing about surgeons is this: They have gone to the head of the class their whole lives; skipping grades, taking AP classes, testing out of math and English, and generally leap-frogging into a future peopled with other adults who rule the school. Sure, they're working for it, but since they're so successful, they don't have to manage as much loss as do regular mortals. The individuals who don't win every spelling bee and merit scholarship learn about disappointment. They acquire a coping skill or two. They try yoga, self-talk, read *The Little Engine That Could*. And when they get up after a blow, they graduate to *Dealing* and *Life 201* and so on. But not surgeons. Not people like Lucy Peterman. So while she may have been a postgrad when it came to memorizing cranial nerves, she was still in kindergarten when it came to coping.

"I changed my mind, Charlie. I don't want to go to the cemetery today."

"This was a good idea, Luce. We're almost there."

"The counselor didn't say I had to go immediately, she just said soon." Lucy gripped the door handle of her brother's sedan. "I said I'd never go back. I know other people visit, but I don't need to. I know he's dead."

Charles pulled under the archway of St. Ann's Cemetery. "If you do this for me, I'll stop bugging you about moving back into your room."

"What am I supposed to do here? Talk to him? Pray?"

"I don't know. Go to his grave. Then maybe you can eventually go into your bedroom, and after that, pack up the stuff you stole. It's a process."

Unfailingly practical Charles. You'd think that Lucy the brain, the med school grad, was the grounded, practical planner, but no. She was more the romantic dreamer. The one who wanted to go to school to learn how to save the world, one breast at a time. But once Charles dealt with the truth of being gay, he's had to create his own blueprint of what the American Dream would look like for him. He majored in computers, saved for adoption in case it factored into future plans, and saved for retirement.

Now he stayed in the Volvo and waited while Lucy slogged across the bumpy ground of the cemetery. She noted the forever-bloom of plastic chrysanthemums in their plastic holders, tilting as if they were exhausted by the work of continually honoring the dead. She imagined them saying, "Enough already, can't I just lie down?"

She straightened a particularly lazy wreath that was missing most of its synthetic blooms. She gave off a little grunt, shoving the spike farther into the ground. "Everybody's got a job to do," she muttered to the wreath. "This is yours."

Taking a left at an obelisk that should have been marking a famous Kennedy instead of the very un-famous Orcus Farmer, Lucy saw the hydrangea tree she'd planted in the spring. It had bloomed splendidly then, but now it sported beige paper tears for the winds of fall to scatter in sadness across Richard's grave.

Richard Lubers. Lubers was the reason Lucy hadn't taken his name in marriage. Lucy Lubers was more than even she could stand, even for loyalty. Nineteen seventy to two thousand thirteen. He'd been clear in his funeral planning that the only other thing he'd wanted on his headstone was the proclamation I LOVE LUCY.

"Ricky, you got a lotta 'splainin' to do," she said to the grave as she stood there, unsmiling and quiet. There had been so many things he'd prepared for *in the event of his death*. Insurance, estate planning, even funeral decisions. It's as if he'd known his days were numbered, as if he'd known that people—that *she*—*would* need direction, and soon. More likely though, it was just his way of thinking ahead and forever caring for her. He was that kind of man. A one-in-a-million man.

They'd met in residency. Richard, an only child, raised by a single mother who then died of breast cancer, was as committed to caring for women as any man could be without a uterus of his own. Earnest, careful, and completely devoid of subterfuge, Richard didn't know how to flirt, woo, or flatter. He would have made a terrible spy, but he made a wonderful partner. "You have got to get a hobby," she used to say to him. He would respond, "You, my love, are a full-time job." This really wasn't true because all of Lucy's bristles were smoothed like spackle on drywall when he was around. But now he wasn't around anymore, and Lucy's life had a Richard-shaped hole in it that she needed to figure out some way to fill.

She brushed off the rugged top of his headstone and traced the writing on its face with her finger. LOVE. She looked around. The only other person in sight was the groundkeeper. When they'd arrived, he'd been on the far side of the cemetery on a riding mower loud enough to double as a rocket ship. Now Lucy saw him steadily making his way over to where she sat as she tried to conjure up the feeling of Richard's hand on the back of her neck, his lips on her ear. The mower was a kind of grief-seeking missile finding the quickest path to her side around all the headstones and monoliths in its path. Trying to think reverent thoughts amid the irreverent sounds of a rabid grass clipper made Lucy, even in her sorrow, laugh at the absurdity.

"All right already," she said to no one in particular. "I'll get out of here and spend time among the living, for Christ's sake."

Back at the car she plopped herself into the passenger seat. "There. Check that off the list."

Her brother buckled his seat belt. "What's with the grass guy?"

"I know; what was that about? It might have been some weird ownership thing." She deepened her voice to sound like a radio announcer. "'This is grounds keeping time, mourning time is after work or at night.' Or else it was Richard in his usual no-nonsense fashion telling me to get the hell out of here."

"A little harsh on both accounts; but not bad advice, overall."

She glanced at her brother. "I wish I could remember the accident."

"Why? The witnesses kind of filled in the blanks, didn't they?"

"Yeah. Deep shoulder, overcorrection, ditch, roll, death, miscarriage."

Charles lowered his eyes, giving a respectful moment of silence for his sister's loss. "Shit, Lucy."

"I keep thinking if I say it like that, I'll believe it. Get over it."

"I would think it was a blessing, not remembering."

"I want to know what we were talking about. His last words."

"If I know Richard, it was probably, 'Fuck!'"

Lucy laughed and then laughed again harder. "That would be so Richard. Mild-mannered, bespectacled Richard. Never a harsh word until there is, and then it's a doozy." She gulped, making a sound somewhere between humor and sorrow. "I only remember one thing: him reaching across me, arm out, like Dad used to do if he stopped too fast and we were in the front seat."

"He was something, no question." The groundkeeper made another pass around the graves directly in front of them, his tractor's engine roaring in great crescendos with each row mowed.

"I'll figure it out, Charles. This grief thing. I'll figure it out."

"It's not a puzzle, Luce. There's not going to be a final exam. Think of it as an art project. A time to create something new."

"That's not how I see it. If you lose an arm, you don't grow a new one. You tie off your shirt sleeve and clean your house with the other one. You figure it out."

"Coming from a reconstructive surgeon, that's a pretty brutal assessment. You do see my difficulties with your belief system, right? Listen to your therapist: You've got to let people in."

Lucy laughed. "What do I need other people for? Other people wouldn't make me laugh when I want to knife a groundkeeper. I don't want any other people getting all up in my business."

Charles took his sister's hand. "You still need to meet new people. Promise me you'll try."

She smiled at him. "Okay. Maybe only for a minute. But I'll try."

9

Happy Ain't Just a Town in Texas

When Charles dropped Lucy off, he gave her a salute. "Good work today; carry on." Lucy flipped him a two-fingered sideways gang sign and walked into her house, down the hall, and into the spare bedroom. She'd made a decision at the cemetery. No more helpless Lucy. No more *get-some-therapy* boohooing from people who didn't think she could get it together on her own. It was time to show everyone that she could go into a store without binging on chocolate, offending perfectly nice people, or stealing a stockpile of bandages or jewelry that meant nothing to her. She had to prove she could do this and do it without help.

From her closet, she chose a small leather clutch purse in case she had the urge to shove a toaster into a side pocket. This purse would say, *Get real, don't even think about it!*

She'd decided to head for Walmart, the ultimate quick-and-dirty shopping exercise.

In her car, she turned right onto Main Street, past the strip mall with Fur Flying, a family-owned barber shop/pet-grooming business; Tattoos and Tea, a little Victorian shop of horrors; and a dress store creatively named The Dress Shop. She hated Walmart almost as much as she hated her own hypocrisy. How can the shopper hate her shop? The addict despise the dealer? She had no answer for this, just the typical snooty rationalization of the rest of the population: Alcohol is not a drug; Walmart is not shopping.

Lucy entered the store through silent, obliging electronic doors. Within ten feet of the entrance, she cringed at a rack of waistless maternity wear. Or were they possibly mother-of-the-bride dresses? They'd be perfect for a labor-and-delivery cruise ship event. Adjacent to the dresses were T-shirts emblazoned with rhinestone sayings. UNDER THIS SHIRT I'M BUTT NAKED read one, in a tasteful peach color, size XXL.

Without a shopping list, Lucy marched head up, shoulders back, through the aisles, clenching her teeth with crime-free determination. Standing in front of dozens of rows of toiletries, Lucy saw a grocery cart bearing a little girl who looked the personification of Cindy Lou Who from *How the Grinch Stole Christmas*: lopsided pigtails, two-inch eyelashes, valentine lips. The girl's eyes were closed while she rubbed a pink packaged pacifier over her face and neck. The rapture expressed in her face would embarrass any adult caught in a similar situation—say, a grown man rubbing his new Mercedes car keys across his five o'clock shadow. On this girl, it just looked like devotion, bliss, and the prop for a good afternoon. As Lucy watched, Cindy Lou's eyes popped open. Staring, she appraised Lucy from head to toe and then reached out and offered her the pacifier, smiling with a little crease in her forehead as if to say, *Here, you look like you could use this more than I.*

Cindy Lou's mother stood with her back to Lucy, studying her grocery list. Then she tugged at the cart and moved deeper down the aisle. The child continued to proffer her pacifier until the cart rounded the corner and disappeared. Touched, Lucy's mind wandered back to her miscarriage, like a tongue searching out a rough spot on a tooth. She thought of the stack of supplies she'd purchased once her pregnancy had been confirmed. The baby-wipes warmer, the bright red rattle, the pacifiers. A knot unraveled at her navel and she braced herself on the cold metal shelves right there in the store, shelves holding shower gel, plastic scrubbies on a rope, bath oil. She spotted Richard's favorite brand of soap and lifted the package to her nose, inhaling its scent. Her husband's scent. It filled her sinuses and flicked on every switch in the house that was her brain, illuminating every room, every memory. There, behind her eyes, Richard stepping out of the shower. Richard embracing her from behind. Richard making love to her, while she felt— finally—beautiful.

Someone coughed and Lucy opened her eyes, looked around. No one. She slipped the bar of soap into her tiny purse and strolled to the end of the aisle. Lifting her hand she sniffed again and walked toward the exit, stopping to touch a sweater as if to say, *I'm in no hurry to leave. I could stay all day.* Between Lucy and the exit were the security sensors that announced larceny as if it were an overdue library book, a gentle beeping that was less a call-to-arms and more a sociable *Yoo-hoo.* She had never set it off herself, but she'd witnessed the confusion of the innocent people who did. They collectively stopped and looked around for the handcuffs. Employees, assuming that true larceny would lead to frantic running and not gentle acquiescence, waved at the people with a jolly head wag. *It happens all the time. No worries.*

Without hesitation, she stepped between the white and blue security gates. That was the key, keep moving. No alarm followed her and the electric exit doors opened. She moved into the large vestibule before the second set of doors; freedom was seconds away.

"Lucy Peterman, valedictorian. How are you?"

Lucy started. Near the red plastic toy car where fifty cents got you a ride with a clown frozen in a rictus of fun stood the policeman she'd gone to high school with. The one who knew where she lived.

Her mouth popped open. "I. What? Do you work here?"

He tilted his head indicating his casual attire: ratty jeans, paint-splattered, too-small navy sweatshirt. "No, I am not a cop for Walmart."

"Oh." She smiled politely and turned to go.

"Did you find what you needed?"

"Yes." Over her shoulder, she flashed him a thin smile.

"No bag."

"What?"

"You aren't carrying a bag."

Lucy's face colored. "What's it to you? No bag. Whatever."

"You're not out the door yet." His gaze held her. A knot on a shoelace: stubborn. "Possibly you left something in the soap aisle. Your keys, maybe?"

A feeling of cold water trickled down her spine. She turned and held his stare for an impolite minute. Lucy inched her car keys into her jacket pocket and, looking away, walked an exaggerated arc around him and back into the store. Forgetting any socially appropriate speed or etiquette, she entered the soap aisle, yanked the bar of soap out of her purse, and shoved it onto the shelf. Righteous now, she stalked back to the exit doors and said, "Are you going to arrest me?"

He shrugged. "No harm done, as far as I can see." She rubbed her eyes and the exit doors opened. Time to go. "I'm Mark Troutman," he said, and he held his hand out for her to shake. "Wanna get some coffee?"

She snubbed the hand he offered. "I suppose I have to, right? Look, I know I should be grateful or something, but I just don't want to do this."

He scratched his weekend beard and said, "What do you think *this* is?"

"I don't know. Some kind of intervention. A lecture. A forced conversation, after which I'm going to walk away and need a nap."

Lucy read his pause and frowned. She remembered her father's brand of discipline from her childhood. *I'm going to stand here until you decide that I'm not giving up in the face of your stubbornness.*

But the fight went out of her. As if accepting her medicine she sighed and said, "All right. Let's get this over with." Without speaking, they walked next door, where a small coffee shop/bookstore struggled to survive next to the retail giant, hoping against hope that wireless and an artful latte counted for something in this crazy world. So much so that the owners had named the shop Artful Latte in a Crazy World.

At the counter, Lucy made a show of paying for their drinks, and with their coffees in hand, they chose seats away from the knitting circle, a gaggle of women chatting away in plush chairs.

"What have you been up to since high school, Lucy?"

"You mean other than working the five-finger discount? Just say it, okay? Give me the law talk so I can go."

He laughed and said, "You're angry. I remember that."

"What are you talking about?"

"I've been thinking about you since I saw you at your house. Do you remember me from high school?"

"Sorry. No."

"We had lockers across the hall from each other."

She shook her head. "Sorry, Mark."

"I'm not surprised. I was angry, too. A loner. Into weed. Not your type."

"Ha! Like I had a type."

He took a sip of his coffee with unwavering eyes. His jaw looked tense. It was not an expression Lucy had the strength to fight. But it wasn't an unattractive look, either.

"I saw you come out of class once. Kick the shit out of your locker. Rip something up. What were you so mad about?"

"Puberty, high school. Whatever." She thought for a minute. "No, actually, I do remember. Biddy Bartholemew voted me Best Hair for Senior Favorites—you know, in the yearbook."

"Better than Biggest Stoner."

"Look at my hair. I have always had *the* worst hair in the history of our school and she knew it."

"Why'd she do it?"

"So I wouldn't get the category she wanted."

"Which was?"

"Most Humorous."

"Didn't you get that one?"

Lucy paused. "Wow, you have quite the memory." When he didn't respond she said, "Ugly girl gets Most Humorous, Best Personality. Yeah, that's not a cliché."

"Was Ugly Girl a category you gave yourself?"

"I don't remember 'Stoner' being on the Senior Favorite list, either. What were *you* so mad about?"

He shrugged.

Lucy shoved her chair back. "Oh, I get it: This is a one-way walk-down-memory-lane therapy session. Look, I gotta go."

"Jesus, calm down. I just took a minute to collect my

thoughts. Not everyone thinks at the speed of light." He took a swallow from his coffee. "Shitty home life, back then. These days, I guess because I went from weed to alcohol to divorce before I turned thirty-five. A whole life in just a few years."

Lucy caught a flash of the high school boy she thought she hadn't remembered. The dark eyes, hair hanging in them, acne. "I think I remember you now. You were smaller."

"I bloomed late. That pissed me off, too."

For a second, in her mind, she stood back in the hall outside the high school principal's office. She'd been on her way to work on the yearbook. Teenage Mark had shrugged out of the office, a large hand on the back of his neck steering him into the hallway. His father, saying, "Dumbass. I told you three strikes and you're out." He'd shoved Mark— who worked to appear cool in spite of the bully dad who'd yoked him—down the hall. Lucy had watched the pair all the way out the door, where the father cuffed Mark twice, hard, at the side of the head.

She nodded toward the Walmart. "That wasn't the first bar of soap that's ended up in my pocket, you know."

"Cleanliness is important." He grinned.

"Feloniously important."

"So you're a doctor, and—what? They don't pay you enough?"

"Yeah. And you drink too much because—what? Every day is a gift and you're going to unwrap the ribbons?"

His head snapped back an inch. "At ease. It was a joke." Sighing, he said, "Look, you can go if you want."

"I don't need your permission." She shook her head. "I don't know why I do it, okay? Like you probably don't know why you drank yourself out of your marriage."

He winced. "Not to reduce the enjoyment of this conversation or put too fine a point on it, but I can drink, get divorced, and still not end up in jail. Can you say that about what you do?"

"Are you going to arrest me?"

His face fell. "Does it seem like that's what I'm doing here? Arresting you?"

"I'm not a criminal. I'm not!"

"Denial ain't just a river in Egypt," he said.

"That's another thing I hate about AA—the catchy one-liners that get thrown in your face like they're some kind of solution. Like the receiver will be enlightened and never drink again."

He laughed. "Sorry to use another tired cliché, but you are a ballbuster." He laughed some more. "I love it."

Lucy pulled a face. "I assure you, that is not something people love about me." She spread her hands on the table and examined her short nails. "I get that I have a problem, I just don't think there's any mystery involved. I'm trying to fill a hole in my life with things instead of experiences. But I'm going to counseling just to make sure. The hospital wants me to go to AA."

"It helps, Egypt. Especially in the beginning."

"Don't call me that."

"Next time, you might end up in real trouble."

She dragged her eyes up. "Why not this time?"

"Call it valedictorian dispensation. But get some help. Next time you might end up at my place."

"Jail?"

"Or whatever." He looked away when he said it and Lucy felt something fish-like flip in her stomach. "Either way, it's trouble for you, I imagine."

"I just don't get how AA might help. I don't drink."

"You're a smart woman. I'm sure I don't have to connect the dots for you. If you don't want to see it, though, I can't make you." As she moved to leave he said, "Biddy Bartholemew always was a bitch."

Lucy sank into her car seat and started to cry, another unpredictable impulse she seemed to have no control over lately. Wiping her face with the spare lab coat she kept in her car after the fast-food napkins ran out, she watched as Mark Troutman exited the coffee shop. It was hard to reconcile her memories from high school with this solidly built, confident man. Straight-backed and lean, he pulled a well-worn baseball cap from his back pocket and covered a testosterone-fueled bald spot. She sniffed her hand, looking for Richard's scent; finding only the smell of coffee, she turned the key in the ignition.

As she inched her car forward out of the parking space, a small dog darted out from under the grocery corral. Lucy slammed on the brakes and her eyes met the dog's, and for a moment—a moment right out of a wine commercial featuring attractive young people in a singles bar—she felt a connecting of souls. Then the dog darted away, moving like a Navy SEAL as it zigzagged around the wheels of cars both parked and in motion. Lucy cringed as she heard the screeching brakes of a black SUV.

She bolted from her Subaru and into the path of a honking black Mini Cooper hell-bent on making its small-car way in a big-car world. She dodged a woman pushing a wheeled walker and flinched as the dog ran between the tires of a Holsum bread truck. The dog ran full out, ears flapping for speed, until both it and the woman with the walker exited the parking lot and headed straight into the oncoming traffic. Lucy held her hand out as a traffic cop might do in order to save school children.

Through blaring horns and elevated fingers she shouted, "Dog!" One woman screamed, "Jesus fucking Christ," out her car window in a reaction that would have been more appropriate during a terrorist attack.

Across the street, Lucy jumped onto the grassy boulevard of a Pontiac dealership and scanned the area for the dog. A tiny flash of white and brown rounded the side of a Bonneville and headed for the back lot. She followed, waving at the salespeople behind the plate-glassed showroom, finally catching up with the shaft of a tail connected to a round, furry rump unflatteringly lodged in a wire fence.

As Lucy approached, the dog stopped struggling and peered around at her with the large, buglike eyes of a chronic hyperthyroidism patient, soulful, desperate, unable to sleep for worry of where its next meal was coming from. Lucy let it sniff her hand.

"You've got yourself in quite the predicament. I'm living that same life, metaphorically speaking. I totally have my ass caught in a big gate." The dog allowed her a scratch behind the right ear. "It sucks," she said. "I know."

Lucy was able to push apart the pliable links of the fence so that the dog popped loose. But instead of making a break toward freedom, it stepped right onto Lucy's knees, stretched up, and sniffed her neck, chin, and mouth. There was no overly forward licking or gratuitous wagging, just a gentle and serious snorting coupled with a stare that said something like, *I know all about you; where's the roast beef?*

"You've got some burrs in your ears, little one. And no offense, but you don't smell so good."

The dog opened its eyes and looked apologetically into Lucy's. "You need a bath. And maybe a few less donuts. What's a pretty girl like you doing wandering around, anyway, getting into trouble? Where's your collar?" Lucy's knees creaked as she stood and gathered the dog into her arms. "Let's get you in a tub and sort things out."

The dog sighed and wrapped her tail around Lucy as if to say, *Oh thank God, I'm bushed. If you had some bath salts, that would be nice.*

A fifteen-minute drive later, Lucy carried the dog inside the house and without preamble lowered her into the sink in the kitchen. She stroked the small animal under her chin and tested the water to make sure it was warm enough. Slowly she began bathing her. Occasionally the dog licked Lucy's hand or snuggled into her armpit, but mostly she just gazed into space in apparent bliss. Dirt ran down the drain, and what had been a stiff brown coat morphed into a silky fawn color with white highlights. Her toenails, too long and ragged, changed from mud colored to a pale seashell pink. Lucy pulled several dish towels out of the drawer. When she had finished drying her, she said, "Now let's get you something to drink."

Lucy filled a bowl and set it down near the back door, then mopped up the water from the bath. After collecting the towels and placing them in the laundry room, she turned, searching for the dog. "Here, girl," she called. She followed the wet footprints out of the kitchen, down the hall, and into her makeshift first-floor bedroom. There, in a doggie circle on her bedspread lay the damp bundle of brown and white fur, burrowed into Lucy's powder-blue robe. Her snoring had a slight whistle at the end of each breath.

Ever since Richard's death, Lucy had been unsure of what to do in her own house. It was a feeling she'd gotten used to. But this time, there was another being to accommodate. A being that she found she didn't want to disturb.

She noticed the blinking message light on her phone, but ignored it and crawled into bed next to the little animal. She reached out a tentative hand and rested it on the dog's paw. The dog articulated a very clear, almost human *woof,* and just before Lucy closed her eyes she saw the outraged face of her cat, glaring at her from her bureau. The righteously indignant jut of her tail broadcasted her disapproval, and Lucy mouthed, "Oh relax, Mrs. Bobo. Go lick your privates."

10

Smoke and Mirrors

When Lucy woke from her nap, it was dusk. A wonderful smell floated in the room: bacon. She rubbed her eyes and wrapped herself in a shawl. She called out, "Charles?"

As she padded into the kitchen, her brother pushed an omelet onto a flowered plate. "Happy Halloween."

"Do I need to change the locks?"

"I guess I would if you don't want Meals on Wheels wandering in and cooking you a gourmet meal while providing sparkling, low-conflict conversation." Charles raised his eyebrows and said, "I didn't bring this dog with me, but she seems to know her way around. She said I could stay."

Lucy knelt to pet the soft, downy animal. "She got her ass stuck in a gate," she told her brother. "That's how we met. I gave her a bath."

"Are you keeping her?"

"No. I'll try to find out where she lives. Put posters up or something."

"So Stewart from frozen foods just needed to get his ass caught in your gate and he would have gotten inside?"

Lucy looked up. "Huh?"

Charles gestured toward the phone. "He called while you were sleeping."

"Oh. Ugh. What did he say?"

"Listen for yourself," he said.

The answering machine registered two hang-ups, followed by Stewart's voice. "Hi, Dr. Peterman. Um, Lucy. This is Stewart. From frozen foods? Um. Sorry I missed you the other night. I always do that. Come on too strong, I mean. I—I hope you'll forgive me for putting you on the spot." There was a pause and Stewart went on. "Please don't feel bad." There was another pause. "See you in the frozen foods. No harm, no growl, as they say in football."

Charles grimaced at Lucy. "No harm, no growl?"

"He's got a real way with words." Lucy's face fell. "I am the social equivalent of a chronic dieter. I vow to do better, dream of the perfect friendship, but I'm unable to muster the hyper-vigilance needed to put down the sabotaging behavior and reach out for help."

"Yep."

"I need to go to People Anonymous. 'Hello, my name is Lucy and I suck at interpersonal relationships. It has been two years since my last dinner with someone not related to me.'"

"And Stew was that chance?"

"He was a start, I guess." Lucy rubbed her eyes, "You know, once, when I was flying somewhere to a surgical conference, they had me seated right next to an emergency exit. I asked to be moved, immediately after hearing the three criteria for using that seat." Lucy ticked them off on her fingers: "You must not block the exit, hurt yourself or others, or get distracted. Given what might be occurring at the moment when I'd need to wrestle the door off its hinges, I couldn't make any of those promises. Shit, I get distracted while brushing my teeth. I hurt people while grocery shopping. If the plane was going down, I'm pretty sure I'd block the exit." Lucy ran her hand through her wild hair. "I've gotta call him."

"He sounds understanding."

"That makes it worse. Where's Phong tonight?"

"Spanish class. You know he's running for alderman. Thinks he should be able to speak the language of the people."

"How's the campaign going?"

"He spit a coffee bean twenty-nine feet and one inch at the Coffee Festival."

"So that's a really important skill for an alderman. Also, fairly impressive. How'd he do it?"

"He told the newspapers he just shut his eyes and thought Olympic gold."

A loud, frat-party kind of barking erupted from the living room. Lucy strode toward the front door, calling over her shoulder, "It sounds like I have five breeds in here instead of one smallish, dappled doggie." Seconds later she appeared in the kitchen looking panic-stricken.

"Luce?"

"The cops are here. In the driveway." Charles looked so unaffected by the news that Lucy was forced to add, "Now!" in such a hysterical tone that the dog paused mid-yip.

"Jesus, calm down."

"Do you think the hospital finally called them? Or Stewart, maybe? He probably checked the surveillance tapes, saw me steal that pumpkin. But I put it back!"

"You stole a pumpkin?"

"Charles, go out there. Tell them I'm not home. Tell them I'm in surgery." Lucy looked wildly around. "No, don't. They must know I'm not working. That's why they're here. You're supposed to stick close to the truth when you lie; that's what they say."

"Who?"

"Lie experts. Tell them I'm indisposed. Tell them I want to be alone." Lucy paced around the kitchen.

"Okay, Garbo. I'll answer the door. You try and get your bag of nuts together and sit like a good little squirrel and shut up."

As Charles stepped out of the kitchen, Lucy whispered a loud "I love you."

She stood there, hugging the squirming dog, who chewed a cat-shaped rawhide, until Charles reentered the kitchen. Then she blew air through her lips and rolled her eyes. "That was close."

"There's someone here to see you."

"Hi, Egypt." Mark Troutman strolled into the kitchen

and put his hand up in a casual wave. "This isn't an official call. This is for that rogue cat of yours that terrorizes the neighborhood. I'm dropping off information on how to get her properly licensed." He held out a small pamphlet with a cartoon kitty on the front.

Charles smiled. "I told him you'd never get that cat a license if I gave this to you." To Mark he said, "She needs a strong authority figure." And then he quietly left the room.

"I don't know what to say," Lucy said.

Mark said, "'Thank you' is customary in this country." She just blinked, and after a moment he said, "Okay then, I'm going back to work. Maybe we could have coffee again sometime."

Lucy shook herself. "Why?"

"Why? Because people do that. Have coffee. Talk about high school. Occasionally, pie is involved."

"Pie?"

He smiled at her. "Egypt, you are a piece of work," he said. And then he turned and walked out the door.

When Charles returned, he raised his eyebrows. "He's interested in you."

"Don't be ridiculous. Have you ever taken a good look at me?"

"Aw, Luce." It had been a long road with his sister and her looks. He'd watched her get passed over in everything but math and science. As the years went on, Lucy couldn't get over her high school assessment of her looks. Smart as she was, she'd never been able to see how kinky hair and braces as a girl were the gateway to a different kind of beauty as a woman.

Lucy sighed. "You know, a few weeks ago, I was checking out the indie DVD store on Van Buren Street for an old Hepburn movie. There's this woman in front of me, long, auburn hair, totally high-maintenance. There was nothing about her that said, 'I can get dressed in under ninety minutes.'"

Charles nodded. "Let me guess. French-tipped nails, skintight jeans with heels, lip liner."

"You got it. Fitted white T-shirt with a martini glass on it, and breasts that looked like they would deploy on contact. The *beautiful girl* uniform."

"You think those are her 'lounging in front of the TV' clothes?"

"Oh sure. Just like mine, without the flannel pants and mustache bleach." Lucy shook her head. "So I'm standing there in my sneakers and Brewers cap—your basic loser ensemble."

"Yeah, plastic surgeons are such losers."

"So the woman looks me up and down and says, 'Did this movie get good reviews?' I saw what she was thinking: Here's a woman who spends a lot of nights alone watching TV. She'll be able to give a recommendation for a night with just girls."

"Did you help her out?"

"I said, 'I don't speak English.'"

"As they say in high school, fuckin' A."

"Here's what I want to know. Why is it that the really pretty women are also the ones who try so hard?"

"Maybe when you're that high up on the beauty food chain, the pressure is enormous to take it a step further. To be the overachiever and get out of base camp and make the summit, dammit!" Charles hit his fist on the counter and the dog jumped.

Lucy smiled. "Those women are so far out of the ballpark when nude and without makeup that when they complete the paint job and buff they become untouchable. A completely different species: genus super-female."

"Here's the thing, Lucy. Those women have to work harder than you. They have to wear the red dress and the lip liner because women like you have a brain that's already dressed before you even wake up in the morning. You're the superhero. And they freaking know it."

"So it's all smoke and mirrors to distract from their tiny brains?"

Charles nodded. "Or as Stew from frozen foods might say, 'hoax in mirrors.'"

Lucy rolled her eyes. "Wait, I didn't finish the story. I'm in the checkout line and there's a mother with a really young little girl who's repeatedly asking for *Black Beauty*, but it sounds distinctly like Black Booty. 'Mama, I want Black Booty, Black Booty.' The cashier looked right at me and she said, 'Yeah, you and me both, honey.'"

Charles dropped his head back and laughed.

Lucy said, "Turns out *Black Beauty* was nowhere to be found, but there was one hell of a white one back in the stacks."

"That cop is cute, Lucy."

"I'll admit I'm not as horrendous looking as I used to be, Charles, but *A*: that guy isn't interested in someone like me, and *B*: I'm in love with Richard." Lucy unfolded the forms that Mark had handed her: a one-sheet on how to get a license for a cat. And another piece of paper beneath it: a list of Alcoholics Anonymous gatherings in the area, and a meeting place and time circled in red.

"You should call him."

Lucy dropped her gaze to her hands and twirled her wedding ring, her last connection between the life she wanted and the one she now had. "You know I can't do that, Charles."

"Unfortunately," Charles said, "I do."

Later, tucked in under the large picture window in her living room, Lucy pulled a gray cashmere blanket around her shoulders. The corner of the curtain, artfully placed, allowed for a complete view of her neighborhood while obstructing curious eyes from discovering Lucy's plans for the evening. Passersby would see only a darkened house; no lit jack-o'-lanterns, no bowls of candy for trick-or-treaters.

Autumn leaves papered the streets and sidewalks; front porches held filmy webs with furry chenille spiders. Makeshift graves littered front yards with black Sharpie inscriptions: RIP and I TOLD YOU I WAS SICK. Candles flickered in carved pumpkins with jagged smiles. Only Lucy's house sat dark within her neighborhood's cul-de-sac. Her and her wallflower house, both of them unwilling to engage for fear of a long, arduous hangover, a difficult recovery. She'd been careful to erase all outward signs of life. *The doctor must be working tonight. She works all the time.*

Lucy sipped her tea and watched the family across the street tumble onto their front porch. The mother held the door for the last child, pulling his cape free. Lucy could hear her commands float across the street through the crack in her open window, a reminder of all she had lost.

"C'mon, Jake, be careful with your sword. Marissa, your wing is caught in Jake's sword." Robin Hood stood clear of the fracas and patiently waited while the pirate and fairy untangled themselves, and then all three moved onto the porch swing for a photo. All homemade costumes, just like Lucy would have done.

There was a camera flash. "Taylor, your eyes were closed."

The father strolled out of the house. "Smile, Jake. I want to see that pirate smile."

Another camera flash was followed by three more in quick succession, and Robin Hood wandered off the swing. Clapping his hands, the father said, "Let's hit it, troops."

The town siren sounded, and the children took off at a dead run.

The rest of the night carried with it dragons, ghouls, vampires, baseball players, and ladybugs. Mothers with children in wagons, fathers holding the hands of waddling supermen and dancing queens. There were shouts ("Say thank you!"), encouragements ("You missed this house"), affirmations ("You're fine, honey, brush yourself off").

Two women chatted, trailing behind a flowerpot and a ninja. Momentarily unguarded, the flowerpot stopped walking and looked toward Lucy's house. Her petals flopped comically as she tilted her head and examined the darkened front porch. Straightening, she moved toward the stone path that led to Lucy's door. As she approached, she turned her head and saw Lucy. A slow smile crept along her face and she waved a leafy hand, the fingers curling a hello.

"Lulu. What the heck?" The flowerpot snapped her head around and, with a whoosh of her petals, scurried away.

"There's a lady in there."

Lucy couldn't argue with the mother's response to her little girl. "No, honey. Nobody's home."

The next morning, Lucy stood in her driveway. Indian summer was in full swing, and it mussed her hair and twirled the leaves around her feet. She roused her dog. "Come on, girl. Let's . . ." She stopped; she had no idea what should follow. *Let's stop being addicted? Let's find God in the little things? Let's live every moment to its fullest?*

Lucy never had been one for girlfriends or time off. She'd had so little of either through her life. She'd been too busy excelling, and excelling takes time. Her last best friend had been in grade school. Melanie Strathmore was a bossy, energetic girl to pal around with, and that was good for the intense, overthinking Lucy. Melanie always showed up at Lucy's house with a plan. "Today," she'd announce, "we are drawing a chalk sidewalk map to Mr. Crab Ass Shultz's house, so that the aliens that are watching us will take him instead of our parents." Or, "Do you know the words to 'Endless Love'? We're going to sing it next to Main Street and get discovered and be famous." Lucy followed Melanie's instructions to the letter until she got to ninth grade, when the Strathmores moved away. Besides, by then she had her hands full, planning for her AP classes, ACTs, and a pre-med college major.

Plus, Lucy had failings. Not everyone appreciated her sardonic sense of humor, and she didn't know what to say when talk moved to crushes, dances, and manicures.

Gathering the dog in her arms, she noticed a woman a couple of driveways away, moving in her direction. The woman looked familiar—and as she approached, Lucy realized why. She was the one who'd been sitting in the waiting room of Tig's office. The thin one. The one who couldn't eat what she needed. Even from this half-block distance, Lucy could see her hipless form. The woman waved. "Oh good, you have a dog."

"I do." Lucy smiled.

The woman indicated her own trim black dog at the end of a pink leash. "So do I. This is Chubby Lumpkins, Chubby for short, and I'm Sidney Jenkins." She shook her head. "No, Wick. Sidney Wick. Jenkins was my married name."

"Your dog and I have something in common," Lucy said. "My name is Luscious. Neither of us fits our name."

Sidney frowned slightly and stooped to pet her dog. "She's helping me learn that chubby is just a word, and that love comes in all shapes and sizes."

"A therapy dog?"

"Kind of. Although I don't think most therapy dogs hump strangers as much as this one does."

"That's probably frowned upon in canine counseling circles. You'd have to work on boundaries. This is"—Lucy hesitated, searching around—"um, Little Dog. I didn't know I was keeping her until, actually, right this minute. So I guess I'll name her Little Dog."

"That's a funny name," Sidney said.

"Coming from you, that's a funny thing to say."

"I hope it's okay that I'm here. I looked you up in the phone book." Sidney tugged an envelope from her pocket. "I was going to leave you a note. Thought you might like to walk with us sometime."

Lucy put Little Dog on the ground and immediately she and Chubby went on high alert: guarded, tense, noses working. Slowly, they approached each other's hindquarters and loitered in a socially unacceptable way. "It's fine. Great, even. Where did you walk from to get here?"

"East Gate Heights."

"I'm impressed. That's way on the other side of town."

Without glancing at Lucy, Sidney said, "I like to walk. Helps me think. It's like cleaning house."

Lucy clipped the leash she'd purchased the day before

onto Little Dog's collar and said, "Let's do it. Let's clean some house."

She surreptitiously eyed Sidney as they started to stroll. Baggy yoga pants and an oversized black fleece covered her upper body, but Lucy remembered from their meeting in the waiting room how skinny and frail she'd looked. Still, her full lips, clear skin, and large, round eyes, which were the color of sea glass, held court over her rail-thin form.

"I'm glad you came. Little Dog and I were just trying to figure out what to do today."

"I used to go running whenever I didn't know what to do next. But I wrecked my knees doing that. Now I'm working on being kind to my joints." As they approached the downtown shops, Sidney said, "It's nice how close your house is to the main drag here."

"My husband and I wanted to be able to walk most places. Thought it'd be nice for . . . kids." Lucy wiped her hand across her eyes, and despair caught in her throat.

Sidney briefly touched Lucy's shoulder, acknowledging Lucy's distress. Lucy opened her mouth to speak but the prospect of filling people in on her life, or what was left of it, felt impossible. She stayed silent but stopped to look in the window of a photography gallery.

"That's new," Sidney said, gesturing to a large vintage black-and-white photograph of a bride and groom. It was a Hollywood-moment shot, possibly from the fifties, the couple locked in a kiss for the ages. The groom's hand was at his bride's waist, pulling her in, and his other hand tenderly touched her face. She wore a gown with satin, tulle, and pearls; he was dressed in a white tuxedo. Together they made a perfect "Congratulations on Your Marriage" greeting card image.

"What do you suppose became of that couple?" Sidney tilted her head. "Think they're still married, were faithful to each other?"

Lucy smiled, remembering her own wedding. Richard in a black suit with a sky-blue tie that matched the wide ribbon that encircled her waist. His warm, brown eyes had spent the day gazing on her face.

"Maybe I'll buy that photo," said Sidney. "Whatever the price, it'd be a bargain for real happiness caught on film."

"They look so young."

"You know what I think?" Sidney said, still looking at the photo. "I think people should get married at the courthouse without a single person present and no fanfare whatsoever. Then, if the couple makes it to ten years, they should have a big party. The whole shebang: white dress, flowers, cake of their dreams. After ten years they'd deserve it."

Lucy raised her eyebrows.

"What?" Sidney said. "They would! But if you throw the big Everest-of-a-celebration first, there's no place to go after that but down. The people go home, the presents are shelved, and no one's left to help when there's a dispute about who should wash the car or who balances the checking account. You're setting them up for failure with the big wedding."

Lucy glanced back at the photograph. "Divorced?" she asked Sidney.

Sidney nodded. "You?"

"Widowed."

"Shit." Sidney shook her head. "I'm sorry. Did you get your ten years?"

"No."

"Don't listen to me, I'm bitter."

"What happened?"

Sidney was silent for a long while before saying, "I can't talk about it. But you know when you make a wrong turn when you're driving and the GPS unit says 'Turn around when possible'? I really could have used that GPS on my wedding day."

Lucy started to speak but Sidney waved a delicate hand, swatting away the sympathy. "I try to think of my mind like a bank account. Deposits are the successes, friendships, and happy moments. Debits are the disappointments and losses. I make an effort to do the math. Balance it." She grinned. "But I don't have the key to weigh importance worked out. I mean, divorcing an unfaithful husband and losing your wallet are both real disappointments, but losing the wallet really sticks with you."

Lucy laughed.

"When did you lose your husband?" Sidney frowned, and it seemed as if the muscle fibers in her temple could be counted.

"Almost a year ago. I'm not really interested in moving on. Or getting over it."

"You know what? Me either. If I get over it, I'm liable to get involved again. No, thank you."

The women turned up the street, passing windows that fronted a consignment store—Goes Around Comes Around—and a stationery store called P.S. You're Pretty. A breeze caught Sidney's hair and whipped it up over her ears and down her back. Lucy saw the web of veins encircling her neck. Chubby Lumpkins pulled to the side and sniffed a patch of what looked like squished squirrel. Sidney reined in the leash.

If Sidney were Lucy's patient who had lost her breasts to cancer, she might have said, *Getting over a loss is like climbing a ladder, one step at a time.* She might have said, *Don't think about forever, just think about getting through today.* Or maybe she would have said, *It's important to take care of yourself.* But knowing what she knew about loss, none of these felt right. So instead she said, "We should try to get better, you and I."

"We should."

"If we're being honest . . . you *do* look hungry."

"Don't kid yourself. I *am* hungry."

11

Tru Dat

Lucy pulled into the asphalt parking lot of the Maple-wood Serenity Center just before the 9 A.M. meeting of Alcoholics Anonymous. To her left sat a pickup truck with a bumper sticker that read SEX INSTRUCTOR, FIRST LESSON FOR FREE, and to her right, a VW Bug with one proclaiming THE ONLY BUSH I TRUST IS MY OWN. With one last pat to Little Dog's head, she cracked the windows, locked the doors, and took in a deep breath.

The square, yellow brick building sported the tall windows of an old country schoolhouse. Lucy tugged open a filthy metal door and it swung wide with a screech. The scent of old cigarettes and stale coffee swamped her fragile mood and slowed Lucy's progress. There were meeting notices, schedule changes, and random inspirational thoughts pinned to the bulletin board, and pamphlets—*One Day at a Time,*

Respect Yourself—on an over-the-door shoe holder hung on a conference room door. Tucked into one of the transparent plastic pockets was a stack of laminated, wallet-sized copies of the "Serenity Prayer"; the writing so tiny that it could scarcely be read. Perhaps, Lucy thought, its power to change lives lay in one's proximity to the words rather than the words themselves.

She backed away from the prayer-on-a-wallet-card as if a grizzly bear had suddenly appeared. Turning, she collided with a soft pillow of a woman who was removing a shower cap, the kind that comes free with shampoo and face soap at the Ramada Inn.

Lucy jumped away. "Excuse me!"

"Oh hell, honey, not to worry." She was a walking, talking version of a soft, powdery beanbag chair, wearing a fire-engine-red pantsuit and pink silk shirt. She looked like a confection, Willy Wonka's wife, a sugared donut of a woman with peppermint-stick lipstick and yellow cotton-candy hair.

"I'm only here to pick up some, um, literature. You know, for a friend." Lucy kept her head down and tried not to make eye contact.

With a conspiratorial duck of her head the woman said, "Oh, sweetie, I know an escape when I see one. I can just step right out of your way and you can run like hell." She had a hint of a southern accent. "Or"—and she winked at Lucy—"you can bring your pretty self inside, have a shitty cup of coffee, and spend an hour with a bunch of drunks."

"I don't drink, really. That's not my problem."

"No, of course it's not, hon. It's just like a prison here. Everybody's innocent."

"You don't understand."

The woman smiled, pure kindness, and said, "Come on in and tell us about it. The people in that room are your biggest fans. You just haven't met them yet." She linked arms with Lucy and gently tugged her toward the meeting room. "You will never feel more welcome as when you're at an AA meeting. We love you already. My name's Claire Weezner, and I'm a ton more fun than my name. I'm thinking of changing it to Claire-all-the-rivers-of-Guadeloupe-Saint Barts. I like the implications. It has sort of an all-inclusive beach front with a *we are the world* kind of feel. Don't you think?"

Lucy resisted but not enough to slow Claire's progress. The tired yellow conference room had long since given up being cheery. Grime darkened all the corners, reminiscent of a time when smoking was still allowed on the premises. Mismatched aluminum folding chairs surrounded three gray aluminum tables in a *U* formation. If not for the large windows that streamed sunlight into the room, it would have resembled a Gitmo interrogation facility. The four people already seated there obviously knew one another and chatted away, ignoring Claire and Lucy's entrance until Claire said, "Hi, everyone! Let's get cracking, I've got a Botox appointment at noon."

A lanky woman with striations in her jaw and neck that

looked like they'd been many years and many drinks in the making continued knitting. "Age is coming, love, and no amount of denial, chemical or otherwise, is going to hold it off."

"If I want to smooth out my worry on the surface to better reflect my inner peace, I don't need your craggy-ass wisdom to get in the way." Claire's smile was radiant.

With a frown, the youngest, toughest-looking person in the room gave Lucy a once-over. Blackened nails, eyes, and clothes shadowed her slight frame. She looked, in a word, used. An inked web of ivy covered her neck, roping around to the front of her throat and into her ear. She snapped her gum.

"Now, ladies, remember your manners," said Ron, a man in a motorized wheelchair, with nicotine-stained nails and dreadlocks. A POW sticker occupied the entire side of his chair and he wore a crucifix so large and so naked that Lucy could count Jesus's ribs. "You're late; we started. But you already know that, Claire, because you always miss the readings."

"I'm here, aren't I? Better late than drinking."

As she took a seat, Lucy eyed the only person who hadn't spoken. She was engrossed in reading from one of the several books at the table. Pretty in a soft, dated way, the woman appeared to have chosen her look in high school and stuck with it. She sat, steadfast in her flowery skirt and lacy collar, following the text with her fingers and ignoring the conversation around her.

Lucy felt the floodwaters of panic rising in her chest. She

was not a joiner, and if she were one of those people who could happily enter a group and vent, she certainly wouldn't have picked this immoderate group of movie extras. Alcoholics. These people couldn't hold their liquor. Didn't know when to say when. Had trouble living in a world where a drink meant more to them than family. *And* they must have thought that Lucy was one of them. That she stumbled through her day intoxicated. Drank a bottle for breakfast. Shook her way through the lunch hour, hoping for a cocktail. Lucy pushed back in her chair, thinking her hypocritical, unimaginative thoughts, and considered how she might escape.

Claire said, "What's our topic today?"

Ron tilted his head with disapproval. "We're not giving you a summary, St. Bart's. Get here on time for a change. Participate."

Claire stage-whispered to Lucy, "Ron's my sponsor and can't help himself. He wants me to conform." She turned back to Ron. "I ain't workin' for da Man, my brother." She pronounced it "brutha." Ron rolled his eyes.

The frowsy woman still had her nose in her book. "Tru dat," she said without looking up, and everyone laughed. Ron pointed to the woman and said, "Kimmy knows. Right, Kimmy?" The prim woman lifted her eyes from her book long enough to give Ron a black-power fist.

Lucy reached for her purse as she looked at the exit, and at just that moment, Tig, like a life preserver on the *Titanic*, strolled into the room. "Hi, everyone. Sorry I'm late."

Ron clearly was happy to hand over the reins of what

would soon be an unruly meeting. He nodded to Tig and said, "We're talking about gratitude."

"Thanks for getting everything going, Ron," Tig said, putting an oversized briefcase on the floor and pulling out a chair. "Who wants to start?"

"Right on! Okay, I'll go. I'm grateful for my new friend here," Claire said, indicating Lucy with her thumb. "She's definitely what our group needs. We're a bunch of stereotypes and we need some redefinition." Tig smiled at Lucy as Claire went on. "I'm grateful for having my colors done and finding that this fire-engine red is the cornerstone of my palette. My consultant is single, beautiful, and might be interested in more than just my cornerstone." Claire winked at the group, adding a lascivious element to her candy-store look.

"No relationship for a year, Claire. You know the rules."

"Oh shut up, Ron, I just need a Park n' Ride. I'm not interested in anything but getting my colors done, if y'all know what I'm gettin' at."

"Unfortunately, we do." The dark girl pulled a strand of hair under her nose, pursed her lips, and held it there, looking dastardly and silly at the same time.

"No interrupting people, Sara. Keep your black lips zipped," Claire said in mock irritation. "*All-the-rivers* has the floor! I'm grateful for Starbucks and for the fact that I am thirty days sober as an infant. Over and out."

There were positive affirmations all around. Even Sara gave a grimace of a smile.

Tig said to Lucy, "If there's anything you would like to share, please feel free to speak up."

Kimmy said, "We're very rude and don't follow all of the rules entirely but you will find us very empathetic."

"I don't have an alcohol problem."

Sara rolled her eyes.

"Sara, please," Tig said gently.

Lucy said, "I'm not saying I don't have problems. I'm addicted to my own loneliness, for one thing." Lucy straightened her shoulders and glanced around as if it were someone else who had confessed to having no friends; someone who, in a moment of introspection, had shared that fact with these strangers. She itched to leave before more incriminating information sprang from her lips.

Then, as if reading her mind, Sara said, "This isn't a friendship club."

"Sara Lynn, you will hold your tongue and let our guest speak," said Ron.

"She's not one of us. She said so herself." Sara slammed her chair against the wall and swooped toward the exit. "I don't need this. I'm out of here."

Before the door slammed, Tig was able to say, "Come back tomorrow, Sara Lynn, but with a better attitude." To Lucy, she added, "She is working on her anger, and it gets the best of her at times, but that shouldn't stop you. Go on."

Lucy slid her chair from the table and stood. "This isn't going to work."

"As you wish." Ron nodded. "But remember: Sometimes lonely is as lonely does."

Claire touched Lucy's arm. "Stay. This is partly why our group is so small. We're fringy with manners and protocol, but we're sincere."

"I rarely drink," Lucy said, shouldering her purse. "It's not like I'm above it, believe me." Surprising herself again she said, "I probably don't have the guts for it. Tig knows."

Kimmy looked at her with a peaceful expression. "We all have something a little different to deal with. Maybe we have what you need. Maybe not. But you won't know unless you sit it out."

"Not today. I just can't." Lucy shoved out of the room in the same way that the tortured Sara had done, filled with stubborn resolve. Unlocking her car door, she sat down heavily in the driver's seat. "So that sucked," she said, and Little Dog snorted.

Later that night, Charles spooned white rice onto his plate and said, "You have to go back." Ever since he'd found Lucy sleeping on the floor in a flutter of chocolate wrappers, he had made it his habit either to bring or make dinner for Lucy.

"Nope. I'm going back to my therapist and coming up with a different plan. She'll help. She saw how bad it was."

"What were the people like? I always imagine an AA meeting populated by greasy-haired, shaky people with diet Cokes and cigarettes."

"No, it was nothing like that. It wasn't very big. But the group was pretty eclectic. No different from the mix you see in the grocery store or when getting your oil changed."

"What'd they talk about?"

"I'm not supposed to tell you. It's Alcoholics *Anonymous*. What goes on in the Maplewood Serenity Center stays at the Maplewood Serenity Center."

"C'mon, Luce. You can tell me. Did you forget you were the first person I told when I came out?"

"You used that last month when I wouldn't give you my recipe for chili. Besides, I didn't stay very long." Lucy pulled a folded paper out of the pocket of her jeans and handed it to her brother. "The twelve steps of Alcoholics Anonymous. Look at number three. We're supposed to turn our will and lives over to God. Apparently if we do that, he'll fix things." Lucy stood quickly, and her fork flipped like a catapult, sending a piece of white rice flying onto Charles's hand. "I'm not interested in letting anyone else drive in my life. What if everybody crashes and dies again? I'm already pissed at God for that."

Charles stood and hugged his sister. "I guess I can't argue with that. But can't you kind of modulate the message for your purposes? Maybe it's not about God per se. Can you engage with a higher power that isn't quite so parental and bossy?"

"God *is* bossy! It's always push, push, push with him."

"Right; so pick an entity that feels more supportive. Remember 'Come as Your Favorite Saint Day' at school?"

"That was so weird, wasn't it? Who has a favorite saint in third grade? Everyone wore their bath robe as a costume."

"Lyra Giese wore her mother's pink shorty robe and high-heeled slippers. Maybe God isn't your go-to guy in this situation. Maybe you should pick a saint. Ask for help."

"So when they're praying in the AA meetings I should envision Sister Hilaria?"

"Maybe Joan of Arc. She's feisty." Charles tilted his head and examined his sister. "Should I come to a meeting with you? Grease the wheels?"

Lucy looked at her brother and touched his prominent chin, remembering how often he had stuck it out for her. "I love you, Charles. But this is just another time where you can't do anything to help."

The worst thing for Lucy about her counseling appointments with Tig Monohan was getting into the building. Even after passing through the gauntlet of Reception, successfully dodging volunteers, nurses, and lab assistants, Lucy kept her coat buttoned and her keys in hand, in case fleeing might become suddenly necessary. Choosing a seat by the door, she idly flipped through a *National Geographic* magazine with its smorgasbord of rainforest extinction, general atmospheric warming, and reports of worm shortages in Maine. Once again her anxiety took the stairs two at a time as she waited to be called so she could talk about her shortcomings. She'd spent her whole careful life watching where she stepped, staying out of the fray, and now, this one time, she allowed her impulses free reign, and everywhere she looked, the cosmos seemed to be shouting, *Explain yourself.*

When her name was called she carried the magazine with her into Tig's office.

"Did you leave this particular issue in the waiting room for me?"

"Nice to see you, Lucy," Tig said with a warm smile.

"Seriously, are you trying to teach me some kind of lesson?"

Tig tilted her head and narrowed her eyes. "I'm not following."

Lucy dropped the magazine on Tig's desk and pointed to the photo essay of an African tribe. "This picture here. The little boy with the shoe."

Clad only in a pair of faded shorts held onto his slender hips with a piece of twine, the boy wore one slip-on tennis shoe, the kind surfer dudes wear after a day of catching waves. "Cause I get it. I steal unnecessary stuff while this little guy doesn't even have a shoe for his right foot."

Tig raised an eyebrow. "You think I planted that particular photo essay for you?"

"What am I supposed to do with that image? It's not like I can erase it later with the Uninstall button, the way I do when I'm cleaning up my hard drive. From now on, I have to live with that image, and the possibility of it popping up while brushing my teeth or having a conversation with the guy at the Jiffy Lube."

Tig said, "It sounds like your anxiety is particularly high today. Talk to me about this, Lucy."

Lucy flipped the magazine to a full-page color photo of a grouping of women. "Here's another," she said, as if the lesson-to-learn was inscribed on the page.

The women were all topless, and all standing together, like deer, seemingly unaware of their feral exquisiteness. Their luminescent skin shone without benefit of Clinique's new line of moisturizers or the latest in skin toners. Calm and collected, they gazed serenely at the camera, their quiet attitude made more impressive by their uncovered breasts.

"What are you showing me here, Lucy?"

"Look how beautiful. The only time in my life when I could be *that* composed, nude, and in front of a camera would be in a dream."

Tig gazed at the picture.

"Yeah, and even then my body anxiety would win out and I'd grab a dream bush."

Lucy wasn't finished. "Check out those breasts. In plastics, we say that the *perfect* breast measurement is twenty-two centimeters from sternal notch to nipple. This woman's breasts are easily a glorious forty centimeters from origin to destination with not a trace of anxiety in her eyes, not a date circled in her appointment book for a surgical consultation. No dreams for a perkier twin set. Her culture loves her long, beagle-eared breasts. She's probably the pin-up girl of the tribe. If, say, she had small Hershey's Kisses for breasts, she would cover them in shame and pray at night for breasts that droop toward her middle, hoping against hope that one day she would be able to tuck them into her waistband for the harvest and feed the tribe during breaks."

"What are we talking about, Lucy?"

Lucy dumped herself into a chair. "Maybe my shopping/stealing thing is just my biological drive to hunt and gather, but made crazy by a culture that forces a narrow range for beauty. If loveliness in our society was a saggy ass and shitty hair, I could stay home with my gold medal and stay away from the temptation of free shopping."

"So you're thinking IV bags are the key to beauty?"

"Look, I'm just offering some kind of insight. Isn't that what I'm supposed to do here?"

"Maybe we should talk about why you left the AA meeting."

"You saw me there. I don't fit. And, besides, I don't get alcoholism. First it's a disease, and then it's something we give to our higher power." Lucy emphasized *higher power* like it was a ridiculous notion, made up by children wielding crayons, or well-meaning hippies. "If you have diabetes, you take your insulin, not pray for Jesus. If you drink too much, you should stop drinking so much."

"And if you steal too much, you should stop stealing so much."

"Whatever. Stealing doesn't wreck my liver and ruin my ability to work."

Tig shot Lucy an incredulous look. But Lucy waved her

expression away as if she were returning a serve at the tennis courts. "I *can* work; my hands are steady and my thinking is clear. It's just my decision-making *after* work that's a little sticky."

"Sticky?"

"I'm just saying AA isn't the right place for me. The people at the meeting said as much: that I need to find some place more appropriate for my needs."

"I'm not going to fight with you. I'm happy to listen, try to solve problems, identify issues, and work through them—but I'm not going to fight you."

Lucy seemed to deflate a bit, having been puffed up and ready for the debate. She had fought her way through medical school. She had fought hierarchy and sexism. She had fought disease and illness every single day of her life as a doctor. Her life was all about putting up her dukes. Take that strategy away and what was she left with?

Tig said, "I talked to Stan. It would go a long way to mending your relationship with him if you'd return some of what you took."

Lucy stood. "I offered to bring it all back! He scoffed at me."

"He's less angry now. More willing to listen."

In her mind, Lucy saw herself unlock her old bedroom door, push into the dusty room, and breathe in the scent of what was once her and her husband's refuge. Her chest tightened. She pictured herself filling boxes with all the pilfered supplies and hauling them out of her house.

Tig took in Lucy's pallor. "Lucy?"

"I have every last syringe, every last chux pad. It's all in my bedroom." She considered explaining the details to Tig, but what exactly would she say? "My marriage bedroom is a shrine to my husband except when it's a storeroom for red-hot hospital merchandise"? Would she tell Tig that she only opened the door to the room when she has to make a deposit? That she slept in the home office that was supposed to have been the nursery for her unborn child?

Tig saw Lucy's discomfort and offered, "Do what you can, Lucy, and before long you'll do what you need. Then you'll be able to do what you want."

"Do what I want? I wonder what that will be. I *had* what I wanted." She sighed. "Okay, I'll try. But I'm keeping an IV bag in case I go to Africa someday for a charitable boob-job junket. Don't try to stop me."

"Come back to the meetings, or find another job, Lucy."

Lucy stood and paced the room. At the large picture window she tapped her fingers on the glass.

"Okay, I'm going to pound the twenty meetings out, pack that crap up, and get you to sign me back to work as soon as I possibly can."

Tig started to speak, stopped, and looked at Lucy. "Mourning is not something that you cram for like a med school exam. Changing behaviors and building relationships take time. You can't lasso mental health and punch it into submission."

Lucy checked her watch. "Are we finished? There's a

meeting in twenty minutes. I'm going to get a passport and a stamp and fill that sucker up, then I'm going to come back here and display my shiny new frame of mind and get back to fixing other people's problems the way it should be done: with anesthesia, a scalpel, and a Band-Aid."

12

You're Ugly and Your Mother Dresses You Funny

Parked outside the Serenity Center, Lucy closed her eyes. She tried a relaxation technique she had learned in med school. She clasped her fists, took a deep breath in, held it, then released, shaking her hands out. Her heart pounded. She took another breath. Little Dog crawled across the console, placed her front paws on Lucy's shoulders, and licked her ear. Lucy scratched the dog's back and was rewarded with a face sniff and a sneeze. A knock on her closed window startled her, and she turned to see Claire Weezner waving. "Why, hello again."

Lucy rolled her window down. A thought raced into her head. *This woman thinks I have ruined my life by drinking.*

"I know that look. I've seen it many times. It's so weird being out in the world and knowing." She widened her eyes dramatically. "I promise not to breathe a word. That's the

AA credo, honey. A-n-o-n-y-m-o-u-s." She whisper-spelled it. Lucy opened her mouth to protest and Claire winked. "Aw, honey. I couldn't care less that you know I'm a lush. Love that word. Makes me feel a little sexy. You know, like I'm all about excess and pleasure." Claire reached through the window to pet Little Dog and said, "Of course, waking up in your own vomit is not very pleasurable, so I try not to do that anymore."

Claire smoothed her pink jogging suit and said, "C'mon. Lock up. Time to go inside." She took a step back and said with her kind, soft southern voice that reminded Lucy of wind chimes, "Sweetie, I don't know what ails ya but this place here, it's got a kind of healing mojo."

As they approached the heavy doors of the Serenity Center, Mark Troutman stuck his head out. "Claire. We're waiting for you."

Lucy frowned. "What are you doing here?"

"Same as you, I imagine."

"Don't you ever work?"

"P.M. shift. Sometimes nights. Leaves my days free to stalk AA meetings, Egypt."

Claire looked from Lucy to Mark. "What name did you call her?"

Mark smiled. "Inside joke."

"Not a very funny one," said Lucy.

"Well, butter my butt and call me a biscuit. How the hell do you two know each other?"

Lucy said, "It's complicated."

"I bet it is, sweetie. It always is with Mark. He's tasty-looking, though, don't you think?" Claire lifted her reading glasses from a colorful beaded cord around her neck and examined Mark lasciviously. "I'd go for this kind of thing, if I went for that kind of thing. Manly angst." She licked her lips.

"Oh, for Christ's sake, Claire." Mark's neck colored.

Lucy paused at the room entrance. She spotted Ron right away, sitting in his wheelchair, chatting with an elderly woman chewing a toothpick. There were others she hadn't seen that first day. A thirtysomething man in a business suit and an Asian man in a red-and-white-plaid shirt that screamed "picnic" rather than "addict meeting." Kimmy, the soft woman wearing dated clothes, waved Lucy over, patting the gray metal folding chair next to her, and whispered, "Tig called to say she won't be coming today, and the five thirty P.M. meeting had to be cancelled. We have visitors." Turning to her right, she said, "But you know Sara, right?" The angry teen from the last meeting rolled her eyes and said to Ron, "Let's go."

After the initial welcomes and readings Ron said, "Experience, strength, and hope. Anyone have anything to say on these topics?" The businessman consulted his watch. Lucy glanced at Mark, who looked away. The elderly woman cleared her throat and said, "Used to be able to smoke in these meetings. Gave people something to do. I don't have much to say about strength and hope, but I got lots of experience. More than enough for one person." She flipped the toothpick to the other side of her mouth and fixed the collar on her faux denim shirt. There was a daisy appliqué on the collar. "I don't know why I come to these meetings. They don't do me no good. Been drinking since my teens. No hope for me now. Breaks up my day though, these meetings. I like that."

"Well, that was cheerful," said Sara.

"Sara," Ron said in controlled admonishment. "We do not offer commentary. We offer support and hope. If you cannot abide by this rule I will ask you to leave today and come back tomorrow."

Claire spoke up. "Leave her alone, Ron, she's just a girl."

Sara slumped in her seat and glared at the table.

Kimmy put down her knitting. "I had to learn that strength can be about doing something but also about doing a little less. Every night my father falls out of bed after drinking himself into a stupor. Every night I haul his butt back into bed. Hate the behavior, not the drunk, right? Last night he fell out of bed and I walked into the room, gave him a pillow, and went back to bed."

"When you move out, you won't even have to toss a pillow his way," said Claire.

Kimmy picked up her knitting. "And when you quit butting into people's testimony, Claire, you'll give us all hope."

The Asian man spoke up. "Why isn't there an Al-Anon group during the week?"

"More drunks than non-drunks, I guess," said Claire.

Mark glanced at Lucy, raised a knowing eyebrow, and gestured for her to take the floor.

Lucy said, "I'd rather just listen if you don't mind. There are things I don't feel like sharing."

"You're only as sick as your secrets," Sara said while searching for split ends in her jet-black hair.

"Lucy, you don't have to say a thing. Just soak up the support, baby," said Claire.

Twenty minutes later, Lucy jiggled her foot. As soon as the clock hit the hour she slipped her purse onto her shoulder and fled. At the door of her car, Mark caught up.

"There's always an informal social time after the meeting, you know. That's when you get the real stories. Like, apparently Ron was a Marine."

"I don't want anyone knowing my story."

"That, my high school friend, is abundantly clear."

"Alcoholism at least has the status of a disease. Like there's some kind of brain-chemistry hook. But stealing stuff is just greed. Or arrogance."

"I don't think that's totally true. There's brain chemistry involved in stimulating people's reward centers, and from what I've read, stealing can be as intoxicating as drinking alcohol."

Lucy started to say something, but stopped. "Did you have to learn about that as a cop?"

"Uh, no. Wikipedia."

"You Wiki'd my issue?" Warped as it was, Lucy was momentarily touched. She pictured this man—who was probably more comfortable with driving or woodworking—with his computer open, typing. She considered the reason for his interest, then cracked open her car door, intending to leave, but said instead, "So Kimmy lives with her dad."

"Yeah, she's got some effed-up sense of loyalty to the guy."

"She talks about it in the meeting? In front of all you strangers?"

"That's how you turn strangers into friends, Lucy. I'm not a joiner, but if I'm gonna join any group it's gonna be a group with problems."

Lucy swung her car door wide just as a small spotted stray cat darted across the parking lot. Little Dog barked and dove from the front seat. "No! She's a runner. She doesn't always come when you call her."

Mark sprinted after Little Dog. The cat skittered up a tree, leaving Little Dog at its base, and Mark stomped on the red leash still attached to the dog's collar. As he reached Little Dog, the cat leaped from the tree, landing on Mark's shoulder for a split second, then darted off and into the brush. Little Dog went wild while Mark grasped the leash with one hand and his eye with the other.

"Hang on to her! Do you have her?" Lucy grabbed Little Dog by the collar and scolded her. "Since when do you do that? Run off without warning, chase a cat. What were you thinking?"

Mark dropped the leash and put both hands up over his eye. "Shit."

"What happened?"

With his jaw clenched he put one hand out. His lips were white. "Judas Priest. Can you just not talk for a second?" He tried to open his eye but only succeeded in causing it to tear up in earnest. He moved over to his beat-up pickup. "That cat hit my eye."

"Let me look. I'm a doctor."

"I know," he said in measured tones. "I know it. But I cannot remove my hand right now." Lucy put Little Dog in her car. The gravel crunched under her shoes as she made her way back to Mark.

"Just let me see. *Quickly.* In about five minutes, this lot is going to be filled with co-dependent do-gooders."

"I'm going to drive myself to the eye doctor."

"I'll take you."

"Lucy. Respectfully. No."

He opened his car door and sat. Wiped his eyes. Lucy watched while he fumbled, putting his keys into the ignition, then tried to shift. Lucy said, "Oh good God. Stop with the manly act and get into my car."

The door to the Serenity Center opened and the man in the suit walked out, checking his BlackBerry and moving with the full importance of someone who believes his work keeps the world spinning. Mark slammed the door to his truck.

Fifteen minutes later, Lucy paced in the waiting room at South Central Wisconsin Optics. When Mark emerged an hour later with a patch on his eye, she frowned and said, "I'm so sorry."

"Scratched my cornea. Have to take a few days off. Hurts like a son of a bitch."

"I'll take you home. We can get your truck later."

In Lucy's Subaru, Mark rested his elbow on the armrest, keeping his palm over his injured eye. Little Dog snuffled into his lap, burrowing her head into the crux of his elbow. With his free hand he scratched behind her ears.

"Dogs," Lucy said. "They're the only beings that can cause you nothing but trouble and then get you to give them a backrub."

"Dogs and women."

"I wouldn't know about that, I guess."

"Sadly, that was a joke, not a history report."

"So do you have a dog? A German shepherd named Sidekick?"

"Dave."

"Your sidekick's name is Dave?"

"My pug. His name was Dave. He was old. I got him in the divorce. He really liked me. Couldn't ever think of replacing him. You probably think that's stupid."

"Not stupid. I only just started with Little Dog. She's a stray. The posters I made to find her owner have been sitting in my car for the past two weeks. I've no intention of putting them up. If her owner didn't think enough of her to get a collar, he doesn't deserve her." She touched Little Dog's tail. "Already, I can't imagine what I'd do if something happened to her."

Mark nodded, looking at Lucy, and said without a trace of self-consciousness, "Happens fast, sometimes."

And Lucy, as usual, missed the entire moment.

On her own after Mark closed the door to her car and climbed into his truck, Lucy was left to puzzle out what he'd said as he left the vehicle.

Thanks. I don't usually let people help me.

Her doctor-self smiled, having heard these words before. *You're different than other people, Egypt.*

When Lucy thought about herself, she saw what she thought others saw: someone who didn't stand out unless you had her résumé in hand. In truth, she had cultivated that perception. She loathed superficial judgments and was uncomfortable with overly friendly people looking to share. She liked books, facts, and science, finding they rarely let her down. She had almost no hobbies, few friends, and a sense of humor that could be seen as rude but functioned mainly to thwart interactions that might turn uncomfortable. When it came down to it, she wondered if Mark found her as irritating as she found herself. Lucy was pretty sick of herself lately. She had too much time on her hands.

From the passenger seat, Little Dog looked over at her expectantly, reminding her of the one noisy and impatient box of stolen supplies that she had managed to pack, crowing from the backseat like a redneck comic. *Let's get 'er done!* She dialed Charles, and when his voice mail picked up, she left a message.

"Your job is getting in the way of my therapy. I have man translation needs, for one thing. And I could also use some help boxing up the . . . stuff . . . the supplies. . . . okay, the loot. Whatever." She hung up, then scrolled through her address book.

"Who else can I call?" She bit the inside of her cheek and silently scrolled through her phone list. Charles, Clinic,

Dentist, Dermatology, Domino's Pizza, Hair Affair, Laser Solutions, Massage and Wax World, Pizza Hut, Pizza Pit, Richard. She paused. Closed her eyes, let herself feel the density of longing in her throat. She dialed her late husband's phone number and thought about the bill she kept paying, just to keep his recorded voice a cell tower away.

"This is Richard Lubers. Leave a message."

There was a digital beep and Lucy said, "Come back."

She was scrolling through the rest of her phone list: Phong, Charles, Wells Fargo, Sidney, Starbucks . . . Sidney. Lucy thought for a second, then pressed Call.

When Sidney answered, Lucy said, "I have three pizza restaurants and three hair removal salons in my phone. And you."

"Better than porn lines and the Home Shopping Network."

"That is splitting hairs, I'm afraid." She took a breath. "Listen, I know we don't know each other all that well— almost certainly not well enough for me to ask this. But can you come to my house and help me box up some stuff?"

Sidney paused. "I'd be honored. I had a terrible time packing up my ex-husband's things, and it was just a divorce. I can't imagine how hard it must be to pack up your husband's things. But good for you. It'll help you move forward."

"What? Oh, no. There will be no moving forward. I'm not talking about Richard's things. I'm talking about the stuff I . . . the hospital stuff. The stolen stuff."

"Oh, I gotcha. Whew. I was thinking, *Shit, this girl's getting too healthy for me.* But if you're talking about the crap you took—I'm all in for that. Pathology 'R Us is just a phone call away."

"Nothing of Richard's goes."

"Not a thing."

"No discussion."

"None from me."

"I'll make you a deal. You help me do this and I'll be your go-to gal when you need to go to the grocery store."

"I guess, but I've got no immediate plans to move forward, either."

"Sidney, seriously? Why do you go to Tig?"

"Why do you go? Listen, Lucy, you don't get 'no judgment' from me and then judge my addiction as worse than yours. If that's the deal, then it's no deal on my end."

"Wait!" A silent, sour lemon seemed to choke the line between them. "You're right. Of course."

"You got boxes? I can be there in thirty minutes."

"I'll be ready in fifteen."

13

The Marshmallow Study

Are you sure you want me here while you do this?" Sidney stood inside the door at Lucy's house holding two computer-paper boxes and Chubby Lumpkins's leash. She'd pulled her hair away from her face in a messy ponytail, and her clear blue eyes took center stage.

"Yes. I need you to keep me on track. Remind me of my purpose, and keep me company." Lucy reached for a box, brushing her hand against Sidney's. "Jeez, you're freezing."

"I'm always cold." She pulled the sleeves of her hoodie over her knuckles and yawned. "And tired."

Lucy led Sidney to her old bedroom. "Tig says it's time to give the stuff back."

Sidney shrugged. "So okay. How much could there be? Let's do it."

"Brace yourself." Lucy shooed Mrs. Bobo away from the door while Sidney repositioned her grip on the box, ready to get this therapy session moving forward.

"Don't judge." Lucy unlocked the padlock, slid the lock, and pushed the door open.

"Holy shit," Sidney said.

Lucy remembered reading about an alcoholic who had returned home after treatment as an inpatient. He'd stepped into his old apartment and seen for the first time the extent of his disease. Empty liquor bottles had littered every surface: floors, tables, and countertops. There'd been so many that there was little place to step or sit without being assaulted by the smell and clank of empty glass bottles. Today Lucy saw what Sidney saw: a bona fide hospital supply closet that had seemingly been tipped on its side and scrambled like balls in a bingo wheel. Blue packaged items, flung far and wide, occupied most flat spaces in the room. A larger grouping by the door looked as if they were waiting in line to escape and be put to good use.

"So we'll need more boxes then," said Sidney.

Lucy worked hard to focus on just the things she'd taken from the hospital, and not to make eye contact with the memories in this room. She had to shut down her sense of smell and focus on the task at hand. Occasionally a waft of Richard would get past her defenses and she would abruptly stop gathering rolls of tape and remember his laugh.

"You're no match for my catlike reflexes, Lucy Peterman," he'd say just before tackling her and tossing her onto the bed. She'd attempt to roll out from under him, putting up the weakest of resistance.

"Yeah," she'd said with a sarcastic smile, "you're a real ninja." Then they'd make love.

Today Lucy looked up at the ceiling, searching for the patch of plaster with a tiny moisture stain in the shape of Africa. An overwhelming feeling of loss rushed into her chest and she leaned against a bookcase. Richard's old Army sweatshirt lay tossed onto the back of a chair she'd had since college. It was an ugly thing, filled with horsehair and hard angles.

He used to joke about that chair. "We have a whole museum of uncomfortable furniture in this room. Can we at least get rid of this chair?"

"No, Richard. It reminds me of when I was a poor med student. It's good karma to remember where you came from."

He'd acquiesce like he always did, a bit begrudgingly but ultimately with humor. "It looks like we're opening a branch of Goodwill."

Now Lucy rubbed the sleeve of the sweatshirt against her cheek. Sidney knelt to check under the bed and said, "C'mon, let's get this done so we can take a nap. I've been up for like three hours." She lay her head on the floor and lifted the dust ruffle. "Hey, what's this?" She slid a gift-wrapped box out from under the bed. It was rectangular, covered with a black and white fleur-de-lis wrapping, and tied with a deep-red bow.

Lucy looked at the box and caught her breath. "Oh." She clutched the sweatshirt to her chest.

Sidney touched the gift card where Lucy's name was written in black ballpoint pen. "It's for you."

Lucy stumbled over an IV bag to get to the gift; she fingered the beautiful paper, the thickly tied bow. "My birthday was a few days after the accident. I haven't been back in here except to toss stuff into the room and grab a few necessities." Lucy ran her fingers over her name, her husband's handwriting, a fusion of print and cursive—a lover she hadn't seen for a long time.

"Open it!" Sidney said, eyes wide.

Lucy shook her head, closed her eyes. "I don't think I can right now. It's too much. All this." She gestured around the room. "Now this, too." Hugging the box, she felt her throat close and she began to cry: the silent, adult cry that women cultivate in the marriage bed after a fight, or when stuck somewhere where crying is considered an admission of defeat.

For a few moments neither woman spoke. Sidney reached to give Lucy an awkward head-hug. Chubby yawned, dropping his tongue like an anchor.

Lucy said, "You must have gotten a little sun yesterday. Your freckles are showing."

Sidney touched her nose. "Bane of my existence."

"They're charming."

"They make me look like I'm twelve."

Lucy touched her own hair, stood and tugged at the waist of her jeans. "Can I ask you a question?"

Sidney nodded.

"What's it like to look like you do? You know, sort of effortlessly beautiful."

"Effortlessly beautiful? You've got to be kidding me."

"Not at all."

Sidney's hands fluttered to her face; skeletal butterflies, knobby and webbed. "Have you seen this nose? My hair's so thin . . . and don't get me started on my quicksand abs."

"God, what must you think of me?"

"You! With that to-die-for thick, curly red hair and your perfect skin? Besides, this isn't a competition."

"That's for sure. I'm not even in your division."

Sidney said, "Oh, I get it now. I'm your first eating-disordered friend." She chuckled a little mirthless laugh. "You don't get it. We only hate ourselves."

Lucy opened her mouth to speak but Sidney put her hand up. "Everything good about you, you get to keep. I only use it to highlight my own inadequacies. My counselor says I self-loathe to give myself something to do when I should be eating."

Lucy stroked the gift box. "Richard thought I was beautiful. I never did all that well with men," she snorted. "Obviously."

"Men are overrated. Besides, I didn't earn my appearance like you earned your degree."

"I just have a great memory for facts," Lucy said.

"And I just have culturally acceptable cheekbones that

my mother passed on to me, along with her fear of failure, perfectionistic tendencies, and pathologic fear of adipose tissue. Fucking lucky me."

"Richard was my chance at love. This gift is like the governor's call before the execution," said Lucy.

"I get that. Take your time." Sidney brushed her hands on her pants. "Let's leave this for today." She led Lucy out of the musty room, walked her into the kitchen, poured her a glass of water. "Tig gave me an assignment, too. I'm supposed to cook for a friend and actually eat what I prepare." She locked eyes with Lucy and said, "You're my friend. I could maybe do that with you." Chubby let out an exhausted whine that sounded a lot like, *Oh for God's sake, eat already.* Sidney put her hands on her bony hips and stretched back. "I'm working on packing my shit up into a box, too, but it's just a lot more shit, and a lot smaller box."

Lucy waved as Sidney and Chubby Lumpkins began their walk to the other side of town, having refused her repeated offers to drive them. Hugging Richard's gift to her chest, she returned to the bedroom she'd shared with him, the bedroom she'd abandoned almost a year earlier. Its noisy silence bombarded her: Richard's cologne bottle waving to be picked up; his coin jar asking to be upended, its contents spent; a brand-new baby rattle bought before the accident, making it superfluous. She stepped inside just far enough to snatch the box Sidney had filled. Hoisting it onto her hip, she stepped into the hall, breathing hard, as if she'd run a great distance from a frightening animal.

With both the carton of supplies and the wrapped gift in tow, she marched to her car. She shoved the supplies into the backseat, dropping the gift and tearing a corner of the wrapping paper. She gasped, retrieved the gift, and rushed back inside. Sucking her bottom lip, she lifted the torn wrapping and, like a peeping tom, both excited and afraid, peered past it. Then she snatched her hand away and put the gift down.

"Luce!" Her brother's face appeared at her door. Butting his head into the screen, he called again, "Luce, I have my toothbrush, and I brought plenty of big boxes. Phong is gone, we can pack all night."

"You're too late. I've already started, fallen apart, given up, and moved to the maudlin-recluse part of the evening's program." Lucy held up the gift, wagging it a little.

"And that is . . . ?"

"It's my months-ago birthday present from Richard. It was under the bed."

Charles's eyes widened. "Open it, Luce. What are you waiting for?"

"Something . . . I don't know. If I open it, it's over. My last conversation, so to speak, with Richard, will be over. I didn't know this existed, and now that I do, I don't want it to go away."

Lucy thought about the marshmallow study. A well-known experiment in delayed gratification, it was conducted by researchers at Stanford in the late 1960s. A series of children were placed individually in a room with a marshmallow. They were told that if they waited to eat the marshmallow instead of devouring it right away, they would get a second marshmallow.

Delayed gratification. Lucy had invented delayed gratification.

Charles sang a thready tune. "An-tic-i-pa-tion," he crooned.

"Carly Simon knew all about it. If I open this, Richard will be gone."

Charles touched his forehead to his sister's temple. "Luce," he said softly, "he's already gone."

She sighed. "He's ruined me for other shoes." Charles pulled his head back, squinting at her in puzzlement. "He was like the best pair of shoes I ever tried on: perfect color, no pinch, in my size, and on sale. I had him just long enough to imprint his soul onto mine. Now nothing in my life fits."

He nudged the box. "You think he gave you shoes?"

Lucy sighed. "The thing is, no matter what's in here, it's going to be a disappointment."

"It depends on what you're expecting. If you think Richard is in there, then, yes, you will be disappointed. But if your heart is set on slippers, this could be a dream-come-true day." Charles cleared his throat and walked to the kitchen. "I'm going to get a glass of water and then we can decide what to do: open the mystery gift, pack hospital supplies, or exorcise your bedroom."

"Those are the worst multiple-choice options ever! That's like saying, 'Today is your day: You can get a root canal, eat dirt, or drink colonoscopy prep, you choose!'"

"This is therapy, right? Returning the stolen hospital supplies? Mental health isn't a giveaway. When you're a nutcase, you've got to work for your sanity."

Lucy shook her head. "You're secretly loving this, aren't you? All those years when you were crushing on your GI Joe, and trying to get team manager positions so that you could hang out in the guys' locker room, you were just waiting for me to screw up."

"I knew you had it in you." Charles swallowed the last of his water and glanced at the telephone. "You have messages. You want to get them?"

"I do? Yeah, whatever."

Charles punched the button on Lucy's answering machine and Claire's southern sweet-tea drawl filled the room. "Good seeing you today. We're meeting again tomorrow at eight A.M. It's AA new-member day. I'm bringing donuts with sprinkles, and I just know someone will volunteer to bring the coffee. You need a pickup?"

Charles shot a glance at his sister. "New-member day?"

The machine beeped again. "Hi, Egypt." The man cleared his voice and said, "Yeah, this is Mark. Since I have to take a few sick days for my eye . . ." He took a deep breath and said, "I'm going to the pound tomorrow. Need a dog. Call if you want to come." The connection remained intact, as if he were going to say more, or was hoping for an automated reply. He cleared his voice again and hung up. The machine beeped a final time and they heard Mark's voice again. He rattled off his telephone number. "Ironically enough, it's an acronym for GAS HOLE," he added.

"That's two invitations for my sister the hermit crab. Way to go, Luce. And here I was thinking about maybe pushing you onto an online dating site or enrolling you into a scrapbooking week at Memories Made with Scissors, just to get you out of the house. But here you're doing it all by yourself."

Lucy lifted her chin. "I'm a very busy surgeon. People need boobs; I don't have time for scrapbooking."

"You know what I love?" Charles asked her. "I love that Little Dog is your pimp. If this dog hadn't shown up, you'd be eating Ramen noodles and watching old *Friends* reruns. I can't remember when you've had a message that wasn't from the cable hookup guy or the dentist. So are you going?"

"To AA? Sure. Didn't you hear? There will be donuts."

"I'm more interested in Gas Hole."

"You're always more interested in the guy. Maybe. No. I doubt it."

"Listen, Luce, a little relationship advice from me to you. After you help him find a dog, don't bring him back to open that box."

"He's not interested in me that way, Chuckles."

"I'm just telling you. That would be a real buzzkill."

Lucy nodded. "Gee, thanks for the heads-up," she said with mock gratitude. "I'd never want to kill a man's buzz."

After dinner and a Netflix movie, Charles woke, stiff from falling asleep in the leather recliner, Mrs. Bobo snoring in the crux of his arm. He gazed at his sister, stretched out under the big picture window on the overstuffed couch. Years of sunscreen protection, moisturizer, and scrupulous skin care had left Lucy's skin remarkably unlined. Her wild curls framed her face and in the golden light of the street lamp she looked like a softer, prettier version of her younger self. Charles removed her glasses, pulled an extraordinarily soft afghan up to her shoulders, and tried as gently as he could to lift Richard's newly found birthday gift off her chest. Lucy grumbled and dropped her arm across the florid bow, and Charles pulled his arm back. He rubbed his eyes and gazed at his usually insomniac sister, until she rolled onto her side, repositioning the gift in her sleep.

14

A Watch Goose

As she stood at the living room window, Lucy buttoned her navy pea coat and fiddled with her keys. She watched as the family from across the street piled into their car, the old Dr. Seuss rhyme in her mind. *Father, mother, sister, brother, this one is my other brother.*

The boys juggled into the van, bouncing past each other, the girl ignoring their attempts to pull her into the fun. They jiggled and settled into their preassigned seats like eggs in their carton. The father loaded backpacks, lunch boxes, and a briefcase into an open hatch back, then got into the driver's seat. The mother helped buckle the little boy into his car seat and adjusted the buttons on his coat. She pushed his hair out of his eyes and leaned in for a kiss. Then she stepped aside as the vehicle backed out of the driveway. Lucy, from an opposite vantage point, watched as the carload of kids moved down their street. The mother blinked into the sun, and before returning to her house, she caught sight of Lucy watching her. Startled, Lucy waved, first with uncertainty, then with more conviction. The mother raised her hand with less enthusiasm. Maybe she was unnerved to be seen tending to her family by one so obviously single and unencumbered by children. Or maybe she was judging. Lucy couldn't tell. As the woman pulled the collar of her jacket close, Lucy turned from the window.

"Hey, sunshine. Whatcha doin' up so early?" Charles shuffled into the living room with his hair mussed and his brown horn-rimmed glasses askew, clothed in boxers and a white V-neck T-shirt.

"I'm going to AA. Then I'm going to walk Little Dog."

"You look kinda perky."

"I feel a little perky." She grabbed her keys, Richard's gift, and Little Dog's leash, and headed for the door.

Charles caught the screen before it slammed shut. "Cool," he said. "But, Luce?"

"Don't say anything negative. I feel good, and I don't need your snarky little-brother humor to give me any reason to slow down."

"You gonna attach that leash to your box there, or consider taking Little Dog with you?"

Little Dog sat at Charles's feet, looking quizzical, her head tilted, her nose quivering in overdrive.

"Oh! Of course! C'mere, girl." Little Dog sprinted down the steps and into the front seat, where she looked gratefully back at Charles. Lucy positioned the seat belt around the dog and said, "You'll get used to it. It's for your own good." Out the window she said to her brother, "Thanks. Have a good day at work."

The gray day soothed the colors in the trees, which were hungover from a summer of partying. Lucy pulled to the shoulder of the road as the first drops of rain hit her windshield, thinking that maybe the gray day and AA might be too much for her tenuous good mood. Little Dog leaned in, responding to the car's abrupt change in direction, and Lucy glanced at Richard's gift, as if it were a reminder that AA should come first and she should stop making excuses. Lucy turned the car back around and headed toward Serenity Center.

"I'm indecisive," she said to Little Dog. "Aren't you glad you're buckled in?"

Another mile with only one more unplanned turnaround and Lucy pulled into the Serenity Center parking lot. Cracking the windows for Little Dog, she stepped into a spitting rain. Lucy noted Claire sitting in her car and watched as the woman dropped her head into her hands. Lucy knocked on Claire's window and Claire's pale, drawn face shifted as if a theater curtain had been drawn and snapped into place.

"You okay, Claire?"

"Well, of course, dear heart. Here, grab these donuts.

Every single one is pink, frosted with pink sprinkles. If Claire is buying, Claire gets to pick."

"You looked a little, I don't know, tired a minute ago."

"Fighting the good fight sucks you dry some days." Claire hauled herself out of the car, staggering a little. Lucy thought she spotted a copper-colored cane stuffed against the passenger-side door. "We better get inside. Ron has been a stickler lately for punctuality. Easy for him. He gets to ride everywhere."

Lucy lifted her hand to touch Claire's back but she stopped before making contact.

Inside, Tig, Ron, and Sara were already seated, heads turned inward, deep in conversation. Mark stood with his back to the group with his hands in the pockets of his jeans. Claire announced, "I brought the donuts. If there ain't any new members, can we eat a donut, skip the readings, talk about something important that will change my life, like a Macy's sale on Spanx, and go home?"

"You know the rules, Claire."

In an uncharacteristically weak tone Claire said, "Please, Tig?"

Sara rushed to Claire's side, shooting a glance at Tig. "Here, sit." She pushed a metal chair over to her. Claire fell into it gracelessly, and Lucy watched as Sara's usually sour countenance softened into girlish worry. "Can I get you some water?"

Claire took Sara's hand and said, "Honey, what I need is

you right by my side, eating a pink donut and telling me about your night last night."

Mark was wearing glasses over the patch on his eye. He turned to the group and frowned at Claire.

Sara said, "Last night was fine. Boring, mostly. Had to meet with my caseworker. The anniversary is coming up." She looked at Lucy. "What are you looking at?"

"Okay, Sara. You don't get to pick a fight because you're entering uncomfortable territory," said Tig.

"When's she gonna tell us her stuff?"

"Sara," Mark said, "it took you a month and a half to tell us your name."

"Screw you, Troutman. Just because I don't blab like a little girl, like you do." She laughed and for the first time to Lucy, she looked her real sixteen years instead of sixteen going on forty.

"Don't make me come over there."

With a black fingernail Sara flipped Mark off. Claire whispered to Lucy, "It's like watching *True Grit*, ain't it? They've been friends a long time, those two."

"That's interesting," said Lucy. "You wouldn't think they'd have much in common."

"Loneliness is the great communicator, my dear. Everybody speaks that language *and* understands it."

Lucy examined Mark from her quiet corner of the metal folding table. She pictured him alone, not drinking, no dog, no spouse. It was a familiar snapshot.

"He and Tig work hard to keep Sara out of the system. I know she stayed with him for a short time. She moved out when some dickhead from a meeting implied a biblical relationship between them. She gave the guy a black eye, was put on probation, then took her backpack and disappeared. She's only been back six months. She won't even talk about where she's staying."

Then Kimmy pushed through the door and silently sat in her usual spot. Taking out her knitting, she began working on a skein of yarn, examining each stitch before poking her needle into a loop. Claire glanced at Kimmy, did a kind of double-take, and said, "Kimmy?"

Kimmy didn't look up. "Claire."

"Is that a bruise on your chin, darlin'?"

"Dentist."

"Y'all went to the dentist after we had dinner last night?"

Kimmy brushed her hair forward. "Leave it."

Sara said, "What fucking good is this group if we can't help our own people?"

Kimmy looked over her reading glasses. "The meetings are good for me, Sara. They help me."

There was a beat of silence. Then Tig spoke up. "Lucy. You don't have to talk about anything difficult, but maybe you could tell us just a little something about you."

Lucy's heart jumped to attention and she immediately felt like the little girl in class who's called on to answer a question about a subject she knows nothing about. If there had been a tiger in the room, she'd have been ready. Her body was bathed in adrenaline, ready for fight or flight.

"I . . . I haven't prepared anything." Her eyes darted around. She looked at her hands and opened her mouth.

"She was the smartest girl in the school. Not the class, but the entire school."

The group turned their attention to Mark, who still stood by the window. "For homecoming she was in charge of making a poster. Lucy and I are both townies, you know. We went to high school together. We were around before they changed the mascot from the politically incorrect Warriors to the now ridiculous Hodags. So you know most posters were pretty straight. Go Warriors! Or Hilltown Warriors are Number One. But not Lucy's. She had this long ream of paper where she painted an Indian chief with a flowing mane of feathers and a spear poking a skirt-wearing gladiator in the butt. You know what the caption read? WE'RE GONNA POKE-A-UR-HAUNTUS. Get it, Pocahontas? Half the school didn't even get it! It was classic." He threw his head back, laughing at the memory.

Kimmy stopped knitting, Claire looked between Mark and Lucy, Ron stared, and Sara, unimpressed, said, "Dude. Seriously?"

Even Tig blinked, surprised by the view Mark had provided of the secretive Lucy.

That's when Lucy saw again the younger Mark of her high school days, keeping his head down, hiding his intellect quietly, appreciating a kindred square peg, while she secretly tutored the idiotic prom king, hoping he might say hello to her in the hall.

On her usual dart-out-the-door exit of Serenity Center, she'd suggested to Mark that they meet at the Humane Society the next day, after lunch. Hardly waiting for him to answer, she moved quickly into the parking lot. By now she had almost perfected her exit: keys in hand, then ignition, then reverse. Nonetheless, Tig had caught Lucy just in time to say, "Nobody's normal, Luce." And then, inexplicably, "AA is serious about no relationship for a year, and definitely not with someone from AA."

Lucy had looked at Tig with a blank expression for a beat too long. Tig said, "Mark."

Lucy widened her eyes. "Mark and Claire?"

"No, Lucy. You and Mark."

Lucy inadvertently covered Richard's gift with her hand as if it were a child listening to the cursing of adults instead of a gift-wrapped box sitting on the front seat of her car. Then she said, "Dr. Monohan, you could not be more off base."

It had been a full twenty-four hours since that last meeting and now Lucy waited, tapping her steering wheel while watching a group of dogs play in the side yard next to the South Central Wisconsin Humane Society. She checked her

watch and fiddled with the clasp, unlocking the silver link-
ing mechanism, locking it back, finally pinching the tender
flesh of her wrist after the fourth time. It was as if the watch
had slapped her and said, *Enough.*

Lucy didn't know if Mark worked, slept, or polished his
guns in the afternoon. She figured the less she knew, the
better. If he showed, fine. If not, she could breathe a sigh of
relief, pick up an application to volunteer at the shelter, and
report back to Charles. She tried to silence all the fussbud-
gets in her mind.

One thing she knew for sure, though. Waiting around by
herself for ten minutes in a parking lot was a whole lot better than riding with Mark and trying to make unscripted
conversation with him as they drove together to the humane
society. Twenty-five minutes of tongue-tied driving and
self-conscious stuttering would likely undo her. She'd probably steal his pine-tree air freshener and then have to do
hard time for it.

Lucy touched Richard's gift, riding shotgun next to her,
and fished out a CD from her glove box: *Speak Mandarin in
500 Words.* She shoved the CD into the player. A woman's
musical voice came loudly through the car speakers,
"Huānyíng."

"Huānyíng," she said aloud, matching the woman's volume.

There was a rap on the window and Lucy whipped her
head around. She opened the window and the voice said,
"Nǐjīntiān? How are you today?"

Mark stood smiling, his face unguarded, a little boy

expecting a puppy at the end of the day. "How do you say 'excited' in Chinese?" he asked.

Lucy shut the volume off on the CD and opened her car door. "You look like Christmas morning."

Mark gave her a bashful look. She'd read him too accurately. "Nah, I'm a hard-hitting cop. Takes a lot more than a dog to soften this hide."

"Okay, tough guy. Let's go pet some puppies."

Notices for classes of all kinds papered the glass doors of the Humane Society: TEACHING KIDS KINDNESS, BIG DOG AGILITY TRAINING, and one with large block letters that advertised placing old dogs with old dogs. Lucy stopped to read a handwritten notice on a page from a yellow legal pad. It was taped slightly askew, as if its author had been rushed—and maybe a little conflicted, too.

FIVE-YEAR-OLD MALE GOOSE, VERY GOOD WATCHDOG, NOT FRIENDLY, NOT GOOD WITH KIDS, NOT GOOD WITH ANYBODY. JUST A GOOD WATCHDOG (GOOSE). NEEDS A GOOD HOME IN THE COUNTRY. NEEDS TO GO SOON. FREE.

"Hey, this one looks like it's for you! You're kind of a watch goose yourself."

Mark read the note and turned to her in mock outrage. "How do you know I'm not good with kids? For your information, kids love cops. We're the good guys. I always do career days at the elementary school. Let them sit in the cruiser. Let them feel up my steering wheel with their sticky hands. Check their parents out in the system."

"You don't, not really."

He smiled at her. "Not the parent-check thing, okay, but the rest of it, yeah. I don't let them wear the hat anymore, though. Learned my lesson the hard way, combing my hair for nits."

"Ah, lice. The gateway STD. Show me a kid with lice, and I'll show you a future herpes sufferer."

Mark gave her a sidelong glance and Lucy added, "Nah, I'm kidding."

"Dr. Peterman, you're a few clicks off."

"You are speaking from a glass house."

Mark winked. "And you're just the rock to break it."

A tiny thrill ran up Lucy's spine.

A woman sat at the front desk. "May I help you?" she asked. A tiny puppy sat on her shoulder, its eyes closed in blissful sleep. The woman wore pink hospital scrubs and long, dangly earrings resembling fishing lures. Her eyelashes were thick with mascara and her yellow-blond hair looked like it had been styled that way since high school. Lucy wondered if she'd been homecoming queen. Her nametag read MARILYN.

Mark smiled. "We'd like to take a look at the adoptable dogs. Please."

"Very nice. We're a little shorthanded today, so we aren't giving any tours, but you can wander back in the kennel and visit our friends. We ask that you keep your fingers away from the cages, and if you have any thoughts of feeding the dogs, you leave that thought with me."

"No, ma'am. I wouldn't dream of feeding them." Mark gestured with his thumb over his shoulder at Lucy. "I can't vouch for her, though. She's always got something in her pockets."

Lucy shoved Mark. "Not true," she said. "I follow all dog rules."

Marilyn frowned. "This is serious. You can't feed them. These dogs are going through a tough time right now. Many of them have separation anxiety and post-traumatic stress syndrome. They haven't a clue where their next home will be. You feed them something you think is *no big deal*"—she emphasized her words with an outrageous expression, widening her eyes—"like a Slim Jim or a Vienna sausage, and we're cleaning up a shitstorm at two A.M."

Both Mark and Lucy blinked, assured Marilyn that neither of them had even the smallest of sausages between them, and walked into the doggie viewing area. "Shitstorm," Mark said. "Is that the clinical term, Dr. Peterman?"

"We call it a code brown at the hospital."

Past the front desk, Lucy peered into a room with a large picture window. Inside sat a worn, overstuffed couch with bites taken out of each foam-filled arm. A panel on the door read PRIVACY/SEPARATION ROOM. There was a chew toy tossed in the corner and a box of Kleenex perched on a small shelf. *Probably all kinds of tears being mopped up in that room*, thought Lucy. She felt Mark's eyes on her and met his gaze. He nudged her with his shoulder. "Don't go getting soft on me already. I need you to yay or nay my selection. I can't be going home with some basket case because you got all weepy looking at an empty room."

"Bring it on, pal; I'm tougher than I look." As she spoke, Mark pushed his way into the room that held the kennels, and her words were completely drowned out by barking dogs.

They passed the first kennel, empty except for a steel water bowl. The space, lined with cement block, was clean, spacious, and shut off from the viewing area by a chain link fence. The second kennel held a ginger scruff of a dog that resembled a loofah in Lucy's shower that she just hadn't gotten around to throwing away. The dog stood within an inch of the chain link and let out a series of ear-splitting yips. The index card clothes-pinned to the fence read, TRIXI, STRAY, NO TAGS, AWAITING HEALTH CLEARANCE.

Lucy pushed Mark forward to the next dog. "Keep moving."

The next kennel held a black Rottweiler with a head the size of a Volkswagen. He lay with his enormous cranium on flatbed paws, with his hind feet daintily canted to the side like a woman riding sidesaddle. After a moment Lucy noticed his other distinguishing characteristic. He had a penis and scrotum so large it looked like a wrinkly toddler nestled against his side.

Lucy cleared her throat and said, "This guy's for someone suffering from small-man syndrome."

Without taking his eyes from the dog, Mark said, "I'm here to tell you that we can move right along. I'm good." Lucy tore her eyes from the dog's package just as he gave her a trucker-in-a-stripper-bar grin and dropped his tongue in a yawn, as if to say, *You just say the word, baby.*

Lucy said, "I feel a little violated."

Mark laughed. "So do I."

The card on the next fence read, BELLA. RELINQUISHED IN HOME FORECLOSURE. NEUTERED, CLEARED, READY FOR ADOPTION. Inside stood a full-grown dog with a tennis ball in her mouth, holding it up as if waiting for her owner to come and play. Her tail was in full wag, her throat stretched and accommodating as if to say, *Here, let me get this.* She might have spent her lifetime posing this way, waiting for the loving approval of her owner. Lucy's breath caught.

"This one would drag you from a fire, call 911, and give you CPR until the ambulance came." She dropped her gaze and noticed a bandage on her dewclaw. "Oh, she's got an injury. What'd you do to your paw, Bella?" She glanced at Mark, started to speak, and then looked more closely at him. His eyes had a special brightness to them—a misting before a sun shower.

"So, I'll go tell Marilyn this is the one, huh?" Mark nodded. Lucy tugged at Mark's sleeve and said, "This one'll break your heart a hundred times before Sunday. If you like that kind of thing."

Mark smiled and said, "Turns out I do."

15

Stop, Drop, and Roll

In her Subaru, following behind Mark's car, Lucy reconsidered her impulsive acceptance of a sandwich and new-dog orientation at Mark's house. She'd been swept up in the love story of dog and man, his ease about the decision he'd made to take Bella. But it was too late now. She'd already agreed. As she stepped out of her car in front of his house, Mark said to her, "So you signed up to volunteer at the Humane Society."

"The days get kind of long when you're used to working. I'm thinking it will keep me out of trouble."

"Sublimation. A good strategy for a lot in life."

As they approached his Cape Cod, Lucy noted the brown-striped awnings that resembled long eyelashes on the dormers, giving the house an "Aw-shucks, who-me?" kind of look.

"This is your place? I expected, I don't know, something more policelike."

"What, with bars on the windows and a Harley in the driveway?"

"Actually, yeah."

"It was my granny's place. I inherited it, and have been restoring it for the last eight or nine years." As he spoke, Bella walked through the front door with the tennis ball still in her mouth. Then she dropped the ball, trotted to the couch, and fell asleep.

Mark raised his eyebrows. "Apparently being adopted from a dog shelter is exhausting."

"Little Dog did exactly the same thing. Canine life must be terribly taxing."

Lucy looked around. Next to a brown sofa, a huge flat-screen TV was mounted against the wall. There was little else in the room besides a recliner, a fireplace, and an intricate Persian carpet.

"This place screams boy-bachelor," she said.

"Better than girl-granny. That kind of puts the ladies off."

Lucy felt the comment in her chest. *Ladies*. She swallowed and realized where she was. In a man's home. A not-Richard man.

"Lucy, I'm kidding. I couldn't resist the ridiculousness of me and *ladies*. It's the funniest punch line I could come up with."

Lucy tried a breezy smile. She took a step back and inadvertently kicked a rubber wiener in a bun. It was when it squeaked that she noticed a large basket filled with colorful ropes, rubber squirrels, bones, and balls. There were collars, leashes, and an impressive assortment of hard and soft dog toys.

"You having a party?"

"Obviously not, or I would have hidden my obsession."

"Rubber squeaky toys?"

"And other important dog-intelligence stimulators."

"What are you training him for, the CIA?"

"You need a lot of teaching materials when you home-school. I need someone to do my taxes."

"Seems like you picked the right dog for that. As soon as she wakes, she could put in a good ten minutes before the next nap." Lucy laughed and impulsively touched his arm. Mark turned; they made eye contact and held it just long enough to be too long.

Lucy blushed. She looked at her feet, started to move away, but instead turned and opened her mouth to speak.

Mark touched a curl of her hair, then placed a sure hand on her waist as he guided her face toward his. It was the sureness of his movements, his ease and decisiveness that jump-started something inside her. Something that said, *Yep, I remember.*

His lips were soft. He touched his tongue to the center of her lip and she opened her mouth. He slid his hand down her forearm and pulled her toward him. Lucy, unable to stop herself, reached around his waist. She felt the leanness in his body, his lithe, muscled back through his T-shirt. He gently guided her back and against the sofa. She touched the bristle of his dark hair, felt his bare neck, and tugged him closer.

The rest of it was quick undressing, opening, and hot breath. When he entered her, she marveled briefly how it was possible to hyperventilate so long without passing out. But that was the only part of her medical-trained brain that was working. Her inner mammal had effectively shut her up.

"Lucy, oh my God."

Hearing her name, uttered with such shameless ardor, made her breath catch. "Yes," she said as he slid his fingers against her. With her eyes closed, she arched her neck and he kissed her in the hollow of her throat. If she had been thinking, she'd have been mortified by her uncontrolled movements, her unhinged pleasure. His hand made the luxurious journey up her spine until he cradled the base of her neck. He breathed her name into her ear.

And then came the unsurprising, inevitable, Lucy-like response: shame. Shame, embarrassment, and guilt. The top three in the Fortune 500 list of "feelings after having sex with a near-stranger." They hadn't even had dinner and a movie.

"God."

Misunderstanding this call for the divine was a good thing. Mark laughed a little and said, "I know. My thoughts exactly."

"God. No. I . . ."

He leaned back to look into her eyes. She pushed at his shoulder and avoided meeting his direct gaze. Quickly, she reached for her underwear—her white cotton, no-chance-of-a-visitor pair—that now were rolled on the floor. Lucy imagined them angry and disappointed. This was not their plan for the day. They had expected a walk at the dog park, maybe a late morning nap, certainly not a shove and roll. *What were you thinking?* her underwear seemed to say. *Let go of me.*

She turned her hip away from him, buttoned her jeans. "I gotta go."

"Luce, I . . . Wait. Don't leave."

"I'm married. I don't do *this*. Ever." She said *this* like it was the worst possible thing she could do. Worse than staying in bed all day, shutting people out, stealing, and giving up hope.

As Lucy yanked the front door open, she heard Mark's words behind her.

"Lucy. I'm sorry. I thought . . ."

She was out the door before he finished his sentence.

Lucy sat in her car and started the engine. Her thighs were wet. *Richard. Not Richard.* She slammed into reverse and drove over the curb. The car bumped and lurched, setting off her no-seatbelt alarm. She gunned the engine, turning each corner like a race-car driver. As her cell phone rang, it skidded off the passenger seat and joined Richard's birthday box, demoted and lonely on the floor.

Once home, she shoved her way into her house. Little Dog jerked to attention. Hopping to her feet in full-out parade mode, she wagged, sniffed, and panted, sensing infidelity. *Other dogs?* she seemed to be thinking. Lucy ignored her and flew into the bathroom, stripping her clothes off as she went. The shower hit her skin with a raking, hot spray, and she started to cry.

Richard's face came to her. His smile, his gentle doctor's hands. His body had been so unlike Mark's tight, wiry, athletic build. Her fingers had tingled when she'd touched Mark's ribs, his firm shoulders and sinewy arms. She involuntarily shuddered, guilty again. Little Dog's nose popped past the shower curtain and examined Lucy with subdued interest. Lucy pulled it closed.

When at last she turned the shower off, she grabbed her robe and trailed water out of the bathroom and into the hallway outside her bedroom, veering at the last moment into the would-be nursery. Dumping herself on the bed, she let the water drop from her curls to collect in her clavicle and run down her back.

She wasn't naïve; she watched television. She knew the world was consumed by sex and that she was mostly alone in her almost chastity. Every network seemed to have a thousand series detailing romantic teenage escapades, hawked like Coney Island sideshows. But it wasn't prudish beliefs that had held her back from engaging in hookups like her roommates had in college. It was this: After getting past the mechanics, she had matured from repulsion, to cringing embarrassment, to wonderment after accidently having an orgasm during a dream in the night. Lucy liked to savor beautiful things: a perfect white chocolate Easter bunny; a handwritten letter collected from her mailbox, like the thank-you notes she received from gracious patients. And Richard had been her savored one. She'd drawn comfort from that fact that she'd been faithful to him even before she knew him. But now, after his death, she'd been unfaithful. She needed a mulligan, the sort of free shot given to golfers when they needed a do-over. A do-over for the day; that would be good. Hell, make it for the year and she wouldn't be holding her cell phone right now, about to call someone for support.

Pushing her hair away from her eyes she considered her options. She couldn't call Tig, who'd already vetoed the behavior she'd engaged in. She considered Claire; she considered her new friend, Sidney; she even considered Mark.

Sighing, she picked up her phone, and when her brother answered, she said, "You'd better come over again."

Charles was standing in her kitchen. "Now what, Luce? I love you, but if you tell me you're going to prison or halfway across the world to free Tibet, I don't know if I'll be able to take it. By the way, you look like crap."

Lucy pushed her hair behind her ear and tried to rub the smeared mascara out from under her eyes. "I did something really stupid and irresponsible today."

"Yeah? Worse than stealing?"

"Yeah."

Charles leaned against the refrigerator. "Okay, lay it on me."

"I slept with the cop."

Charles slapped his hand on the kitchen table. "Good for you!"

"No! Not good for me. I didn't just make a goal in a soccer match. I had sex."

"Yeah, I got that. *Slept with* is a euphemism for sex. How was it?"

"I don't even know him."

"I had hetero sex one time. As I recall, it wasn't that complicated."

Lucy slammed a cupboard shut above her head. "I'm not that kind of girl. I don't have sex with strangers. I'm married."

"What era do you live in, Lucy? Sex is not taboo anymore. Two consenting adults, a condom . . . it's a national pastime. And P.S., sista, you aren't technically married."

"Wait. What?"

Charles stood and folded his sister into a hug. "You're not married, sweetie."

"Condom?"

"Yes. A condom. He did wear a condom, right?"

"There wasn't time. It happened too fast."

Charles frowned. "Fast, condomless sex is oh-so-eighties, honey. What were you thinking?"

Lucy pushed away and put her fist to her mouth. "I . . . it never crossed my mind. I never had to think of it before. Richard and I tried to get pregnant right away."

"If I wasn't so cool, I'd be really grossed out by this flood of unwanted information. I hate to say this, Luce, but you need to get tested."

"What?"

"For bugs. I take it that if you didn't converse about condoms, you probably didn't chat about past history, either."

"Bugs?"

"My God, Lucy. You're a freaking afterschool special right now."

Lucy sat heavily at her kitchen table and dropped her head into her hands. Just as quickly she popped up and ran to her car. She yanked the passenger-side door open and swiped her birthday present from the floor. When it slipped from her fingers, she grabbed the red bow and pulled it from the car like an unruly weed. Back inside, with Charles standing next to her, she ripped the paper from the box. She was breathing hard. She wrestled the tape from the Nike shoebox and lifted the lid. Then she plunged her hands into the tissue and stared at what she'd uncovered.

"This is too much," she said. "It's just too much."

Charles abandoned his earlier jocularity. He put his hand between his sister's shoulder blades and said, "C'mon Lucy. Breathe. Take a deep breath. Let me in. What's happening?"

"Call Sidney," she told him. "I need a girl."

All sharp chin and angled shoulders, Sidney sat next to Lucy on the couch in the living room as Charles stood nearby.

Lucy said, "Thanks for coming."

"Talk to me."

"I opened the box."

"That's not the big news," Charles nearly shouted.

Sidney glared at him. "Go ahead, Lucy."

"I opened the box, and this is what was inside." Lucy handed Sidney an old-fashioned ice-cube tray from the sixties; silver with a handle that dislodged the cubes when it was pulled back. That, and a pamphlet with a Post-it on its front cover. Hand written on the yellow square in jagged script was *Just in case. R.*

"Do you know what it means?" Sidney asked, taking the pamphlet and lifting the note for a closer look.

"It was an inside joke," Lucy said miserably. "I was always so afraid I wouldn't get pregnant. Or that something would happen to Richard before I did. I just loved him so much."

"I used to say, 'Can you just fill up an ice-cube tray with your genetic material and we'll save it *just in case?'* I would use our code phrase in public, *Whack a mole,* and he'd crack up."

Sidney winced a little.

Lucy gave a weak smile. "I know, crass. Richard used to say I was all gingham on the outside and Naugahyde on the inside." Lucy pulled the ice-cube tray apart. "After I got pregnant, I used to say, 'Get the tray. Baby needs a sibling.'"

Charles said, "Sorry, Luce, but that's a little fucked up."

"Oh yeah? It's no different from you putting money into your Alzheimer's fund." Charles looked around guiltily, and Lucy turned to Sidney. "He's got like a million dollars in a fund specifically for a full-time male nurse when he forgets all his zip codes."

"All his zip codes?"

Charles nodded his head. "I used to work in the mailroom, and I did a lot of sorting. I know all the zip codes for south-central Wisconsin."

Sidney said, "Whitewater?"

"Five, three, one, nine, zero."

"Belleville?"

"Five, three, five, zero, eight."

"Orfordville?"

Lucy snapped, "Shut up, Charles. Jesus."

"You shut up, Lucy. Sex is not an emergency. It's a leisure activity."

"Not for everyone, Chuck-up."

Sidney looked first at Lucy, then at Charles, and shook her head. "You both just turned into eight-year-olds right in front of my eyes."

Lucy took a swat at Charles's knees and he jumped away.

Sidney pulled the flyer out of the box and said, "This is a sperm bank. Do you think he made a deposit?"

"Oh my God, do you think that's possible?"

Sidney smiled. "Well, why else would he give this to you?"

"Wow," Lucy said. "Wow. Let's call the clinic." She grabbed the receiver and hit Power just as it rang. Confused, she lifted it to her ear.

"Lucy?"

Lucy froze. She looked at her brother like she'd come

upon a rattlesnake on a walking path, halfway between hot coals and a steep cliff.

"Lucy?" Mark's tinny voice came through the receiver. "Are you there?"

Without turning her head, Lucy darted her eyes from Charles to Sidney and back again.

"Okay," Mark said. "You don't have to talk. Just listen to me. I know. It wasn't how I pictured it." He laughed an uneasy laugh. "But you're great. Lucy. I think you're, uh, great."

A thrill traveled up her spine. She hung up.

There was a silence in the room. Lucy blushed.

Sidney said, "Charles, get your phone and call the clinic. Ask for information."

"And say what? I can't just call and ask if Richard Lubers made a sperm deposit and if we can keep it in the freezer at home."

Sidney nodded. "We should go down there in person. But it's too late today. It's already six o'clock. Look on that pamphlet. Is there account information, or a receipt or something?"

Charles laughed. "Do you think they give you one of those little bank books we used to get when we were young? Before everything was done electronically? You know, for deposits?" He paused. "You know, this gives new meaning to the term 'withdrawal method.'"

Sidney looked at him. "You're being kind of a douche bag, Charles."

"Yeah, Charles," Lucy said.

"Sorry, girls, but this is the most exciting time in Lucy's

life since . . . I would say ever. Pardon me for enjoying it a little."

"You just got upgraded from douche to dick," said Lucy.

"Fine," Charles huffed. "I'm leaving. Call me when you grow up, Lucy." He swept out of the room and slammed the screen door. Twice, for drama.

Lucy shouted, "God, Babs, you are such a queen." She looked at Sidney. "Forgive him. Usually he eschews stereotypes, but occasionally, he goes in for the theatrical entrance and exit." Miserably, she added, "He'll be back tomorrow with an offer of hummus and a board game." She sat back on the couch and rubbed her face with her hands. "Am I that far out of it? Does everyone have sex at the drop of a hat now? I mean, is it really no big thing to 'stop, drop, and roll' in the middle of the day with all the lights on, and your skirt hiked to your waist?"

Sidney turned to her. "Now that's an image. Okay, so listen. What part's not okay with you? You're not . . . uh . . . involved with anyone else, right? And you like him."

"Sure, I like him. I like my pastor, too, but I'm not gonna bang him in his living room. Do you think Mark does that a lot?"

"I don't know him. What do you think?"

"I haven't any idea. He sure knew what he was doing, though." Lucy remembered the feel of Mark's hands on her skin, on the small of her back.

"Is that what you're worried about? That he's done this before?"

"I don't want to be a number to anyone, or a screw-the-ugly-widow mercy fuck."

Sidney squinted. "Have you looked at yourself since high school? There's nothing ugly about you, and I would venture a guess that there never was."

"You wouldn't understand."

Sidney sat up straight. There was an edge to her voice now. "Do you see anyone but yourself? Wake up. *Everyone* is the walking wounded. You don't have the corner on suffering. Not by a long shot." She grabbed her crocheted bag from the couch and swung it over her shoulder. With her knobby fingers she pulled her thinning hair out from under the strap and then took out her keys.

"A man finds you desirable. And your beloved late husband really loved you. Poor ugly you, Dr. Peterman. Poor smart, gifted, independent, financially secure you."

Lucy inhaled sharply and Sidney went on. "Your brother's not the only drama queen in your family." Turning, she slammed out the front door, then opened it again and slammed it a second time.

Little Dog trotted over and propped her front legs onto Lucy's knees. Her large brown eyes said, unequivocally, *When's dinner?*

"I can see that you really want to be fed," Lucy said. "But what you're really saying is, 'I will never leave you.'"

16

Mr. Blue Sky

The next morning Lucy lay in bed and listened to the kitchen faucet drip. An hour later she was still listening. Little Dog sat by the front door, whining. The days were getting shorter and shorter, and sometime during the drama of her life in the past weeks, she could sense the sounds and smells of Indian summer giving way to the ones of winter. There was more of a snap in the air, and the imminent promise of snow.

In her pajamas, she leaned on the front doorjamb and eyed a potted mum on her front stoop: gloriously orange and yellow with green foliage and a grosgrain plaid ribbon encircling the gold foil-covered pot. A grinning burlap scarecrow reinforced by a shish-kabob stick held a sign that read, I'M SORRY.

She touched the card, flipped it over. Mark. The memory

of his hands shoved Richard's face from her mind. The memory lingered for a moment until shame, like her old high school principal, put that memory into detention, where it belonged.

Her neighbor's garden gnome, fat in his blue-belted top and Santalike beard, smirked at her as if to say, *How the mighty have fallen.* It was true she had felt a little superior to her neighbors. She'd holed up with her husband, her job, and her pregnancy like the member of a Waco, Texas, cult. Now it seemed the gnome was gloating—a tubby sentry, keeping track of the number of people who wandered in and out of Lucy's life. Lucy grabbed the pot of mums and turned to the gnome. "Oh shut up, you little shit," she said under her breath, and walked into her house.

The kitchen smelled of onions from the night before, when Charles was over. She scooped up the ice tray, the black and white wrapping paper, and the brochure, and shuffled—for the first time without any palpable anxiety— into the room she had shared with her husband. Climbing into the bed, Lucy stared at the stain of Africa above her. Thanksgiving was coming, then Christmas, then New Year's. *How could she possibly get through another year?* Richard used to say to her when she made fun of his penchant for obsessive organization, *Routine helps you see when something really special is happening. Label your files and alphabetize your folders, and the next thing you know it's strawberry season.* She turned on her side and examined the Post-it. *Just in case. R.*

She sat up with a thought. Maybe there were more things lying around, more messages from Richard. Little Dog scrambled to attention. Dropping to her knees, Lucy looked under the bed and pulled out a rolled sock. Nothing. In the closet she searched through Richard's sweaters, opened shoeboxes, and shoved aside a fleece jacket that had fallen to the floor. Kicking hospital supplies out of her path, she searched his dresser drawers, pushing aside boxer shorts and socks, and pulling out T-shirts by their shoulders. She returned to the closet, going over every inch with the thoroughness of an Iowa tornado. Nothing. Breathless, she scanned the room. On the floor, between the legs of the bedside table, sat a box where Richard kept his reading glasses, his earplugs, and a small pile of abandoned books. Inside it, she saw Richard's iPod, kiwi-colored with a charger forever docked and charging, and ear buds.

She powered it up and stuck the earphones into her ears. The first song was by Electric Light Orchestra, a band from the seventies. "Mr. Blue Sky." "Sun is shinin' in the sky. There ain't a cloud in sight." The song went on its cheerful way all the way to the final verse. Still on the floor, she hit Play and listened again, and then again.

When Lucy woke up, she heard what sounded like a birthday party of birds flitting, tweeting, and flirting outside the window. Mrs. Bobo, perched on her favorite windowsill, watched silently, her tail twitching wildly. It jerked like a broken live wire, that tail, promising any small animal, bird or otherwise, a quick death by cat if caught.

Lucy pushed herself to a seated position. The brochure about the sperm bank was stuck to her cheek with sticky sleep drool. Shaking her head, she peeled it off and watched Little Dog yawn. "It's a new day, girl. I've got you, music, and some potential sperm. What else could a girl want?" The earphones she'd had in her ears lay on her pillow, connected to the now-dead iPod. She glanced around the shambles of her room, plugged the iPod into the charging station, and scooted out of bed into the hall. Grabbing her phone, Lucy opened the brochure and read. *Men commonly choose sperm-banking if about to undergo treatments or take medications that may affect sperm production.*

Lucy pressed a hand to her chest and skimmed the rest of the text, looking for the part where she could learn about defrosting Richard's DNA, using it, and getting on with getting him back into her life. Near the bottom she read the words, *When you are ready to use the sperm, you must notify the bank in writing. The bank then will release the specimen, shipping it to whatever physician you request.*

"Screw writing," she said, and punched the number of the clinic into her phone. Almost immediately she heard a recorded voice in a surprising British accent.

"Thank you for calling Cryobanking Conception Clinics. If this is an emergency, press One."

Lucy considered this option and decided that pushing

the emergency button would be over the top. What would she say? *Help, I need sperm. STAT.* The British woman's voice continued.

"If this is not an emergency, please call back during regular business hours. CC Clinics is currently closed for the weekend." She pronounced *weekend* with an emphasis on the second syllable—week*end*—making Lucy feel as though she were in a movie with Hugh Grant, embarking on an English romance, and that this was a lovely lark of a call, likely to end in happily ever after. She grabbed her calendar. Saturday. She couldn't go back to sleep now, and in vitro fertilization was pretty much out for the week*end.*

She threw herself back into her bedroom and grabbed the wrapping paper. Little Dog peeked in just as Lucy rushed through the bedroom door. "Maybe there's another present," she said out loud. "C'mon, Lucy. You got this. Systematic." For the next hour and a half she searched every drawer, cubby, and cupboard in her cozy, if elderly house. When she found herself examining the space under the basement stairs with an otoscope she'd purchased for her pediatric rotation in med school, she came to her senses. "This is ridiculous," she said aloud. She put down the otoscope and took another look at the loot she'd unearthed: sixty-seven cents she'd discovered in an old pair of jeans, and Richard's pre-exercise inhaler. She took a puff from it, then another, shrugged, and said to Little Dog, "Just for fun."

And then, still dressed in the clothes she'd slept in, Lucy grabbed the iPod, clipped the leash onto the only friend that would have her lately, and walked out the door.

Listening to the music in her new-to-her iPod, Lucy smiled and shook her head, reflecting on Richard's eclectic and almost uncanny music choices: "Everlasting Love" by Gloria Estefan and "Give Me Everything" by Pitbull. "Say Hey (I Love You)" by Michael Franti, and the classic Barry White song "You're the First, the Last, My Everything." Lucy did a little hop step. "My kind of wonderful, that's what you are." She skipped over a crack in the sidewalk. "Your love I'll keep forever more." Whenever Sidney popped into her mind, and Charles, and God forbid, Mark, she visualized their faces and gently pushed them away, actually using her hand to swat the air. Anyone looking out his window would have seen a well-dressed woman performing a kind of tai chi hip-hop. The golden late-morning sunshine felt like a spotlight, and the leaves applauded her enthusiasm.

If "It's Raining Men" seemed like an odd choice, Lucy ignored it and played it again for good measure. "Bad Day," by that Canadian singer she liked but whose name she could never remember, started in her ear. "Where is the moment we needed the most?"

"Jesus," she said aloud, "I'm not loving this one." She turned the iPod over to click past the song and didn't notice the cruiser slowing down, or the open window, or the look on Mark's face.

"Lucy."

Lucy pulled up short, met Mark's eyes, and automatically touched her hair. "Don't you ever work?"

"I am working. See the big car? Can I talk to you?"

You're falling to pieces every time. "No. Just forget it. I'm a big girl."

"What does that mean?"

Lucy gave him an incredulous look and kept walking. He rolled the cruiser forward. "I don't want to forget it."

Lucy refused to look at him. *You say you don't know.*

"I wish I'd done things differently. We could have had dinner."

"And maybe we could have used a condom." Lucy planted her feet on the sidewalk and finally turned to face him. "I'm sure you're not new to this, but I am. I am new to this, and I don't like anything about it."

Mark braked. Looked away. "I'm not gonna lie. That hurt."

"I doubt that."

"What did I do that was so wrong, Lucy? Want you? Is that it? How did your husband ever get past your defenses? That's what I want to know."

Lucy stared at him. Opened her mouth and shut it. The song continued in her ear, like a good musical friend who was just trying to help. She pulled an ear bud out and took a deep breath. "I know I'm doing some things wrong, *a lot* of things wrong. It's kind of a cliché, you know, that surgeons are not good with people."

"Help me out, Lucy. I don't know what we're talking about. I didn't think I was pushing you."

Lucy spoke in a near whisper. "Did it look like I was being pushed?" Before he could respond, she said, "That's why I'm done with people for a while. I don't know what I'm doing."

Mark shook his head. "So you're going back into hiding then?"

"You don't know me well enough to say that."

"I know me, and you and I aren't that different. I know all about hiding."

"I'm not hiding. I've got a dog. My music." She said *my music* like she was Michael Jackson or Elton John, talking about the songs she'd written. "And I've got the potential, finally, for something bigger." She touched the pocket where she'd put the brochure, and imagined the microscopic sperm waiting for her, waiting to bring Richard back.

"Could you just stop walking?" Mark asked. "Could we go someplace to talk?"

"Nope, and I'll go to AA on Tuesdays and Thursdays, just so it isn't awkward."

He shook his head. "You are a piece of work. You know that?"

She pointed to her earphones like they were an important telephone call and turned the corner.

17

Dear Baby . . .

Lucy put her hand on her chest and felt the beat of her heart through her white T-shirt. It had taken her forty minutes to drive to the Cryobanking Conception Clinics and her heart hadn't slowed in the least. She chose the closest parking space in front of a rambling, brown-shingled ranch that resembled a dentist's office or maybe a senior center. Before she even got out of the car, she checked the worn pamphlet a third time to confirm that this was the right address.

Inside, it smelled like new carpet and vanilla. The lights were bright, and there were big bottles of hand sanitizer on the counter blocking the view of the receptionist. Lucy found this a little obvious. *We know where your hands have been, pal,* she imagined the staff thinking. *Gel up!*

"Excuse me." Lucy smiled and stood with her very best posture.

The receptionist pulled her nose from her computer. "How can I help you?" she asked.

"My husband is here. I mean, his genetic material is here." Lucy had not prepared a speech. She'd only pictured herself arriving and leaving with tubes in a nitrogen flask of some sort. That was her fantasy anyway, although she knew that wasn't how it worked. Pulling her doctor-self together, she tried to sound authoritative. "I'm Lucy Peterman; my husband, Richard Lubers, made a deposit about a year ago. I'd like to collect that, if I may."

"Are you the designee?"

"I should hope so. He didn't say. I mean, he died without saying." She swallowed. "He died."

"I'm sorry," the receptionist said, as if she couldn't care less, and tapped on her keyboard. "Did you bring identification?"

Lucy fumbled in her purse. "I have my driver's license, my birth and marriage certificates, and my passport." *Always good to be prepared.* She spread these on the desk and continued, "And here is my husband's driver's license, his birth certificate, and his social security card. I have our joint MasterCard and Pier 1 cards if you need something with both our names on it."

The receptionist scratched her eyebrow with a dark, manicured nail and said, "Marriage license and photo ID should do it. You can put the rest of that away." She tapped again and said, "I'm sorry, I don't see a Richard Lugers in the system."

"Lubers," Lucy said so forcefully that the receptionist blinked.

"Pardon me."

To Lucy, it seemed near impossible that all this keystroking was necessary for such a short name. *R-i-c-h-a-r-d-L-u-b-e-r-s Enter*. What else could she possibly be writing? A telephone rang somewhere.

"Yes, here it is. I found it. It was under Lubers."

"Yes." Lucy blinked. "Can I have it?"

"Well, if you are who you say you are. Yes. But you can't take it with you today. You have to go see a reproductive endocrinologist, and get the appropriate tests. There are fees involved."

"But it's here. He was here. My husband was here."

"It appears so. Yes." The receptionist focused on Lucy. Straightened her glasses. "Now you need to get a doctor's appointment and follow procedure."

"Can I see him? It?"

"No, Mrs. Lubers. There's really very little to see."

"It's here, though. You're one hundred percent certain."

"Get a doctor's appointment," the woman said more gently now. "We'll be here when you're ready." It was the only defrosting Lucy was likely to see at the clinic, and for the moment, that would have to be enough.

Outside the laboratory, with the fall breeze on her face, she dialed her brother's number. "Charles. Please stop being mad. Everything is going to change. You'll see. I'm at the sperm bank. Richard really did come here. From here on out, Charlie. You could be an uncle soon."

She dialed Phong's number. "Tell Charles to call me. Tell him I don't *need* him. I *want* him. There's a difference. It's a good difference." Finally she called her health clinic. That's when she learned that, like most things, nothing was as easy as it seemed. If you want a dimmer switch in your house, an electrician has to replace all your knob and tube wiring and upgrade you to the twenty-first century. If you need a new roof, pretty soon you also will have to replace the gutters, soffits, and struts. If you want your husband's sperm, your personal plumbing has to be mined and your entire infrastructure spelunked.

The appointment receptionist at Excel Health Co-op spoke with nasal clarity into the phone. "First you must see your general practitioner for a basic assessment and referral to an OB/GYN or fertility expert. They will schedule a pre-conception exam, which will include several blood tests, a PAP smear, and possibly a mammogram."

"My God. How long will all of this take?"

"We can book you for your first appointment in three weeks. December first. The rest depends on you, their schedule, and luck."

Lucy scrambled to regain footing on her dream bubble. "Jeez, if I were still in high school I could go under the bleachers and get pregnant without a single appointment." She added a thready laugh to make sure the receptionist got the joke. "I'll take that December appointment," she added.

"That would be my advice."

"But," Lucy said, "if there is a pep rally there's no telling what I might do."

Appointment made, Lucy walked back into her house with new eyes. She went in search of the file folder she kept of general decorating ideas: paint colors, upholstery, furniture. Tucked deep into her old wooden file cabinet she spotted something she had purchased after finding she was pregnant that first time: a hardcover artist's sketch book, a set of calligraphy pens, and a roll of double-sided tape. She'd intended to use the book to chronicle her pregnancy: monthly changes, details about the delivery, gifts. Ultimately, she'd hoped to use it to write notes to her baby that she could read as he grew up. Notes about his graduation, his wedding, the birth of a grandchild.

"Perfect," she said. Spreading out the magazine clippings from her file, with crib styles and paint samples, she began sketching ideas for the perfect baby's room. With Little Dog curled at her hip, she turned the page and began a letter. *Dear Baby*, she wrote. *I can't wait to meet you.*

With the prospect of a baby back on the agenda, Lucy felt euphoric. She wanted to move on with her life. Get back to work. With her iPod in place, she marched into the Maplewood Serenity Center. She consulted her watch. Right on time. Inside the usual dingy room, Kimmy, Claire, and Sara stood in a triangle. Tig was on the phone, standing in the corner. When Lucy entered, Sara rolled her eyes in tiresome disgust.

"What's up? Where is everybody?"

"You tell us," said Sara. "Mark says he's got some new shift schedule and he can't make it on Wednesdays any more, which we all know is bullshit. He's had the same schedule, for like, ever."

Claire, looking as usual like a pale confection of spun sugar said, "Mark's fine, Sara. He'll come back when he's ready."

By now Tig had finished her call. "It's Ron," she said.

Kimmy put her arm on Claire's shoulder. The bruise on her chin was the color of a jaundiced liver. "Ron went on a bender. Drove his wheelchair off an embankment. Spent the night in a ditch."

"My God." Lucy shoved her iPod into her pocket. "Is he all right?"

Tig said, "He's stable. We can't get any more information on the phone. It's good to see you, Lucy. Does this mean you're working on the goals we set?"

Lucy ignored Tig. "Ron seemed like the most stable of all of us. Pissy but stable," she said.

Claire, Kimmy, and Sara traded glances. "Sometimes he is. Sometimes he's not. We were just going to visit him. Do you want to come along?"

At the veteran's hospital, as Tig spoke with the nursing staff, Lucy and the other three women formed a mismatched quartet just outside Ron's room. When the nursing assistant finished helping him brush his teeth, they entered.

"I should have known you birds would show up," said Ron.

Lucy moved to his side, checked his IV drip, and hefted the water pitcher for fullness. "Are they treating you well here, Ron? I can talk to someone if there's something you need."

"At ease, Super Girl." Sara walked to the opposite side of the bed. In a voice Lucy had never heard, she said, "Ronnie? What happened?"

His large black hand covered her pale white one. "A bad night. Nobody's perfect. Claire, you're looking tired. Take a seat." He nodded at Kimmy. "On the other hand, you're looking well."

"Stop taking care of us for a second, Ron, and tell us what happened," Claire said.

Ron exhaled. "My son, Eric, took the baby. Nothing I could do. He's irrational. Police say I've got no rights. The boy's grandpa, but no rights. He'll keep that baby until he doesn't want him anymore and then I'll get him back. No telling what shape he'll be in. Hoping he's too young to remember any of this."

Kimmy said, "What were you doing out rolling around after dark? You know you can't do that."

"I wasn't drinking, if that's what you think. When Eric put my grandson into the car, I saw his stuffed bunny go flying into the weeds. Heard that baby howl. I thought I could get it, but the embankment by my apartment was steeper than I thought. Lost my damn traction and spent the night on my back. Opened that old scar in my leg and now I'm back in this old barn. Goddammit."

Claire laughed. "It was just your crazy driving that got you in here? Don't that beat all hell."

Sara grabbed his hand. "Idiot."

"I am still your elder, Miss Sara. You will speak to me with respect."

Kimmy breathed a sigh of relief. "You scared us, Ron."

"I keep telling you all to worry about your own selves. You people are so ready to jump into anything that isn't about fixing yourselves. I don't need you trying to rescue me. I don't want to hear another word about any plans that don't include separating yourself from your addiction." Ron trained his eyes on Lucy. "What about you, Lucy? How have you been?"

The group turned to her in unison. Lucy said, "Busy."

As they were leaving the hospital, Tig put her hand on Lucy's arm. "I wondered when you were going to get back into therapy. I haven't seen you on my schedule, and the group isn't talking."

Lucy's smile was radiant. "Thank you. Thank you for keeping track of me but you'll be happy to know that I am better. So much better."

Tig looked at her with an unreadable expression. "Tell me about that," she said.

Lucy cleared her throat. "It's true that I went through a

terrible time. You saw me at my worst. I don't blame you for wondering where I've been." Lucy touched Tig's arm, as if she were reassuring a patient.

"Then make an appointment. Come to my office. Tell me what's changed."

"Okay, I will. I have your number. I'll call." Lucy moved away like an expert operator in a singles bar, but not before she saw Tig narrow her eyes.

18

Risk Management

Every day Little Dog watched the transformation. Lucy began by clearing her things from the room she had been camping out in for almost a year. "A suite, that's what this baby needs. Her own place. I'll put in a bathroom. A walk-in closet. Push the walls out."

Little Dog thumped her tail and rested her head on her paws. Mrs. Bobo, disdainful of all things, lifted her tail. Over the next three weeks, with Richard's iPod charged, Lucy worked as hard as she had in medical school, like her hair was on fire. She hauled old clothes to Goodwill, brought workmen in for estimates, and cleaned every corner of her old Victorian. She bought plastic toilet-seat locks, cupboard door locks, and outlet covers without a thought of illicitly pocketing a pacifier. She shopped for eco-friendly paints, carpets, and baby furniture, stealing nary a tooth-pick.

In between her shopping excursions, she deleted answering machine messages by the score. From Claire: "For heaven's sake, get your butt to a meeting and get to work, hon. We won't ask what cha' been up to. But jus' between you 'n me. What cha' been up to?" From Sidney: "I'd love to have you over if you'd like to come, hang out a little. We could talk." From Mark: "Hi, Lucy."

Ron even tried once.

"I'm going against my own better judgment, calling you like this, but Claire is bugging the hell out of me. We'd love to see you again." She didn't delete that one.

Three weeks went by. Lucy occasionally called her brother. "Painting the baby's room soon," she said to his voice mail. And "I know you'll call when you're ready." And "C'mon, Charlie, you're about to break your last silence record." And, finally, "You are not going to bum my high, Charles. You are not!"

She even booked a couple of sessions with Tig, thinking of her future as a single-mother breadwinner, knowing she would need to work, be a role model, come to a future class-room for career day.

"Aren't you supposed to be happy for me?" she asked Tig. "I'm out of my slump. I'm moving forward."

"Are you?"

"What do you mean, *are you*? I'm going to have a baby.

It's actually perfect timing, to have this time off to focus. I have a lot of work to do on the house."

"Time off. Is that what you're calling it?"

"I've stopped stealing. I'm back in my bedroom. I'm rebuilding a life for myself. I see that as progress."

"You *were* making progress. Going to AA, making friends."

Lucy scoffed. "Friends? A bunch of alcoholics and an anorexic. I'm leaving crazy land behind."

Tig was silent. She wrote something down on her legal pad.

"I just don't get you counselors. Sometimes happiness is just happiness, and not avoidance in disguise. Sometimes people get better. Sometimes you people are wrong."

Tig nodded. "Sometimes, yes. So you're serious about having Richard's baby?"

Lucy, in her most obnoxious incarnation of herself said, "Duh," and Tig put her pencil down.

"I will be here for you, Lucy. No matter what."

Grumbling, Lucy went back to her plan with even more conviction. Her daily routine now included a cup of coffee and a to-do list, followed by a brisk walk with Little Dog. She spent the rest of her morning talking to workmen, cleaning out snarled junk drawers and basement boxes; but always, always, she carefully left Richard's things untouched. Evenings were spent cataloging the day's accomplishments and writing to the child of her dreams. *Dear Baby, Your father was perfect. We're going to be great friends.* In the moments when she paused in her decision making—single or double breast pump, baby sling or carrier, plastic or silver spoon?—she napped. Sometimes she napped when she was in the middle of reading about the pros and cons of epidurals, or doulas versus midwives. When the contractor came at noon to estimate the cost of adding a bathroom, Lucy had been asleep.

"Wow, I'm tired," she said, uninspired and bleary-eyed. The *caw-caw* of a black bird flapped into the room.

"Sleep is good," he said benignly.

Full of good will, she thought. *What a nice thing to say. So supportive.* She considered setting the record straight, telling him about the sperm bank, but thought instead, *soon enough*.

Finally, alone and seated on a hard plastic chair in the clinic's exam room, Lucy held a gauze pad in the crux of her elbow. She extracted a blue latex glove from the box mounted on the wall and pulled it over her right hand. There was a quick knock at the door and a man entered, wearing gray pleated pants and a white-and-gray-striped shirt.

"Dr. Peterman. I'm Brian Ballwig. Nice to meet you." He extended his hand, and without thinking she offered him her own glove-covered one.

"Oh! I was just being nostalgic, I guess," she said, ripping the glove off.

"You're in plastics, I understand."

"Breast reconstruction, yes. But not today," she said with a little laugh. "Of course, unless you need a little lift." She laughed again. "I'm a very reasonable person when I'm alone. It's only when I'm nervous and people are present that I lose my mind."

"No need for nerves here." He sat at the computer terminal in the exam room and typed in his password. "I understand your usual GP is Dr. Geevie." Several screens popped in and out of sight until her chart was before him.

"He wasn't available for weeks. You had the soonest opening. I just need a referral, really."

"So it's just a preliminary check today. The nurse's notes say you and your husband are pursuing pregnancy, is that right?"

"Technically, yes."

"I guess it does seem a little technical. It's all about risk management these days. Let's take a look at your vitals and blood panel first." There was more shifting on the computer screen and Lucy looked around. There was a collage of baby announcements tacked to a corkboard over the doctor's shoulder.

"Nice blood pressure. And look at that. I wish I had a cholesterol level of 170," he said.

The babies on the bulletin board winked and blushed. Some slept on the chests and laps, or in the arms of their parents. One had a tiny set of reindeer antlers perched on her perfectly round head. Another wore nothing but angel wings and a strategically placed cloud. It was like looking at the offerings in a fruit market at the height of summer. Each child's face ready to be plucked from the photo, ripe and ready for kissing.

"Oh," Dr. Ballwig said. "I didn't realize you were pregnant already. I thought this was a pre-pregnancy exam."

Lucy tore her eyes from the photos. "Huh? It is a pre-pregnancy exam. I'm not pregnant."

Dr. Ballwig frowned and pushed back from the computer. "Your blood test clearly indicates pregnancy. Your hCG is elevated. You had your blood drawn an hour ago, right?" He refocused on the computer and tapped through to another screen. "Your urine test confirms it." He rolled his stool back and said, "Well! Congratulations. I guess we can skip a few steps."

Lucy's face froze, then she stood. Looked again at the babies and then at the doctor. "I'm pregnant," she said. The color drained from her face and she put her hand to her forehead.

Dr. Ballwig took her by the elbow, helped her find the chair behind her. "Why don't you take a minute? Give your husband a call. I'll get you some apple juice and we can start over."

Lucy swallowed and nodded. Dr. Ballwig moved into the hall in a clean *swish* of lab coat and competence. Lucy stood, grabbed the box of gloves from the wall, shoved it into her purse, and swept out of the exam room like 007 from a Soviet submarine.

Little Dog lay asleep on the backseat, whapping her tail

twice as Lucy threw herself into the front seat. Throwing the box of gloves into the back of the car, she yanked her phone out of her purse, opened the calendar, and squinted at it. Her last period had been the day after Halloween. It'd been seven weeks since then. She counted the days back to the afternoon she'd been with Mark. Four weeks. The horror hit her like a tidal wave. She hit a button on the car door and all four windows slid open. She gulped in air.

"This is too much," she said. Then she threw her head back and screamed, "This is too much."

A man in a hard hat stared as he lit a cigarette. "What are you looking at?" she shouted at him as she gunned the engine and screeched out of the parking lot.

It was a short drive from the clinic to the cemetery. An elderly couple watering a large patch of golden mums around a headstone didn't look up as Lucy's car tore through the gates. She slammed it into park, opened the door a crack, stopped, and put her head into her hands.

"This isn't working," she said. "I can't make this work."

She watched as the older woman deadheaded a shriveled mum; the man filled a silver watering can from a spigot. They didn't speak, but instead went about their business of loving by creating a garden for one.

"I'm not going to do this," she said to herself.

After three days alone, wallowing and chewing the inside of her cheek until it was raw, Lucy decided she had to talk to someone. Someone who understood difficult choices. Someone who continued to reach out even in the light of Lucy's gracelessness.

Sidney had given Lucy her address that first time they'd walked: 516 Serendipity Lane. At the time, Lucy had laughed at the irony of meeting this likeable woman at the office of obvious obsessions: Tig Monohan's counseling clinic. It didn't feel so ironic now. She needed a friend.

Lucy had a picture in her mind of where Sidney lived: a house covered in pale pink paisley, with gingerbread dormers and minty-green shutters. Not this tired bungalow with the canted front porch. She checked the address scribbled on the back of a car wash coupon and pulled her coat in tighter against the winter wind. No, this was definitely the place. The dove-colored paint on the front door was what Lucy associated with Maine, with faded clapboard shingles and the sound of seagulls flapping overhead, but that's where the poetry stopped. There was no railing near the bare, hastily constructed front steps. A combination of red and white trim circled half of the weathered front porch, but petered out unevenly as though the painter had run out of money, motivation, or maybe just the will to live. The doctor in Lucy would have diagnosed the whole place with chronic fatigue syndrome.

She pulled herself from the car just as Sidney, in full winter running gear, jogged up the side street with Chubby Lumpkins trotting easily next to her. Lucy lifted a tentative hand.

"I'm sorry—" she began.

"No," Sidney said. "I'm self-absorbed in the best of times, and these are not the best times for me. I've made self-absorption an Olympic sport." With one hand clutching Chubby Lumpkin's leash, she gave Lucy a quick hug. Lucy felt the knobs in Sidney's spine even through the heavy sweatshirt the woman wore.

Sidney stepped back. "I'm trying to get better, but I'm afraid I'm only patient with my own troubles."

"I'm pregnant," Lucy blurted before she could stop herself. "It's Mark's, not Richard's. I . . ."

Sidney blinked. Started to smile and checked herself. "You're fricking kidding me."

"I am such an idiot."

"You can say that if you want, but it won't help a thing. Besides, you know it isn't true."

"What, then?"

"Human, maybe." Sidney put her hand on Lucy's shoulder. "I've been thinking about you. I bet before the accident, you were never limited by anything. Not brainpower, money, or energy. But the universe got you anyway, didn't it? It found your weak spot and yanked it. Now, like Pinocchio, you're a real girl. You're human."

Lucy's eyes were glassy with tears. "I made a big mistake here, Sid."

"We all make mistakes." Sidney pulled up the sleeve of her long, gray sweatshirt and showed Lucy her wristband.

"I wish I could say this band is from a water park but it's not. I just got back from the hospital."

Lucy put her hand over her mouth and Sidney said, "Come in, there's coffee inside."

The interior of her house felt stark and orderly, in complete contrast to the disarray outside. But it felt famished, too. Clean to a fault, with spare furniture aligned just so, the carpets plumbed, the dull colors devoid of character. Sidney opened the refrigerator and Lucy caught sight of its contents. There was a twelve pack of diet Cherry Coke, a square of tofu, a jug of catsup, and every kind of mustard imaginable. There were also six cans of Ensure. Sidney caught Lucy's stare and said, "I know. I promised I'd buy groceries."

Lucy said, "I'd go with you, but I'm afraid I'd steal them from you."

Sidney cracked a can of Ensure. "Cheers," she said and took a sip, swallowing it like she had the worst sore throat in the history of the world. Then she took a sip of her coffee. Once they settled in the living room, Sidney repeated the routine: She sipped from the can again, and followed it up with the black coffee chaser.

"I have to eat three meals and finish three cans a day. It's God-awful, but measurable."

"What happened?"

"I passed out. I'd never done that before. My neighbor got me to the hospital."

Seated in Sidney's stark, dour living room Lucy said, "It seems like when disaster strikes you should be able to hit a Pause button. Put the news on a shelf and look at it. But it's not like that, is it? You have to keep talking to the people in your life, wash the dishes, feed the dog, go to the bathroom, fill your gas tank. Life goes on. After the doctor told me I was pregnant, I had to say something socially appropriate. But I couldn't. It was too much to ask."

Sidney nodded. "Anorexia is my pause." She gave Lucy a weak smile. "But I wouldn't recommend it." She took a sip of coffee. "I haven't always been this sick, you know. Although I have always been weight-conscious."

"What woman in America isn't?"

Sidney nodded. "I had a pretty man: Bobby. God, stay away from a man with a little-boy name like that: Bobby, Tommy, Joey. They carry a lot of heavy baggage. When we met, he was a hockey player slash physician's assistant. He'd given up his skates, but still looked capable of surging for a goal if pressed."

Lucy smiled. "I know the type. ESPN is tattooed on their brain as the ultimate cultural experience." She put her hand on her abdomen.

"Yep. He married me for himself. I was his pet wife. He'd play with me, take me out if *he* needed it, otherwise I could just piss in the basement waiting for him between watching sports events. I made a great prop: I was successful, pretty enough, reasonably smart."

"So you left him."

"Ha! You'd think, right?" Sidney dropped her ear to her shoulder and cracked her neck, a move Lucy had seen her do several times before. "No. A bunch of old jocks got a hockey league together, started playing on Wednesday nights. The Skates, they called themselves. Had an artist design a logo with a stingray on it, a stingray with devilish eyes. Just another thing for Bobby to do without me. One night, when I was home painting the bedrooms, he tripped on the ice and rammed his head into the goal. Broke his neck."

"God, Sidney."

There was a rueful smile on Sidney's lips. "Don't worry," she said. "He lived. He lost the use of his legs, though. It was a long recovery. Physical therapy, nurses. We both had to learn to get him in and out of the chair, into the shower. I went to every therapy appointment, learned everything I could from the nurses. Until he told me to stop."

"He told you to stop?"

"Said I was no good at it. Suggested I join a gym. Get in shape, lose weight."

Lucy's mouth dropped open and Sidney continued. "I used to have kind of big boobs." Sidney pulled the sleeves of her shirt down over her wrists. "I was enrolled in school at the time, taking classes in social work. So I dropped out. Got to work on my abs. And on this house." She stood and motioned for Lucy to follow her. Down a hallway Sidney opened the door of the master bedroom.

The walls were a honey yellow on top of glossy, white

wainscoting. The floor was painted a Mediterranean blue, waxed and sparsely covered with sisal throw rugs. Jute blinds hung in each window. The sky-blue bedspread was strewn with red poppies. And on the wall, at the head of the queen-sized bed, hung a vintage life preserver with the words S.S. *Happy* printed on it. Sidney opened the door adjacent to the master bedroom and walked inside. This room's white walls and white bedspreads made Lucy feel like taking in a big, clean breath. It had a light-blue ceiling with clouds painted in the corners, and twin beds with red paisley pillows on them. The windows were hung with curtains made from the same flirty paisley material. "Bobby left me for his physical therapist. Told me they had a great sex life. She was pregnant," Sidney added. "Apparently that part of him still worked."

"Oh." Lucy let the word escape like a bird flying from its cage. She paused to gauge the expression on Sidney's face. "I'd been decorating for the happy years to come when Bobby would spend time at home, hoping *we'd* have a family."

"My gosh, I did the same thing!"

"I guess I still believed in fairy tales, then. It took a long time to edit those stories, but eventually they became less Disney, more the Brothers Grimm, and I lost more and more weight. I finally realized that the only consistent characters in my house were fantasy, disillusionment, and me." Lucy flinched as she watched Sidney talk, bony-kneed, deep in recollection.

"I want to finish the house. Sell it, but I don't have the energy."

"Where's Bobby now?"

"No idea. There wasn't much protesting when it ended. 'No hard feelings,' he'd said." Then as if to herself, "No hard feelings."

"Sidney. I'm sorry." Lucy leaned in closer to her friend. "But it's not over for you. Bobby isn't the only man in the world."

Sidney snorted, "Where would *I* find a man? One that I could trust? It's a long process. Besides, whenever I think about it, a cuckoo clock chimes in my head: 'Old eggs, old eggs.'"

"You just described me."

"Not so much anymore, kid." Sidney turned and moved toward the living room.

Lucy said, "Did you ever hear that joke, the one where two little kids are in the backyard playing? The little boy pulls his pants down and wags his penis at the girl, saying, 'I have something you don't have. A penis!' and the little girl says, 'Oh yeah? Well my mommy says that I have a vagina and that means I can have a penis anytime I want.'"

Sidney laughed. "How do you feel?" she asked.

"I have to think about that." Lucy grew quiet as she followed Sidney back from the beautiful bedrooms into the sparse living room. "I feel ashamed. Disloyal. Embarrassed and ridiculous. I feel like I'm pregnant at my prom and the father is from a neighboring town and nobody likes that town. I feel like from here on out it's going to be all true confessions and conflict."

"So you feel like the high school slut."

"You know, I loved Richard, and wanted a family with *him*. I wanted to have *his* baby. I didn't just want *a* baby, any old baby, Mark's baby."

"I promise not to quote you on that, no matter what happens."

"I know. It's terrible. I've always wanted this. I wanted to bring a pan of lemon bars to my birthing class, discuss epidurals, and compare overpriced designer diaper bags. I wanted to join the labor and delivery club, talk about episiotomies and insensitive doctors. You know, laugh at the jokes about how if babies were left to the male species there would be no population growth. I wanted to be a Girl Scout leader."

"And now you're going to get all that."

"I don't think so, Sidney." A cold wind hit the outside of the house and it seemed to shudder.

"Maybe we could talk about something else, then," Sidney said. The two of them sat breathing in each other's air, wondering what could be considered safe territory for a hopeless anorexic and a kleptomaniac unwed mother. "Want to sleep over?"

19

Sleep Sweet

In the spare bedroom, Lucy lay beneath the girlish comforter staring at the painted blue ceiling, with Little Dog at her side. She lifted the overlarge T-shirt Sidney had lent her and ran her hands over her abdomen and up to her breasts. They *were* fuller. That very morning, she'd chalked it up to premenstrual tenderness, but it was actually a call to arms. *Man your battle stations, glands! This isn't a drill!* It was like watching the disguise come off an old, complicated friend who had plans, a map, and was taking over.

It would be several weeks and many thoughts before Lucy would feel the baby move inside her, but she tried now to sense the change within. Just before getting into bed she'd placed the Cryobanking Conception Clinics pamphlet under her pillow. Now she slid her hand under the cool surface and tugged the once glossy pamphlet out. The top page tore free from the trifold and she gasped. Tears welled up in her eyes and leaked onto her pillow. She tried to be silent but to no avail. Her body released a great wracking sob, and then another.

Sidney tiptoed into the room and, light as a paint stick, sat on the edge of the bed and rubbed her back. "Let it out," she said. When Lucy quieted, Sidney moved to the second bed and slipped between its covers.

"We need some rest because we're doing this all again tomorrow. It's going to be better tomorrow."

"How?"

"It just is. Sleep sweet."

Just as Sidney predicted, life went on. The newspaper had been delivered and Lucy sat in the living room holding a down comforter around her shoulders and sipping coffee. Beneath an item about a rash of petty thefts from a string of convenience stores in Iowa, Lucy saw a diminutive headline: "82-year-old woman survives three-story fall." She leaned in to read the article. "Police say a Winona woman had unspecified injuries after falling out of her window and landing on several potted plants. Bethany Anderson, a first-floor resident, upon hearing a 'thud' at 10:30 A.M., looked out and saw a woman lying on her side, covered in potting soil."

"What's happening today?" Sidney asked, sipping from her can of Ensure.

"Not sure. This one's either a suicide attempt, inner ear instability, or a mere gardening misadventure." She pointed to the article.

Sidney read it as she leaned over Lucy's shoulder. "How bad could your day already be at 10:30 A.M.?"

"I guess it depends on how well you slept. It seems this reporter is more interested in the potted plants than the woman. The real story here is how an eighty-two-year-old woman was able to wrestle a window wide open, get past a screen, and fling her old self through it onto the plants below."

"Yoga for oldies?"

"In med school, during my ER rotation, I took care of an eighty-year-old man with a cucumber stuck up his butt."

"Shut up!"

"When I told my mom the story, she said, 'Do you think he fell in his garden?'"

"Did you ask her why she thought he might be naked in his garden?"

"It would have ruined her world."

Sidney nodded and took another pained sip of her Ensure. "Must suck to be eighty."

"You think we all spend our lives missing the point?" Lucy asked her. "You think *I'm* missing the point, that I should be grateful for what I have and try to focus on the bigger picture?"

"Um, I think we all just focus on ourselves. And truthfully, that can be a pretty small picture. I mean, when I'm faced with breakfast, a bathroom scale, or a can of Ensure, I'm not thinking about the world's suffering. I'm just focused on the next sip."

"I'm thinking today we should put grocery shopping on the calendar for you and an AA meeting for me."

The women stood. Lucy said, "Thanks, Sid." She didn't add, "For everything." But she didn't need to. Sidney nodded, started to take another sip, then stopped.

"Most people, when I talk about my eating disorder, say really stupid things. Like, 'It's not like cancer, all you have to do is eat.' Or, 'I wish I could get anorexia for a few days.' Or, 'You have the most amazing willpower.'"

"It's the mental health bias," Lucy pointed out. "If you had a rotted tooth, no one would say 'Just get over it.'"

"You know what's gross? It's only the women who talk like that. The men think I look like shit and the women all want to be me."

"I suppose that's true."

"This last visit to the ER got to me. I saw my reflection in the mirror and thought, look, a walking skeleton, before I realized it was me. Fresh eyes tell the truth."

"So?"

"So I'm starting with Ensure and then I'm going to the grocery store. It's inpatient next, and I can't go there."

"Good. I'd hate to see you there."

"Thanks for not saying 'Why don't you just eat something?'"

Lucy said, "Thanks for not saying 'Why didn't you use a

condom?' You know, I decided something last night. I'm not going to do this. I'm not going to have it." And just by saying it, Lucy knew she was lying to herself again.

Lucy waved at Sidney, pulled her hand inside the car window, and placed it on her abdomen. It took only ten minutes for her to pull into the lot adjoining Charles and Phong's condominium. In the vestibule she hit the buzzer for Peterman-Luong and waited. Checking her watch, she realized that Phong might not even be awake after working the night shift at the hospital, and Charles was almost certainly at work. But then a tinny, static hello came through. "Phong. It's Lucy. I need to talk to you."

Before she could get inside the outer door she said to Phong, "How can he still be mad at me? He never stays mad this long. What is going on?"

"He's not mad, Lucy. He's hurt. He's frustrated. And no doubt he'll be furious at me for saying so, but he's the ultimate enabler."

"What are you talking about? He's always yelling at me. Always telling me what to do. He never just sits back."

"That's what codependency is, Lucy. Focusing on others so you don't have to focus on yourself."

Lucy tugged Little Dog into her brother's condo. "No," she said. "We're close. Good friends. He holds my hand and I hold his. If that's codependency, then everyone is codependent."

"When's the last time you held his hand?"

"He doesn't need me to, does he? He's got you. Plus, what could he possibly be struggling with?"

Phong paused for a beat. "Did you know we want to adopt a child? That we're thinking of moving to a more sympathetic state that would make it easier to do so?"

"Moving?"

"That's all I'm saying, Lucy. This is between you and your brother. I will say this, though: You should open your eyes."

20

A Puppy Is a Big Responsibility

As she drove home from Charles and Phong's condo, Lucy thought about her parents. Her mother had been the colorful one, her father the balanced administrator. It had been that way with her and Richard, and now, she saw, with her and Charles. As dysfunctional relationships go, this didn't seem so bad. People put their kids in cages, killed their spouses, had affairs with their nannies. How could a little energetic caring be a problem? But the answer to that question was not as simple or easy as it sounded. Lucy knew it was time to fix her life and move back into a realm that had worked for her for years—energetic caring.

A note pinned to the front door reminded her that she wasn't going to be alone in her house like she wanted. The construction crew, due back at noon, planned on sanding drywall. Lucy read the note from Ray's Remodeling. *Probably a good day to go shopping.*

Once inside the house, she pressed her palm onto her chest, held it there, then moved it to her belly. Her thoughts were muddled. She tried to push them from her mind. Without thinking, she hit the blinking button on the answering machine.

"This is Dr. Ballwig's nurse. Dr. Ballwig asked me to call and follow up. We'd like to reschedule your appointment. He is only in the Capitol office on Tuesdays and Thur—"

Lucy pressed Delete.

There was a message from Baby Bean, the retail giant for all things newborn. "Your crib has arrived. Please call to schedule a pickup or delivery."

Lucy rubbed her eyes. "I am not picking up that crib," she said aloud.

A final beep brought with it a message from the Humane Society.

"We have an opening for a volunteer position. Your application has been cleared."

Lucy couldn't get to the shelter fast enough. She pushed through the tall glass doors, suddenly remembering her last visit, the one that resulted in a new puppy—well, a new puppy for Mark—and a baby. The baby's for Mark, too, she thought bitterly.

That's enough of that, she thought to herself. At the front desk there was a large poster featuring dogs, hearts, and a grandmotherly looking person holding a cat. VOLUNTEER! it read.

Lucy made eye contact with the worker behind the counter and pointed to the poster. "I'm here to volunteer," she said. "I received a message that my application had been cleared. I can start today. Where do you need me?"

"Good," the woman said. "Enthusiasm is good. We'll get some paperwork signed, go over our policies, and get you oriented." She handed Lucy a laminated card. "This is our basic agreement. Take a minute to look over the list and be certain you can manage these responsibilities, while I get a clipboard."

As Lucy focused on the typed rules, a woman and girl of about seven approached the counter holding a Stride Rite shoebox. Lucy could hear faint chirping inside. The girl said to Lucy, "We found a birdie. She has a broken wing. I caught her with my butterfly net. What's your name?"

"Lucy."

"That's my dog's name," the girl said, and gave Lucy a once-over. She took a seat. The small laminated card she held listed the characteristics of a successful Humane Society volunteer.

Communicate professionally. Check, Lucy thought.

Take and follow directions. Check.

Work independently. Check.

Commit to six months of service. Absolutely check.

Understand and accept philosophies regarding admission and euthanasia. Lucy paused then read on. *Euthanasia is used only as a last resort when an animal is unsuitable for adoption.* Lucy walked back over to the desk, where the little girl and her mother were busy with their injured bird in the Stride Rite box.

"Excuse me," she interrupted. "As a volunteer, I'm not responsible for euthanasia in any way other than, say, not picketing or calling the governor, right?"

The worker opened her mouth to speak when the little girl piped in again. "Sometimes a puppy is mean or sick, Lucy."

The girl's mother put her arm around her daughter's shoulder and said, "Honey, I'm sure this woman knows that."

The woman behind the counter started to speak, but the little girl beat her to the punch. "Sometimes it's best for the animal."

Lucy glanced at the girl's mother, a frazzled-looking woman clearly worn down by the job of mothering such a precocious child.

The mother said, "We'd just had *the talk* on the way over because of this bird. She likes to spread the news."

Lucy winced and turned her attention back to the Humane Society worker. "I just want to know that I won't be asked to be around that kind of thing. That's why I went into plastics, if you know what I mean."

"Um," the volunteer said, "I'm going to get my manager."

"My mom says plastic is what is wrong with America."

The little girl's mother looked sheepish. "I also said, sweetie, that not everyone needs to know everything that's in your head." To Lucy, she added in a low voice, "I was referring to plastic grocery bags."

Lucy waved her off. Her attention was focused on a stately German shepherd being led to the side play yard by a scrawny volunteer who couldn't possibly have held the dog back if a squirrel or criminal came into view.

"What's the story with that shepherd over there?" she asked the worker.

"That's Coltrane. He's a flunky from service-dog training. It's a real shame, too. He's a lovey."

"He failed?"

"He has some kind of issue with escalators. Won't go near 'em."

"Is he mean or sick? Is he going to make it? Will someone adopt him?"

The worker scratched her forehead.

A light bulb went on in Lucy's brain. "Can I adopt him?"

"You want to volunteer *and* adopt a dog today? Um."

The little girl said, "A puppy is a big responsibility," and the mother shrugged as she dragged her out the front door.

When the clearly overwhelmed woman behind the desk gratefully answered a ringing telephone, Lucy sat down next to an older man, who was also waiting for help from a better-informed employee. Out of the side of his mouth, he said, "Listen, if you want that dog, you gotta play it cool. Don't show too much interest. Put down twenty bucks to hold him and come back tomorrow with a collar, leash, and license. If you already have a dog, don't tell 'em and—whatever you do—don't mention that you're planning to give the dog as a gift to someone else." As the manager approached, he stood and leaned back to whisper to Lucy, "It's easier to buy a house than adopt a dog around here."

The manager said to the man, "Arthur, am I right? You're here for Taffy, our shih tzu, I believe?" Arthur winked at Lucy. "Yeah," he said. "I haven't had a dog in years. I figure it's about time."

After touring the entire complex and meeting the resident horse, ferret, and exotic bird, Lucy touched her temple.

"You look a little ashen," said Gale, the director of the center.

"There are a lot of strong smells here, and I just realized I didn't have much to eat this morning."

"Why don't we call it quits for today? We can start orientation tomorrow." She looked at Lucy's application. "You've asked to work primarily with the dogs, I see." Lucy nodded and watched Arthur as he led Taffy the shih tzu out the door to a minivan. When he slid the side door open, a black and white dog peeked its head out. Arthur shooed the dog back in and looked over his shoulder as Taffy hopped in.

Lucy started out the door, but before completing her exit she turned and said, "Oh, by the way, I'd like to put a hold on that German shepherd, Coltrane. I don't have a dog yet, and I think he'd be just perfect for me."

* * *

Lucy was, for once, grateful for her appointment with Tig. Seated in the overstuffed chair with her back to the window, she felt a deep sense of relief after having confessed her secret and admitted to her shame. First Sidney, now Tig. Still, she was worn out with the melodrama of it. "Does every day have to include a discussion of life or death? When do I get to talk about what happened on *The Bachelor* or when the next Tom Cruise movie is due out?"

Tig tugged a chair over to face Lucy, sat back, and crossed her legs. "We can talk about anything you want to talk about." Outside Tig's office window, the wind dragged wet leaves across the pavement. December clouds threatened flurries and people hurried to their cars.

Lucy shook her head. "I haven't told the father. For all of about five minutes I considered not telling him at all. Figured if I wasn't going to keep it . . ." Lucy straightened. "Aren't we supposed to focus on the stealing? I'm not ready to talk about this."

Tig smiled and waited.

Lucy stared into the distance. "I'm way too old for this. For mistakes like this. It's like I was such a grown-up in high school and so focused on college that I didn't allow myself to screw up in an age-appropriate way. Now I'm making up for lost screw-up time."

"You want to talk about why you're not perfect?"

"Believe me, Tig. I know I'm not perfect."

"Do you? Do you know that everyone makes mistakes? Everyone has inadequacies? All of us have things we don't share, can't face, or dislike in ourselves?"

Lucy made a skeptical face. "Not like this."

"I suspect, as a physician, that you already know this. You take other people's failings in stride, holding yourself to a higher standard of daily perfection. Other people can gamble away fortunes, get into car accidents, and end marriages, and you're fine with those things. You understand their humanity. What you don't understand is your own humanity."

"You make it sound like I think I'm infallible. I know I'm not. That's why I've always been so careful."

"Is keeping people out being careful?"

"Richard was the love of my life. I wanted a child with him as a natural extension of our love. That's how it's supposed to work."

"Could that be one possible reality? Could another reality be that Richard was *one* of the loves of your life? Could it be that you're carrying what could become another? That maybe the father could also be someone special?"

Lucy's face crumpled as she tried to reject this possibility.

"Maybe love is shaped like a pyramid. Instead of looking for the one, the only that sits on the top, your job on Earth is to invert that pyramid and fill the plateau with dozens of loves. Dozens of chances to feel as deeply as you did with Richard, but maybe in dozens of ways."

Lucy wiped her nose with a tissue. After a moment she said, "Did I tell you I have a dog?"

21

No Dog Left Behind

Lucy stood in the center of the pet exercise area watching a Great Dane named Zeus lope after Sassy Parker, a golden retriever. Marilyn, head of volunteer training, pulled a wool cap over her blond curls. "I remember you, you know. You came in with that guy who adopted Bella."

Lucy touched her abdomen through her parka as she looked at Marilyn.

Marilyn continued. "These dogs are my family. You don't forget family." She tucked a lock of hair up into her knit cap. "I didn't want you to be one of our volunteers. Couldn't figure out your deal."

"My deal?"

"You're a smartass."

"Yes." Lucy pulled her zipper up to her chin and said, "Why'd you take me on, then?"

"Dogs can sense a phony a mile off, and Bella went right to you. I trust dogs."

"Ah. I see."

"And sometimes you get a look on your face like some of our strays do. Like you just don't know what's next. I still don't know what your deal is, but I can tell you're good with dogs."

Sassy Parker ran with abandon, dodging her fellow dogs at every turn, while Zeus cut each corner by taking only a stride or two to cover significant ground.

"How did these two come here? They are so sweet. Who wouldn't want them?"

"People suck," said Marilyn without a trace of apology. "They can't pay their bills, or a dog pees inside because no one bothered to let him out, and boom; dog's gotta go." Marilyn nodded to another volunteer entering the exercise area with a floppy-eared basset hound. "That hound's name is Candy. Her owner got pregnant and dropped Candy here because she said she didn't want to deal with two poop-producers. If you ask me, someone should take that baby from that coldhearted bitch."

Lucy watched Candy jump into the play area with the bigger dogs. With every gallop it looked like her ears would get caught underfoot. She was all wagging tongue, tail, and ears. Marilyn said, "She's been here a while, actually, in the infirmary. They get ear infections, so people don't want bassets. I don't know what's going to happen to her."

Beyond the exercise area Lucy saw an open field filled

with areas of mowed grass and prairie. "What's that over there?"

"A dog park. A farmer donated the land. There's almost thirty acres of fun for dogs over there. I like that it runs next to us. It's like it gives the dogs something to work for. Something to look forward to."

Lucy said, "Can I ask you something, Marilyn?"

"Shoot."

"How do you deal with the hard cases? The screw-ups? The ones that can't get along with anyone?"

"Oh, I never give up on a dog. It's no-dog-left-behind every day here."

Lucy waited in case Marilyn had more to say. A cloud covered the sun and a late flock of geese flew in formation overhead. After a long silence Lucy said, "Can I take Coltrane home today?"

Marilyn leashed Zeus, saying, "C'mon big guy, let's go get something to eat." Lucy followed the two, dragging her eyes away from the ungainly Candy as she tried to keep up with the beautiful Sassy Parker. Marilyn called over her shoulder, "Today's as good a day as any."

After she left the dog park, Lucy sat in a gray folding chair at the Serenity Center, looking around the room at Ron, Sara, Kimmy, and Claire. A Christmas wreath hung over the clock, and on a table that held AA literature stood a large electric Santa that swung his hips like a metronome

Ann Garvin

to "I Saw Mommy Kissing Santa Claus." Someone had pinned a note to the fur of his coat that read, "Hi, my name is Santa and I'm an alcoholic."

Tig started the meeting with the usual readings. Then she looked at Lucy. "Lucy and I've spoken," she said, "and she would like to start today's discussion." Everyone sat up, looking alert, except for Sara who, in her usual sulky pose, began examining her hair for split ends.

"I know it's time for me to talk."

Sara scoffed and Claire put her arm around her to shush her up. Kimmy relaxed in her seat by the window, turning so that the winter sunshine fell directly on her face. There was no longer any trace of the bruise on her chin. Ron looked slightly less commanding in Lucy's eyes since she'd seen him hospital-gowned and out of his element.

Lucy took a saltine from a package of them in her purse and nibbled on a corner. "I've been holding back for a while. I didn't want to admit anything to anyone."

Sara pushed back from the table.

"I know the topic for today is 'Asking for Help.' I don't have much to say about that. My dad used to say help is for sissies. I guess I believed him. And to make sure I never asked for help, I became the person people come to for help."

Sara heaved a deep, angry sigh, and Lucy decided she'd had enough.

"Sara," she said. "Could you just shut up for a second?" Lucy went on. "I don't drink. I steal. I stole a whole lot of stuff from the hospital where I work. And it got me in trouble. And . . . I'm—" But before she could make herself finish her sentence, Mark walked into the room.

"You're what?" Mark asked.

"You're entitled, is what you are," Sara said with venom. "And you're selfish. And you're a bitch. You have no idea how good you have it." She looked fiercely at Lucy, then shoved her chair back and pushed past Mark, knocking his coffee to the floor on her way out the door.

Mark seemed torn. As was his habit, he turned to follow Sara, but stopped and examined Lucy's distressed face. "What were you going to say, Lucy? You're what?"

Kimmy pulled her face from the sunlight at the window and stood. Then Tig spoke up. "This is not our conversation, people. Ron, Claire, time to go. Let's convene outside."

Kimmy gathered her coat and slipped out the door, holding it steady for Claire, who against her nature, moved out of earshot. At the door Tig said, "Take a deep breath, you two."

Lucy exhaled and turned to Mark. "Boy, when Sara gets it right, she doesn't pull any punches." She dipped the toe of her shoe into the puddle of coffee on the floor and wrote a *B* for baby on the dirty linoleum. "I didn't think I'd see you here anymore," she added.

"I figured if you weren't speaking to me, what did it matter where I was?"

Lucy shook her head. "I don't know. I don't know why I never . . . called after the last time I saw you." It was hard for her to talk.

"You treat people like garbage."

As if this thought had never occurred to her. As if the thought of Mark in any capacity had never occurred to her. She opened her mouth to speak when Ron rolled himself back inside. "Forgot my hat," he said in a gruff voice.

"Wait. Ron, I have something for you in the car." Lucy slipped through the door. When she hit the exit she took a deep breath. In the driver's seat of her Subaru sat Coltrane. Dignified, watchful, patient. Lucy pulled the door open and Coltrane stepped out just as Ron exited the building.

"I know you are never supposed to give a dog as a gift but . . ." Coltrane, like the lion king, stepped into the center of the parking lot, surveying the people standing there as they clustered around their cars. "He almost graduated as a service dog but couldn't get over escalators. I figure since you never use escalators . . ." Ron opened the palm of his hand and Coltrane moved to his side, nudged his hand, and gave Ron a quick, gentle lick.

"I'll be dammed," Ron said.

Breathing hard, Lucy said, "I was just thinking. You know. You could use a companion."

Lucy saw Sara standing half hidden by the Serenity Center door. The dark dye in her hair did little to mask its filthy texture. Her nails were characteristically black, and she wore a huge skull ring on her middle finger.

Claire gestured to Sara. "Come here, honey. I thought you left."

"It's a public place," Sara said, moving in the opposite direction from the group.

Mark stood in the doorway clenching his jaw while Kimmy and Ron made a fuss over the beautiful dog. Lucy warily approached Sara, aware of Mark's eyes on her.

"I get that you don't like me," she began.

Sara pulled the sleeves of her shirt over the heels of her hands and stepped away.

"I don't think anyone's ever taken such an extreme dislike to me without cause," Lucy went on.

"What do you care?"

"I don't know. I'm just trying to understand. To see what you see."

Sara scoffed. "What's the big mystery?" She shook her head in disgust. "I'll tell you what I see. Comes from a happy family, money, smart. A doctor. You have a place to live. How bad could your life be?"

Lucy felt the heat rise from her breastbone and spread through her jaw. "Here's what *I* see," she said. "A young girl calling negative attention to herself because negative attention is better than none."

"Go fuck yourself." Sara turned away. "C'mon Mark— let's go." But Mark didn't move.

"I shouldn't have said that. I'm sorry, Sara," said Lucy.

Sara snapped her head around. "I hate you!"

"I'm doing the best I can." Lucy felt the prickling in her throat and gulped.

That admission seemed to snap a switch in Sara. "Don't you fucking cry, you baby."

"You don't understand," Lucy said, wanting to show this outraged girl her own résumé of suffering. Wanting her to understand she wasn't the only one who knew what it felt like to lose things, to feel nothing, to want to feel something again. "I lost my . . ."

Sara covered her ears. "Shut up, I don't want to hear it. Everyone's lost something. That's how the world works. But you think you deserve something because of what you lost. And you don't. You don't deserve anything."

Lucy felt like she'd been slapped. "I don't deserve anything?"

Sara spoke to her as if she were a child. "I suppose you think you do." Her voice was mocking. "You think you have what you have because you worked hard. College, med school, residency. You people don't get it." Sara took a deep breath; let her words gain some speed before she hit them out of the park. "Because of some lottery you won before you were born, you got a home, real parents, brains. So because your life started that way, you think it should always be that way."

Lucy blinked. As she stood there, Little Dog leaped out of the open car door and sat at attention. She looked from Lucy to Sara to Lucy again, waiting for the answer from her beloved. *Is it true? Is there nothing we deserve? Not even bacon?*

Sara whirled to leave, and as she turned she tripped over a large pothole in the gravel drive. Unable to catch herself, she fell backward then rolled to one side, clutching her wrist. Lucy was at her side before she even caught her breath. She dropped to her knees and put her hand on Sara's shoulder.

"Are you okay?" Claire shouted and started to her side, but Tig held her back. Ron touched Kimmy's forearm.

Sara was still holding her wrist and grimacing. "No, I'm not okay," she said through clenched teeth. "Mother-fucker."

"Let me take a look," Lucy said, automatically in doctor mode as she gently touched Sara's arm.

Sara shrugged her off. But Lucy was accustomed to reluctant patients. She grasped Sara's upper arm with authority, easing her wrist and hand into view. Even in the fading light of the day, it was easy to see the scars. A series of parallel marks of varying length, depth, and healing disfigured the pale skin of Sara's arm from wrist to elbow. One of the cuts oozed a milky greenish fluid. Lucy cataloged the evidence in her mind: clammy hot skin, inflammation, and swelling already collecting at the girl's tiny wrist.

Sara winced. "Let go," she said.

"Sara, we need to get you to the hospital. I'm sure your wrist is broken, and you have an open, infected cut."

Yanking her arm away, Sara awkwardly got to her knees. "Forget it."

"No, Sara, we need to have it X-rayed and casted. And we need to deal with the infection." Thinking of the scars on Sara's arm, she added, "You need some help."

"Leave me alone," Sara insisted. By now she had stood up and was moving away.

Mark said, "C'mon, Sara, I'll take you."

Sara wheeled around and confronted him angrily. "Why don't you find someone else to help? Help Claire. She's got cancer. Or your *girlfriend*. Whatever. I don't want your help."

Lucy stopped short. "Cancer? Claire?"

Sara continued ranting at Mark, as if her words tasted of dirt and she had to spit them out. "Except your *girlfriend* doesn't want your help, does she?" Then she turned to Lucy and snarled, "You're the grown-up. Fucking grow up."

Dumbfounded, Lucy watched Sara stumble out of the parking lot and into the darkness. Mark, who was already at Sara's side, tried to put his arm around her shoulder, but got nothing but a shove in return. Lucy watched the two of them as they disappeared into the night. The wind had picked up, and it whipped the birch trees, making them look like cheerleaders waving pom-poms, even after the game was clearly over.

Claire moved to Lucy's side and put her arm around her shoulder.

"She's right," Lucy said. "I've been so caught up in my own problems. I saw how pale you were, but I never even thought to ask." But Claire said nothing, just steered

Lucy toward her car as they watched Kimmy, fearful of conflict, drive carefully out of the parking lot. Ron nodded a thank-you to Lucy as he and Coltrane reentered the building.

"That was really nice of you," Claire said to Lucy. "Coltrane is perfect for Ron."

"I'm trying."

Tig broke into the conversation. "I can see that," she added. "You're trying to solve your problems by focusing on others."

"I didn't focus on Claire."

"Know this," said Claire. "I don't need your help, then or now. I have help, and Sara's right in some respects, Lucy: You're a train wreck. It's time to start thinking like a grown-up."

Lucy unlocked her front door, dropped her car keys on the table, and walked into the kitchen. She turned on the water faucet and stuck her head into the cool stream of water, letting it run over her face. There was a loud knock at her door, a pause, and then more, louder rapping. Mopping her face with a dishtowel, she moved to her entryway.

Mark stood under the porch light, clearly on high alert. "I can't find Sara. She got away from me at the hospital." Lucy hesitated. Mark said, "Claire's too sick to help me with this, Tig would have to call Sara's caseworker, and Kimmy . . . well, she's got her hands full. It looks weird, a man searching by himself for a teenage girl. I need your help."

Lucy pulled on a long down jacket and followed Mark onto her front stoop. "Mark. I . . ."

"I know," he said. "We need to talk. But first, we have to find Sara. She's got nobody."

Little Dog moved to follow the two of them but Lucy turned to her and said, "Not this time, pal," and pointed inside the house. Little Dog gave her a look. *Praise the Lord, I can't take any more drama*, she seemed to be saying.

"Where should we start?" Lucy asked Mark as they sat together in his car.

"I already tried the place she said was her foster home. I guess she hasn't been there in two weeks. There's a group home she goes to sometimes. They hate cops. I don't blame them. Doing the right thing and following the law aren't always the same."

"Anywhere else we should check?"

"She camps out sometimes when the weather's nice. But it's way too cold for that now." Lucy frowned as she tried to visualize Sara somewhere, huddled in the dark. "There's a trailer park where she had a friend, but the woman was a small-town dealer. She left town."

"Christ," Lucy breathed.

"Yeah. Her father lives down south somewhere. We try and keep her out of the system so she doesn't get sent back there. But she doesn't trust anyone. Gets in trouble. She stayed with Claire until Claire got sick, and then she panicked. She wants to stay with me, but I'm a guy. And a cop. I'm not a foster parent. It's impossible. She doesn't understand."

"I had no idea. I mean . . . until today, when I saw the scars on her arm."

"She's just another terrified kid. The truth is, I could have ended up like her." Then, without warning, Mark pulled the car to the shoulder. "I just had a thought," he said as he executed a U-turn. "I think I might know where she is."

He turned onto the road that Lucy usually took to get to the Humane Society, and for the first time, she saw the DOG PARK sign posted with only the smallest of arrows pointing the way. An asphalt drive circled around, leading into a clearing and a gravel parking lot. Mark put the car into park and stepped out, as Lucy followed close behind. A sharp wind blew her hood back and she grabbed it and held it at her chin.

"Sara!" Mark called, moving quickly toward the gate.

Lucy said, "I'll check the bathroom and catch up to you. Do you have a flashlight? It'll be dark soon." Mark nodded, and headed back to his car while Lucy stepped onto the gravel path to the brick building that housed the restrooms.

"I don't know if that's open in the winter," he called out to her.

At the door, Lucy yanked the large metal handle and was

assaulted by the smell of urine, overlaid with a chemical odor. A tiny dog bounded forward, yapping furiously. He seemed to have springs attached, and Lucy jumped back, letting the door slam shut. "Sara?" she called through the din of the barking, made exponentially worse with the hollow echo of the bathroom. "Are you in there?"

"Larry, shut up," Sara said to the dog. And to Lucy, she said, "Get out of here. I'm fine."

"Mark! She's here." Lucy pulled the door open a crack. "Sara, I know you don't want me here. But Mark's here, too. We're worried. Let me take a look at that arm."

Mumbling now, Sara said again, "Get out of here." But her voice quavered. The dog had quieted and was now sitting in Sara's lap. Lucy opened the door wider. And in the fading light of day, she could see the sweat on Sara's forehead.

Mark rushed up to the door. "Sara, what the hell?"

Lucy knelt down. She could hear Sara's teeth chattering, and when she felt the girl's forehead, it was hot. "We've gotta get her out of here," she said to Mark. "She needs medical attention."

Sara arched her back when Mark leaned down to pick her up. "No. No hospital."

"We can take her to my house. I've got everything we need there," said Lucy.

"Okay, no hospital," Mark agreed. "Lucy is going to take care of you."

The fight seemed to leave Sara's body and she went slack.

"I'll drive," Lucy said. Mark folded himself, Sara, and Larry into the passenger seat of his truck and let Lucy take the wheel.

At Lucy's house, Mark ran Sara through the front door while she clung to her whining dog. A filthy sleeping bag, a damp wool blanket, and her grubby army knapsack fell to the hallway floor outside Lucy's bedroom. "I need my bag. Where's my bag?" she said, but her voice was weak. Mark bumped her elbow as he returned to the hall to retrieve the backpack, and the girl went rigid with pain. She whimpered.

Lucy asked gently, "Can I move Larry?"

"No!" Sara cried. So Lucy worked around the dog, removing Sara's coat to inspect her arm. It had doubled in size in only an hour, and the skin was shiny and hot to the touch.

Lucy riffled through the piles and boxes littered on the floor of her bedroom. She yanked out a bag of Lactated Ringers IV solution, some tubing, and a couple of syringes. She found a vial of antibiotics and a roll of bandages. She selected a needle for starting an IV and pulled a tourniquet off the floor.

"What is all this stuff?" asked Mark, but Lucy ignored him. Before long she had an IV hanging from the bedside lamp, and antibiotics were being pumped into Sara's vein along with fluids to combat shock. Lucy stabilized her arm with bandages and a rolled towel and helped her to swallow some Vicodin for pain, left over from Lucy's own injuries in the accident that had derailed her life.

"You're going to feel better in just a minute, honey."

Sara shut her eyes. But not before handing over one final insult. "You suck, Mark," she said.

Lucy lured the miniature pinscher, Larry, onto the floor with fresh water and food, and after he ate, Mark lifted him into the sink and carefully bathed him, watching filth run into the sink and down the drain. Little Dog watched with interest from her perch in the kitchen. Remembering, Lucy thought, a similar night in her own dog history.

"Have you ever seen her this bad before?" Lucy asked him as they toweled off the dog.

"Oh yes. When she was using." He scratched his chin. "We came to AA around the same time. Her caseworker had just placed her with a foster family. She didn't want to be at AA any more than I did. But you heard her. She's good at naming your issue. Telling it like it is. She got close to all of us."

"What'll happen to her?"

He shrugged. "She's a kid. Homeless. Broke. What chance does she have?"

"She could stay with me."

Mark leveled his gaze at her.

She dropped her eyes and nodded. Gesturing for Mark to follow, she led him into the almost-completed addition. "I started the renovation when I thought I was going to try and get pregnant with my husband's frozen sperm. I wanted the baby's room to be perfect."

Mark looked around the newly painted, restful room and nodded. "I get that."

Lucy shook her head. "No, wait. There's more." She stepped into the room, putting distance between herself and this man she knew so little about. "I'm so far away from who I was when I was with Richard. I'm not the kind of person who has sex with someone she hardly knows." Mark looked like he was going to protest but Lucy dropped her hand to her abdomen before he could speak. "I'm pregnant," she said. Then she added awkwardly, "I got pregnant when we . . ."

Mark's jaw dropped like a marionette's on a hinge. Mrs. Bobo sauntered into the room and rubbed her body against Mark's leg, her tail winding around his calf like a flirty admonishment. *What did you think would happen, stupid boy?* she seemed to be saying.

"I think . . ." he started, then turned away from Lucy and moved down the hall to the bathroom. Lucy heard the water come on.

After what seemed like an eternity, Mark walked back into the nursery and eased himself onto the floor. "When my wife and I were in counseling," he said, "the only thing she wanted to talk about was my drinking. After a few visits, the counselor spoke to my wife about the struggle to give up drinking. You know, from the alcoholic's perspective. I suppose he was trying to create a connection between us. He talked about the temptation of alcohol. The chemical hook. The pattern of behavior that's so difficult to break. How challenging it can be to live with someone who is trying to get free of it." Lucy sat on the new wheat-colored Berber carpet. Mark unbuttoned the top button of his uniform.

"My wife listened to all of this and then said, in a flat voice, 'That's just it. He hasn't tried, not even for five minutes, to give up drinking.' Then she looked at me and said, 'We're done here,' and walked out the door. She filed for divorce the very next day."

"Is that when you gave up drinking?"

"I wish I could say yes, but no. I didn't give up until they warned me at the force that I was going to lose my job. That was rock-bottom for me: not losing my wife, but losing my job. Coming in third—after beer, after work—isn't what any woman wants. It's a hard sell for anyone. The truth is, I didn't deserve her."

"I hit bottom after the accident, when I lost Richard and miscarried the baby. I've been clawing around in the muck ever since. No offense," she added, casting a quick gaze his way.

"I'm not offended by that. But I've been hurt by other, less honest things you've done." Mark stretched out on the floor, his back against the wall. "When I was a kid, I used to think about how I'd be with a son. The ways I'd be better than my father. How I would talk to someone in high school. But then I started drinking and nothing became as important as the drink. After rehab, I just kind of wondered if I'd ever get the chance again. I've got to ask, Lucy. Is this what this is? A chance to be a father?"

"You're already a father. I'm going to keep it. I just don't know if we get to keep each other."

22

Who Said She Wasn't Good with People?

Little Dog hopped onto the couch and nudged Lucy. She pushed the dog's wet nose away and pulled an afghan up over her shoulders. She'd fallen into a dead sleep on the couch after Mark left the night before, both of them having decided to get some rest. Put off any major decisions until they'd each had some time. Mark's night-shift schedule provided the perfectly timed break for both of them. Lucy groaned and Little Dog wagged a good morning, her tail hitting both the couch and Lucy's hip with solid precision timing. When she heard the front door close, Lucy snapped to attention. Out the front window she saw Sara inch down the driveway, slowed by her unbundled sleeping bag and her injured arm. She sprang off the couch and yanked the door open.

"Sara?"

The girl stopped mid-stride, as did her dog. Although her face wasn't visible, Lucy could almost see her close her eyes, exhale, and think: *Caught. Shit.*

"I wonder if you and Larry would like to stay for breakfast. Mark had to work night shift last night. He said you like eggs."

"I don't need your help."

"No," Lucy said, "but I could use yours. You were right. I've been acting like an idiot. Come eat."

Sara was unfazed. "That's how it works in the movies, isn't it? Some reverse-psychology bullshit."

Lucy's only parenting experience was from the perspective of her own childhood. Her mother used humor, and her father used bluntness. *I'm not trying to manipulate you. Nobody's here to win.* To Sara, she said, "Right now I'm talking eggs, not therapy."

There was a long silence in the quiet morning. Then Sara said, "My arm hurts."

In the kitchen, Lucy pushed eggs, toast, and fried potatoes onto a plate for Sara just as the girl stepped out of Lucy's room wearing Richard's clothes. She had on a red-plaid flannel shirt and his old Wisconsin Badgers sweatpants rolled at the waist, and she held her arm protectively against her chest. With her pale skin and her dark hair wet from the shower, she looked like a bedraggled chimney sweep from a Disney movie.

"Would you like something for pain?" Sara shook her head no. "Even Tylenol would help. And you're due for another dose of antibiotics."

Sara ignored Lucy and began eating her breakfast. She moved like an ordinary teenage girl who lived in a home with people who loved her but who aggravated her to no end. She covered her mouth when she chewed, anchored a lock of hair behind her ear, smeared catsup on her eggs, and glowered. She snuck Larry a bite of egg.

"I fed Larry what I feed Little Dog," Lucy said. "Hope that's okay."

"You and Mark a couple?"

"No! Good God, no."

She saw fury flash across Sara's face as she leaped to Mark's defense. "Why not? Cop not good enough for a doctor?"

"We hardly know each other."

"You are such a liar."

Lucy considered the waif of a girl sitting before her. "Okay, you may be right that we . . . we know each other. But I can only see myself with my, um, with Richard."

Sara finished her eggs. "Larry and I walk in the dog park in the morning. He can only poop if he's walking. And he prefers the dog park to pretty much anywhere else."

"First more antibiotics and Tylenol. Then I'll take you."

"Why do you have all this stuff at your house? Are you sick, too? Claire's got a ton of this stuff at her house. Has this white tube coming out of her chest. She's always putting a needle into it."

Lucy looked at Sara and took a deep breath. "I stole it all from the hospital. That's why I go to AA. Remember when I said I don't drink? I got caught stealing, and now I'm not allowed to work until I get my shit together."

Sara raised a pierced eyebrow and said appreciatively, "Dude."

After her shower, Lucy walked without hesitation into her old bedroom, where she'd set Sara up with the IV. "Ready?" she said before realizing that Sara had fallen asleep. At rest, the girl looked almost lifeless, wrapped in Richard's clothes and bundled up in the bedcovers Lucy had once shared with her husband. Almost lifeless, and yet clearly more at home in this bedroom than Lucy herself had been for a very long time. Lucy backed out of the room, pulling the door quietly closed.

In her living room, she rested her chin on the back of the couch and watched a little girl across the street trying to pull an old-fashioned woman's roller skate down the icy sidewalk with a long, dirty shoelace. She was wearing a fabulous gold snowsuit with a rainbow hat, and every time she placed the skate upright and tugged on the lace, the skate rolled an inch and toppled over. With the patience of a neurosurgeon, she righted the skate and tried again. Lucy wanted to call out to her and say, "Keep at it, honey, this is perfect training for life. But remember, as soon as you master it, somebody will take off two of those wheels, add a man, and make you hold down a full-time job." She held her tongue, though. *Who said she wasn't good with people?*

She grabbed her phone and considered calling Charles, or maybe Tig. Instead, she decided to call Sidney. Anything to avoid dealing with her own future.

23

Because Shoplifting Steals from All of Us

White knuckled, Sidney gripped the armrest in Lucy's Subaru. Sidney said, "We don't have to do this today. You've got too much going on to worry about me right now."

"No, it's fine. Great, actually. I had to get clear of my house. I don't really know what to do with myself there. And to be honest, Mark could stop by at any moment, and then I'd have to talk about the future."

Riffling through her purse, Sidney said, "I don't think I have my rewards card." But she said it like she might have said, *I'm having a heart attack.*

"We've been talking about getting groceries for a month," Lucy said. "A carton of eggs, maybe some milk. Just a few things to put in your fridge. We're not shopping for the apocalypse."

"Don't joke."

Lucy touched Sidney's hand. "I need to get some things for Sara. And I need more dog food, too. You're doing me a favor. You are accompanying me to the store in my hour of need."

"Here are the rules," Sidney said. "You can't follow me around and make suggestions about what to buy. You can't put things into my cart. I have to do the aisles alone, and if you so much as *tsk* about my choices, I will leave without making a single purchase."

Lucy nodded.

Once they were inside the store, the women separated. Pushing a shopping cart, Lucy avoided the toiletries, namely Richard's favorite Irish Spring soap, and moved to the bakery section. Poppy-seed cake, Charles's favorite. An apology to her brother in the form of sugar, fat, and lemons. She selected the largest one she could find, then grabbed a fudge-glazed Bundt cake for Sara, thinking of her slim hips and pale face.

After fifteen minutes of searching the aisles for basics—coffee, cream, veggie burgers, bread—she put two cans of soup into the cart and strolled, unprepared, into the section that carried baby supplies. Diapers filled the shelves along with plastic bottles, cans of formula, teething supplies, and rubber nipples. She hefted a tiny package of thirty-six newborn diapers and examined the cartoon baby on the side of the green and purple plastic. As she shoved them back on the shelf, she heard laughter and glanced down the aisle toward the register. Sidney, with her perfect posture and her killer cheekbones, stood chatting with Stewart, who was handing her a slab of what Lucy recognized as frozen lasagna. Clearly a slab that could serve four or two on Lazy Park Lane.

With the stealth of a Mrs. Bobo, Lucy peered behind an end cap of canned black beans and twelve-packs of diet Coke. Sidney was smiling. "So this is the entrée you'd ask for if you were stranded on a desert island?" she asked Stewart.

"Oh yes," he said. "It's magically salacious."

"You mean magically delicious?"

"Exactly." Nodding, Stewart strolled away, a good Samaritan who'd done his job well, providing tasty food to the hungry. He would sleep soundly tonight.

Lucy slipped to Sidney's side, surveying her cart. Coffee, diet Coke, fat-free milk, fat-free tofu, a bunch of grapes, and a yellow box of artificial sweetener. And the fat-filled rectangle of frozen lasagna. "So you met Stewart," she said.

"He's the only reason I can even get through this grocery store. Every time I come in, he greets me with a new idea for dinner. He is the nicest man. Absolutely adorable."

"You think?"

"He's like a small stuffed man. I want to put him on my mantel at home."

"Not in your bed?"

Sidney seemed to consider this seriously. "I don't know. I'd want him around all the time. I'll bet he'd adore you like it was a calling. You can't go wrong with that kind of man."

"Really?" Lucy asked. *"Really?"*

Sidney headed with her cart to the checkout line and placed her carefully chosen goods on the conveyer belt. "Lucy Peterman, you have not had enough love-knocks to judge. Your first love was a bingo. I'm not saying Stewart is a love connection. He's not the kind of guy you lust for. But he's obviously a good, kind man."

"You don't think he's a little . . . odd?"

"You're a little odd, Lucy. Hey, hold my place, will you? I'm going to get some garlic bread. I used to love garlic bread."

Lucy selected a package of gum. The rectangle fit squarely in her palm. It would easily fit in a pocket or purse. She stood there watching the items in Sidney's cart sitting on the conveyer belt until Sidney returned, empty-handed.

Lucy checked her face for anxiety. "Are you really having dinner with Stewart?"

Sidney spoke in a hushed tone. "These cashiers should have to take some kind of oath of silence before they're allowed to work here. Can you imagine what they know about people? The woman ahead of us bought an EPT test and, like, fifteen Lunchables. She probably has a houseful of kids and is scared to death she's got another one on the way."

As Sidney paid for her purchases, Lucy replaced the gum she was holding and picked up a box of Tic Tacs. Then she glanced at her friend. A florid network of splotches had climbed from Sidney's collarbone to her jaw. "I wonder what they think of me?" she said.

"You all right, Sid?" Lucy touched her hand.

"Are they thinking, 'If she eats that lasagna she can kiss her nice, tight ass good-bye'?"

Sidney shoved her minor purchases into a fabric bag, and, leaving the lasagna behind, darted for the door. Lucy hesitated, left her own basket of would-be purchases on the counter, and followed her with the frozen lasagna in hand. "You did great, Sid," she said as they stood together outside. "Take a deep breath."

"Ma'am," said a voice over Lucy's shoulder. "Excuse me, ma'am."

Lucy stopped. "Yes?"

"I work in security. Please come with me. We'd like to talk to you about what you have in your hand."

She held up Sidney's lasagna. "Oh, this is hers. She's already paid for it. I was just bringing it out to her."

"Not that hand."

Lucy froze. Sidney frowned. "Lucy?"

"What?" Lucy looked at the Tic Tacs she was holding. "Oh my gosh! I'm so sorry. I didn't mean to take this. I just forgot to put it down."

"Please step inside, ma'am."

"No! You don't understand. I didn't steal this. I just forgot I had it in my hand."

Sidney's face was registering a confused frown.

"If you follow me, we can talk about this in the office."

"Here. Take it. I don't even like Tic Tacs. They just make me hungry."

"Ma'am. If you don't come with me, I'll have to call the police, and I really don't want to do that."

"Sidney." Lucy held out her hand. The Tic Tacs rested on the bed of her palm. "I didn't mean to take these, I swear." She dropped the frozen lasagna right onto the asphalt, then plunged her hand into her jacket pocket and tossed her phone to Sidney. "Call Charles." Then she put her head down and followed the man into the store.

Stewart stood at the customer service desk as Lucy passed him, accompanied by store security. "Here, Here. Brian, there must be some mistake. My goodness, this is Dr. Peterman." He rushed around the partition toward the pair.

"Step back, Mr. Laramie," the plainclothes security guard intoned. "This is our job."

Amid the rising panic in her chest, Lucy thought, *Stewart from frozen foods has a last name.*

"I'm sure this is just a misunderstanding. No worries, Lucy," Stewart finally said. Stress seemed to have finally sorted his thoughts into a fully organized cliché.

Lucy negotiated the stairs to the security suite. At the top, the guard held the door for her. Inside the mostly empty room, Lucy looked through a two-way mirror and was treated to a bird's-eye view of the entire store. The produce looked lush, the dairy case organized—and she could almost read the coupons in the hand of the woman standing in the chips aisle. Lucy dropped her package of Tic Tacs onto a table. The plastic box made a ridiculous rattle as it hit the tabletop. *Can I keep this?* she wondered.

"Really. This is just a mistake. I was worried about my friend. She has anorexia, and shopping is really stressful for her."

"Do you have anything else in your pockets, ma'am?"

"What? No, of course not." Lucy took one step toward the window. "Look, my groceries are still down there. I was going to buy everything, but my friend was having a panic attack."

"Please empty your pockets."

"I will not."

Brian seemed unmoved and a little bored. "Did you walk out of this store without paying for something?"

"I've explained that."

"Are you refusing to empty your pockets?"

"Oh for Christ's sake." Lucy stood and pulled the lining of her jacket pockets out. She dropped her credit card and grocery reward card onto the table. She yanked at her jean pockets in a frenzy of activity and her ChapStick popped free from the lining, fell to the floor, and rolled to the corner. "See. Nothing. Look, I've been patient with this whole idiotic procedure so far. Cooperative. I don't think you want me to call my lawyer. This is ridiculous."

"Would you like to see the videos, ma'am?"

"Videos?"

"Mr. Laramie has intervened before."

A hot brick of shame sat between Lucy's shoulder blades.

The man pulled out a clipboard and began writing. "I'm going to write a summary of what has occurred today. And you are going to have to answer some questions."

A telephone rang in the room and the man spoke quietly into the receiver. "All right." To Lucy he said, "I'll be right back, ma'am."

Lucy rubbed her eyes while anxiety spread in her chest like the roots of a tree. She took a breath. Tried to calm her thoughts. There was a poster on the wall. National Association for Shoplifting Prevention . . . BECAUSE SHOPLIFTING STEALS FROM ALL OF US.

Lucy put her head on the table, then thought better of it when she imagined the people who might have sat in this chair before her. Criminals with dirty hands.

The door opened behind her and the security man returned with the police. Lucy closed her eyes.

"Egypt."

"Sidney called *you*? Oh Jesus Christmas. I just can't catch a break."

Mark shook his head. "I am your break, Egypt." He turned to the security man and said, "I'll take it from here."

"We have a procedure."

In a voice that said *back off*, Mark said, "You did a nice job. But I got this now."

The man pursed his lips like a fisherman losing the biggest catch of the day, the line having snapped, the silver lure gone for good.

Mark grasped Lucy's upper arm with firm, gentle assurance and helped her stand. Then she said, "I feel sick."

"She needs some air." Mark ushered her out of the security suite and down the steps to the main level. They passed

Stewart, who was wringing his hands. Lucy kept her eyes averted and let Mark guide her out the door.

"I think I might throw up."

"Just relax, Lucy."

"No, I mean literally. I think I might be sick."

Outside, she bent from the hip and took in big gulps of air. He rested his hand on her back. "Okay, now." After a few minutes, he said, "You feeling a little better?" She nodded. "Lucy, look at me. I have to take you in, and you cannot throw up in my squad car. Okay?"

"Are you arresting me? Am I going to have a record? I can't have a record. Oh my God." She bent over again. He didn't say, *I warned you,* or *I told you so,* or *You have the right to remain silent.* Once she caught her breath, they moved to his car and he gently placed his hand on her head and sat her down in the backseat. Before she was able to pull her legs in, she saw Sidney rush over.

"How *could* you?" Lucy said. "You of all people."

"Lucy, I . . ."

"I was here for *you.*"

Sidney bit her lip and backed away from the squad car. A mother with two children walked in a wide arc away from them, and an older man with eyeglasses and an enormous belly glanced their way. A gust of air threw a dusting of snow under the tires.

With her clinical eye for detail, Lucy examined the backseat of the car. Black, dirty, cell-like. The cage that separated driver from passenger looked unbreachable. She couldn't muster even the smallest idea of escape, defense, or irony.

It was a short ride to the police station. Mark opened the car door and knelt in front of her. "You okay?" he said, sounding like a parent comforting a child. She looked into his eyes and said, "You know, I don't think I am."

24

All the Bad Stuff

Mark held the door for Lucy as they entered the Elmwood police station. She hoped that if she stood tall and wiped the guilty look off her face, people might think she was there to file a complaint; maybe report a stolen bicycle. But at the fingerprinting station, she lost all hope of saving face. She couldn't even look at Mark while he donned the same blue latex gloves found in hospitals, maternity clinics, and Lucy's bedroom.

"Life is just one ironic experience after another," she said. "Maybe once you figure that out, you get to move on to the afterlife, which is probably a musical parody." Mark was holding her left hand, rolling her fingertips one by one across the pad and onto the paper with partitioned spaces for each finger. She lifted her eyes to his. "Do I have to do this?" She gulped. "I'm feeling really dizzy."

"I know. I know what this feels like, Lucy. I know what you're going through." Mark handed her a tissue for her fingers.

The whole police department looked remarkably *unlike* what Lucy had seen in movies. The building resembled a school more than it did the battleship gray precincts depicted in television shows. Even so, there was nothing Midwest-friendly about the holding area. Tiled, with a drain on the floor. Lucy imagined the many possible reasons for a place that could be hosed down without un-handcuffing a perp from the bench.

"How can you still be so nice to me?"

Mark walked her into a small private room and gave her a chair. Lucy sat on it heavily, planting her feet on the cracked linoleum. He shrugged. "I feel like I know you."

"You don't."

"Well, I know all the bad stuff. Let's leave it at that." He left the room.

Alone now, Lucy looked around.

In her mind's eye she saw herself sitting there. Valedictorian, early honors graduate from college, chief resident, renowned surgeon, unwed shoplifting mother-to-be. She heard her father's voice dispensing advice for everything from boredom to confusion to self-pity. *Claim the responsibility that is yours, and then go help someone.* She heard her mother's voice. *Get a grip, Lucy.* She rubbed her hands across her face as if they were a washcloth.

Then Charles walked through the door.

"Jesus, you look like shit, Lucy."

"Oh, Charlie. Oh my God, I'm glad to see you." She stood and put her arms around her tall, lanky brother and hugged him close. "I've missed you."

Then she sat back down. "I stole a package of breath mints and now I'm going to lose my job. Breath mints. Not even good ones. They were the orange-colored ones that look and taste like baby aspirin. Yuck. They haven't told me anything yet, but once the hospital gets wind of this, I'm screwed. Do you think I'll lose my medical license?"

She stopped, a little out of breath, and looked at her brother. "Um. How are you? And Phong, of course. How are you and Phong? So you are thinking of adopting? That's terrific. You'd make a terrific father. Just terrif."

Charles handed her a folded piece of paper. "Mark says I can take you home now."

"Really? I'm free to go?"

"Yes, you little freak, you're free to go. God, no more *CSI* for you."

"I don't understand."

"Your good friend Mark—and make no mistake, Lucy, he is a good friend—essentially rescued you from the store. He's not going to bust you for Tic Tacs, but he wanted to make an impression on you by bringing you here. From the looks of your face, he did."

Lucy nodded.

"You have a problem, you know."

"I actually have a couple of problems," she said. "Three, maybe. Or four. Is he still out there?"

"He got called out for something worse than a Tic Tac heist, but before he left, he had your car brought to the station. And he called me from your phone."

"What do I do now?"

"Drive yourself home. Go help someone. Take some responsibility for your life."

Alone in her car, she unfolded the paper Charles had given her. It was her fingerprint sheet, along with a note from Mark written in black ink.

Go to AA, it read.

Lucy pulled into her driveway just as the painter was leaving. He poked his head out the truck window. She noticed the green apple–colored paint she had chosen for the new room swiped across his forehead. "Almost finished, Dr. Peterman," he shouted as he drove away. She smiled a jagged smile, but couldn't bring herself to wave.

Inside, Sara slept, mouth open, on the couch, with Larry cuddled at her shoulder and Little Dog yawning widely at her hip. Hearing the door open, the girl groaned and rolled to her side. Lucy shuffled down the hall to the baby's room and hit the dimmer switch on the wall, turning it all the way up, then down, then up again. The room brightened and dimmed and brightened. She did this several times before Little Dog came in to view the light show. Lucy glanced at the dog. "It's nice to have control of something," she said.

Turning, she left the door open and walked into the room

she'd shared with Richard, and, more recently, Sara, and systematically packed all the hospital supplies into printer boxes and loaded them into her car.

Sara appeared at the front door just as the last box was loaded. A sharp wind had caught Lucy in the face, grabbing her scarf and tossing it over her shoulder as if she were a character in a comic strip being buffeted by bad weather.

"You look better," Lucy said to Sara, but in truth, the girl looked about as awful as she herself felt: wasted, desperate, and out of resources. "How's your arm?"

Sara shrugged.

"I bet you haven't eaten. Let me see what I have in the freezer."

Sara gazed outside long after Lucy went inside, possibly wondering where she'd be sleeping now that winter had come. After a time, the smell of dinner beckoned her back indoors.

Sara chewed her second hamburger, dousing it with catsup, pickles, and mustard before finishing it in what seemed like one gulp. She put her chocolate milk down and said, "So what is going on?"

Lucy looked at Sara as if just realizing that bringing a person into your house was essentially bringing in a witness. A potential judge and jury.

Sara said, "I mean, your room is filled with hospital shit, only now it's not. You've got a bunch of pills, which is kinda cool. Every time the doorbell rings it's either a painter or someone delivering something."

Lucy put down her fork and said, "I'm pregnant."

Without missing a beat Sara said, "Aren't you supposed to, like, glow or something when you're pregnant?"

Lucy winced. "Maybe that happens later."

"You keeping it? Looks like you can afford it."

"I am, yes. But not because I can afford it. Because I've always wanted to be a mother."

"Nice for you."

"Sara, I'm not who you think I am."

Sara licked her fingers without looking up.

"You can believe whatever you want of me, but you should know some facts. While you were sleeping today, I got caught stealing at the grocery store. I had to go to the police station."

"Police stations suck. Social workers are always making your life miserable. Most cops don't give a shit, either. Mark does, though." She pulled a pickle out of the jar, put it in her mouth, pinched her napkin. "What did you take, anyway?"

"Tic Tacs."

"Dude. Stupid." Sara ticked off on her fingers the reasons for the idiocy of Lucy's choice of contraband. "They're noisy. Taste like ass. Cheap. And seriously? You want to risk it all for Tic Tacs? You gotta go for something worth it, something that doesn't need refrigeration, something useful. Next time, try beef jerky—not that turkey jerky crap—or candy. Some-thing with peanuts. Protein is where it's at." Then she pushed away from the table and left the room.

Calling after her, Lucy said, "There's not going to be a next time."

Over her shoulder Sara tossed, "Whatever."

Later that night Lucy couldn't face the cheerful expectation of the new nursery and tried to get comfortable on the couch. Little Dog stubbornly lay on top of her, making each position change awkward for both of them. She grabbed the television remote and surfed through the channels, search-ing for something more appealing than what was in her mind. It was easy to find the dregs of society on television; toddler beauty pageants and reality shows that made per-fectly nice places like New Jersey look like less dignified versions of the primate house at the zoo. She pulled her purse off the antique coffee table that she and Richard had found at the Elkhorn Flea Market. "I love it," she'd said when they'd found it one Saturday.

"It weighs a ton," he said, already taking out his wallet.

"Are you going to buy that huge Coca-Cola sign?"

"This is your thing, Luce. Don't try and get me hooked on this trash-into-treasure fascination of yours." But he *had* become hooked, and the vintage red Coke sign hung in their kitchen above the butcher-block table, right next to the pot rack.

From the side pocket of her purse she tugged out the pamphlet from the Cryobanking Conception Clinics, and her fingerprint sheet fell into her lap. She read Mark's note about AA. Good thing she'd never gotten into scrapbooking, she thought, tucking the form under her pillow. On television, there was a squeal from a toddler who'd just been crowned creepy-queen for a day. Lucy had just enough energy left to hit the Power button and shut it down.

The next morning, during her morning shuffle around her neighborhood with Little Dog, Lucy noticed that it was Christmas season everywhere but inside the house. She remedied this after lunch while Sara was sleeping by hauling home a small evergreen she bought a few streets away to benefit the high school hockey team's fund-raiser. Then, after propping the tree on her front stoop, and in a rare take-charge moment, she changed clothes and drove to the Humane Society, hoping for some doggie optimism. When she returned home, the tree had been moved from outside and now stood in Lucy's red and green tree stand in the picture window. A piece of brown twine had secured it to the curtain rod in the corner, and the chairs and couch were repositioned around it.

Lucy stood in her living room as the wet from December's first snow flurry melted off her boots and left a big wet spot on the carpet. She gazed at the tree.

Sara had her good arm sunk deep into a box of Kashi cereal. "Mark stopped by," she said. "He's the father, isn't he?"

Lucy nodded.

She chewed the cereal, the muscle of her jaw clenching through her thin, pale skin. Then she said, "Dude, this cereal tastes like dog biscuits."

Lucy nodded again and said, "I gotta get some help."

25

Regroup

The painters finished a week and a half before Christmas. The crown molding in the baby's room had been placed, and the December sun washed the walls in a heavenly light. When the crib came, ordered safely from the Internet, Lucy paid the workmen extra to set it up. As she watched men with hands accustomed to hammers and nail guns finesse the tiny screws in the crib, Lucy's throat closed with emotion. She stood in the doorway and listened to their conversation.

"My wife couldn't stop crying, the baby was screaming, and I couldn't get the tape off those tiny newborn diapers."

Lucy thought of Richard and turned from the door.

Later that day she moved her hobo self out of the living

room back into the baby's room. The next morning she lifted her head from the pillow and a wave of nausea hit her along with the smell of bacon from the kitchen. She closed her eyes, felt the rush of her saliva glands, and bolted out of her bed and into the bathroom. She vomited quickly and dry heaved twice before wiping her sweating face on a towel. As Lucy stepped out of the bathroom Sara rounded from the kitchen, munching on a slice of crispy bacon. Lucy put her hand over her mouth and heaved again, waving the girl away.

"Jeez," Sara said, swallowing.

Lucy shuffled back to the baby's room. "Call the Humane Society, tell them I'm not coming."

After five days of throwing up each time she stepped out of bed, Lucy saw it for what it was: a kamikaze-like morning sickness that came and went without a second of warning. The unpredictable pattern wore her down. Sometimes she could get through her morning shower, and sometimes just opening her eyes would have her reaching for the blue bucket she now kept at her bedside.

Chewing on a black nail, Sara watched from the doorway. "Dude, you gotta eat."

When Lucy didn't answer, the girl shuffled to the kitchen. There were sounds of cabinets opening and closing and much banging. And then Sara pulled a kitchen chair into the room. She was holding a glass of ice chips and a slender silver spoon.

"Open up," she said, sitting down next to Lucy. When the glass was empty, she went back into the kitchen and banged out another glassful.

Then the phone rang. Lucy heard Sara's muffled words. "She needs you." Then Sara walked back into the bedroom carrying a can of Lysol, Lucy's laptop, and a look of concern. "It says here that this happens at around six weeks of pregnancy and that's about right, right?"

With a careful nod, Lucy closed her eyes. "Who was on the phone?"

"That skinny friend of yours, Sidney. I gave her a grocery list."

"She can't do it."

Sara rolled her eyes. "I figured. She's picking me up."

"Hi, sleeping beauty," Charles said.

Lucy moved to sit.

"Take it easy. The warden called; said I was in charge of watching, feeding you ice, and trying to get you to eat saltines."

Taking a shard of ice, Lucy whispered, "Sometimes talking brings it on."

"My God, your own personal hell. You have to keep quiet or you'll throw up."

"Please don't talk about throwing up." She swallowed hard, gave a little heave.

"Think it's time to see a doctor?"

Lucy mouthed an emphatic, *No!*

"You look a little gray."

"Just talk to me," Lucy said. "What's going on with you? I gotta close my eyes, but I'm listening."

"Let's see. Phong has got some weird eye thing going on. Has to go in and get his pupils dilated. Maybe an MRI."

Lucy frowned with her eyes closed.

"I'm convinced he's just overtired. Eyestrain from all the work he does on the computer. He's pushing himself on the adoption paperwork, too. What a pain in the ass this international adoption is."

"I'd have a baby for you, Charlie, but if I get through this, I'm done. This is just too hard."

"This is crazy, Luce. Let me bring you to the doctor's."

But she waved him off. "Too tired," she said with her eyes still closed. "Keep talking."

"Okay, well. I know you don't want to hear this, but we all like Mark and think you should give him a chance." Charles held his hand up as if to stop Lucy's argument before she could formulate one. "We know he doesn't look all that great on paper: divorced, alcoholic, impulsive procreation, and all that. But so what? Phong and I would never have gotten together if we'd been matched up online. We're total opposites. Plus, while Richard was great, theoretically—none of that made a difference in the end."

He paused. "Luce?" He waited another beat. "Lucy?"

Then, standing, he pulled a chenille quilt over the shoulder of his sleeping sister. "Just give him a chance, Lucy. Even if it doesn't seem like the smartest idea."

"How's our girl?" Sidney smiled when she and Sara returned from their shopping expedition. Charles had met them in the kitchen.

Sara looked at her list. "Is she sleeping? I think we got everything. We bought her tiny Cokes for her to sip all day. My mom used to give me those when I had the flu. Something magic in 'em." As she pulled items out of a brown grocery bag she listed them aloud. "Crackers—Ritz and saltines. Lemons. Ginger. Lemonade. Potato chips and watermelon Jolly Ranchers."

Sidney said, "The candy is supposed to take the place of real watermelon. Sara looked up all of this online."

Sara tiptoed down the hall to peek at Lucy. Carefully she picked up the glass full of melted ice chips and returned with it to the kitchen. "I got ice from the gas station. There's two bags of it in the freezer. All you have to do is bust it up a little. Oh, and here's what I thought about when we were picking out all this stuff. When I'm out walking the dogs, grocery shopping, and shoveling snow, you and Sidney can be with Lucy. And when I come back, you guys can stay or go. I don't care."

Charles said, "Uh, I can't be here on any set schedule. I've gotta work. Phong and I . . ."

"She needs you. She's your sister!" Sara's petite frame was rigid with indignation. Sidney put her hand on her elbow.

Charles said, "She's not dying. She didn't even throw up when I was here."

A retching sound came from down the hall and Sara scowled at him. Sara rushed into Lucy's room. Sidney and Charles heard her say, "You okay? Can I get you anything?"

Sidney looked at Charles. "Who would have thought?"

"I've gotta go to work."

"Oh, I know. And it's okay, you don't need to be here. Sara's just trying to help. I bet it feels good for her to focus on something other than herself for a change."

"You think Lucy should go to the hospital?"

"I'll keep an eye on her. I'm an expert at this kind of thing."

"Pregnancy?"

"Vomiting."

"My God, we're a bag of nuts."

"You know what they say. You shake a can of nuts and the biggest ones will rise to the top."

Sara reentered the kitchen. "I'm going to walk the dogs. Skinny, you take the first shift."

Charles shook his head. "I'm thinking there's a whole lot of shakin' going on around here," he said.

On Christmas Eve, Sara woke to the now-familiar sound of retching. She watched as Lucy, her curly hair a mass of frizz on top and matting at the sides, hunched back into her room. Wearing Richard's old maroon robe and carrying the telephone, Sara tiptoed into the living room and made a call.

Twenty minutes later, Mark walked in the front door and down the hall, and scooped Lucy into his arms. Sara held the door for him, grabbing Lucy's purse.

In the hospital, Lucy opened her eyes after a B_{12} shot, an hour of IV fluids, and an antihistamine.

"You," she said.

"Yes," he said.

She closed her eyes and slept for two days.

Lucy breathed in the smells of her house, now made tolerable by a week and a half of a cocktail of Benadryl, lemons, and vitamins. As she buttoned her coat, she grabbed her car keys from the hook by the phone.

"You gonna try the dog pound today?" Sara said, holding a coffee cup.

"The fresh air will do me good. I'm feeling a lot stronger."

"Charles brought us some real sugar. I hate that fake stuff you use. Didn't you ever cook? You know, before?"

"Not really. I worked a lot." Lucy pocketed her keys.

Sara picked at her fingernail. "Claire called. She wants to come over."

"Did you tell her to come?"

"Her message is on the answering machine. I didn't pick up." Sara shrugged. "You can call her."

"Okay. Maybe she could come for lunch one day. Hey, thanks for unloading the dishwasher." She paused. "And for calling Mark."

"Something had to be done. You ever going back to AA, or you thinking you're fixed?"

"Eventually, I have to go back. I have to get to twenty sessions or I can't go back to work."

Sara nosed a piece of dog kibble with her toe, picked it up, and tossed it into the garbage. "Can I come? To the dog pound?"

"You'd have to fill out an application. You can't just hang out."

Sara considered this, scratched a scab on the back of her hand. "I'll need an address and telephone number. I sure can't use the dog park." Lucy noticed for the first time something other than defiance or worry in the girl's eyes. She didn't dare name it.

"Use this one. Put me down as a reference. And Mark." Lucy started toward the door. "And get a coat. It's freezing out today. They start everyone new in the exercise area."

Sara wore an old goose down–filled ski jacket that made her appear even smaller than usual. Lucy cranked the heat in the car.

"How come you don't have any friends, except old drunks and Skinny?"

Lucy was too tired to be offended. "Well, I had my

husband, my job, and my brother. I didn't think I needed any friends."

Sara nodded. "I like your brother."

"Everybody does. What about you?"

"When you're trying to figure out where you're going to sleep or how you're going to eat, friends aren't that important."

"I can't imagine your life."

"Yours is kind of boring."

"Hey, Sara. Maybe we don't have to talk."

Sara gave her a thumbs-up and closed her eyes.

They separated at the Humane Society. Lucy headed straight for the dog exercise area with two compatible canines: Candy the basset and Sassy Parker. The dog joy she observed while watching them bowing, dodging, and nipping made her feel lighter. She caught sight of Sara dutifully following another volunteer into the cages, helping to clean them. She'd taken a rubber band and pulled her hair off her face, which was unlined and pale.

Lucy led Candy to her doggie bed at the front desk, and Sara stopped to pet her. She scratched her ears. Candy beat a back leg, grateful.

"You know who would love this dog?" Lucy said to Sara. "Claire."

"Legit."

"Think I should call her?"

Sara nodded. "Yes. Let's get her here, then we can have lunch at our place." Her mention of *our place* was not lost on Lucy. "And Kimmy can be next."

"She lives with her dad, though," Lucy pointed out.

"He can't live forever," said Sara, the ultimate pragmatist.

When Lucy's phone rang, she checked the name. Mark. She hit Ignore and shoved the phone deep into her jeans pocket.

"Why do you do that?"

Lucy met Sara's gaze head-on. "He won't live forever, either."

Sara frowned, and something lifted between the women, as if the barrier they'd both erected had finally been dismantled.

Less than a week later, Claire reentered their lives. Thinner and almost hairless, she approached the doors of the Humane Society, where Lucy and Sara were waiting for her. Sara opened the door and with a worried expression, moved to grasp her arm.

Claire said, "Don't even think about it. I am feeling just fine. The only people I want taking my hand are my lovers, and only for reasons that have nothing to do with helping me through a door."

"Gross, Claire."

"What's trash to one person is treasure to another, little girl."

Claire hugged Sara and kissed Lucy on the cheek. "Look at you two. Frick and Frack." She stood back like a proud, southern matchmaker. "Partners in crime, that's what we have here," she said.

Lucy looked around, hoping to see the typical lack-of-people-interest from workers at the Humane Society. She did not talk about crime with the dog people. "I don't think Sara thinks it's a compliment to be compared to me, Claire."

"Not the worst thing someone's said about me," Sara said, not meeting Lucy's eyes.

They both hustled Claire into the visitors' room, and Sara gave Lucy the signal to retrieve Candy. As Lucy left the visitors' room, she hesitated for a moment at the sight of the unlikely pair: the southern lady and the tough young homeless urchin. Sara placed a pillow behind Claire's back and Lucy felt a flash of envy for the older woman, despite her health struggles.

In the hall, the all-knowing Marilyn had Candy leashed, smelling of lavender, and tied with a trim pink ribbon around her neck. The sound of the basset's toenails scratched the linoleum as Marilyn gazed down at her. "I'd take her in a second, but then my husband would divorce me. Which wouldn't be the worst thing in the world, but still." She cleared her throat. "We discourage dogs as gifts, as you know, but since you are not technically giving this dog to your friend, I am supporting you on this." Lucy nodded. With a quick knock, she entered the visitors' room.

Claire took one look at the dog and squealed. With the energy and intensity of a puppy, Candy flopped up to Claire and nuzzled her leg.

"Well, aren't you a good girl!" Claire said. Candy posed, her craggy feet forever in the first position of a prima ballerina, her ears hanging halfway to the ground. "My God, I have met the mate of my soul. Where do I sign?"

"You gals done good," she said a little later, after she'd signed the papers Marilyn had handed her. "I've been thinking about a dog, especially after seeing Ron with Coltrane, but I just haven't had the energy to go find one."

"What's going on with the group?" Sara asked her. "Do they miss us?"

Lucy glanced at Sara, feeling a clutch in her chest. *Us?*

"You will have to attend a meeting for yourself. I will not kiss and tell." Claire pulled her hat a little farther down and said, "Seriously, ladies. When is that going to happen?"

Lucy looked at her feet, and Sara followed Claire's gaze beyond the fencing of the exercise area. A brisk wind hit Lucy in the face and she turned. "That's the dog park over there," she said, so she didn't have to answer the question.

"I'm all of a sudden very tired, ladies," Claire said. "If you don't mind, I'm gonna pass on lunch. Candy and I are going for a nap." Squinting into the sun, she watched a large black dog romp around beyond the gates of the Humane Society. "You know, Kimmy needs a dog, too. Let's get her here.

Maybe if she falls in love with one, she'll turn her attentions away from that son-of-a-bitch father of hers. And maybe you two will be able to focus on yourselves."

"That was a good idea getting Claire and Candy together," Lucy said to Sara, as she turned the Subaru into her cul-de-sac.

Across the street, her neighbors loaded skis into an overhead container on the top of their van. The husband stretched to get them in place around luggage and boots. He grew testy as the wife stood pointing and giving instructions. Two of the children were outside chasing each other in zigzags across the frosted lawn. When the little girl tripped, her brother stood over her with a stick and proceeded to Taser her to tears.

Sara watched Lucy as Lucy watched the family. "That what you wanted?" she asked.

"Yep. All of it."

"You've got a lot of pictures of your husband in your room. He wore really ugly glasses."

Lucy nodded. "He did. Super ugly."

"You two looked happy in that picture by your bed."

"We were happy."

Sara nodded and brushed a lock of her Goth hair away from her forehead. "My dad loved my mom, but she was a loser. Then my dad became a loser, too. People say I look just like she did." She sat up, rubbed her arm. "I'm better, you know. Lots better. You want me outta here?"

In the driveway, the exhaust from the car's engine rose, obliterating the rear view of the family across the street. "My husband used to chew candy in bed. Hard candy. Anise. Sometimes he'd fall asleep without brushing his teeth. He also took forever to pay our bills. I had to take that job from him because he'd rack up late fees; it drove me nuts. He never got the mail out of the mailbox. He had terrible road rage, too. Awful. He was an only child and thought one child was enough. We fought about that." She thought for a moment. "We weren't perfect. I just like to remember it all as if it was."

Sara placed her hand on the car door lever. Flipped it once. Turned her face away from Lucy's.

Lucy said, "I'd like you to stay as long as you want."

"Think you'll feel better about yourself, living with a homeless girl?"

"Maybe a month ago, I felt a little like that."

"Win the hater over, and you won't have to hate yourself so much."

If it was benevolence Lucy had been feeling, sitting with this bitter acorn of a girl, she wasn't feeling it anymore. The heaviness of the truth settled in her chest. She nodded. "Maybe so." Lucy snapped off the engine. "You can drop the tough-girl act. I've seen you with Claire. With dogs. With me."

"People think I live on my own because I'm antisocial. That's what the counselors call it. Whatever." She shoved her hood back, yanked the wool hat off her head. "It's just that I fucking hate liars. I can spot a lie before it hits the air.

My foster parents, my dad." She shook her head. "Mark gets it. He says I'm an idealist. I expect stuff. That's why I like dogs. They never lie. Dogs and kids. If you're boring them, they yawn. If they hate you, they bite."

"Well, that's what we got here. Two dogs, a cat, and a thief. Stay a while and there'll be a kid, too."

26

Dream Responsibly

In the shower, Lucy let the water run over her shoulders onto her breasts. Now in her third month, they were larger than she had expected. It was one thing to make your living attending to the health of other women's breasts and another thing to see your own morph into someone else's food source.

Her hands ran across her belly. There was a swelling, a tiny tightness. Snapping off the shower, she stepped out of the tub, grabbed her T-shirt, and wiped the steam off the mirror. Tig had told her that women didn't always get a cancer diagnosis in time because they didn't want to face the hard realities of a body that didn't fit the ideal of what they saw in magazines. They didn't touch or look at themselves. But Lucy would not be that woman. She took a quick, hard survey in the mirror, lights on. Then she shut the lights off, looked again, and got dressed.

In the hall, Sara stood in her winter gear with both dogs leashed. "I'm taking them for a walk this morning. Oh, and I won't be back for a while. There's coffee."

Lucy entered the kitchen, and there sat Mark, his hands around a steaming mug. Lucy shook her head. "My God, that girl's a sneak."

"Don't blame Sara. This was my idea."

"Too much longer, and I'd have convinced myself that I'd gotten spontaneously pregnant."

"Immaculate conception, huh?"

She rolled her eyes. "I think we both know there's nothing immaculate about me."

"How are you feeling?"

"Tired, a little nauseous at times, bored, sad, embarrassed."

Mark nodded, sipped his coffee. Lucy added, "Occasionally, when I'm not paying attention, I feel, I don't know . . . expectant. Which sometimes leads to an almost, but not quite, feeling of eagerness." At the sink, she filled a glass of water.

"Sara showed me the baby's room. It's really nice."

"I've kind of taken it over. I figure it's only fair. The baby has taken over me."

He turned away from her. "I've tried to stay out of your way in all this."

"I know," Lucy said. "You've been really understanding."

"No, Lucy. I haven't. I've been really, really angry."

Lucy turned from the sink, considering whether to move so that she could see his expression or leave the room. Her mind flooded her with images: Mark with his arm around Sara after she'd injured her wrist; playing with Bella at the Humane Society; driving her to the hospital. She walked over to him and saw a face filled with fatigue and sadness. But no anger. She sat down at the table, right across from him. "And now?"

"I just want to talk, even though I'm not always the best at it."

Lucy nodded. She waited, and after a long moment she said, "Okay."

"Now that I'm here, I don't know what to say."

Lucy frowned. "Look, I get it. You're a bachelor. A kid isn't in your plans. I can do this myself. I have enough money." Mark started to speak, but Lucy interrupted him. "It's okay. We can work something out. But I don't really need anything, honestly. The truth is that I've always been kind of a loner."

He seemed to change right in front of her eyes. His body seemed to grow larger, his face flushed. "Maybe this was too soon for me to talk." He stood, letting the chair hit the wall as he moved toward the front door. Then he whirled around. "You make people who might want to be in your life feel like shit, you know that?"

"Mark. I'm just saying that I get it."

"You don't know me. You just think you do. You see a cop with an alcohol problem who lives alone. You think now that I have a dog and a social cause in Sara, I can sit around alone and get older."

"I don't think . . ."

"I'm not that kid from high school. I don't date, but not because I wouldn't like to. I'm trying to connect with people. I'm just not good at it. That's not the same as not wanting it." Lucy could see how frustrated he was; watching him was like watching a fly try to get out of a spider's web. "I'm trying to see if there's anything more than this baby between us." She saw a wing break free.

"I know you're a good person, Mark." She walked to the front door and stood in front of him. Took a deep breath. "The truth is that I don't *want* to think there might be something between us and then have it not be true." Mark opened his mouth but she stopped him. "And if there *is* something, and I lose it, I can't afford to fall apart. I'm going to have a baby. I've got to figure out how to get back to work again. Learn how to be a parent."

"I'm not going anywhere, Luce."

"I do a lot of shopping online these days." She stopped, not explaining the obvious reasons for this, that entering a brick-and-mortar store could lead to larceny. "There are these decorative metal signs that you can hang above cribs. BELIEVE. DANCE. DREAM BIG. I like the idea. You know, a piece of advice, for daily reference. But it's a big responsibility, that piece of advice. Do I want an optimistic rah-rah, go-team theme when I know that any day you might wake up, and it might be your last day on Earth?"

"Lucy . . ."

"No, wait. Wouldn't it be better to have less dash-able dreams? Maybe a dream that would straddle GO FOR THE GOLD and BE ALL THAT YOU CAN BE? Isn't that the kind of advice that leads to so much credit-card debt, heart disease, and home foreclosure? People thinking, well, shit, if I might die tomorrow I want a bigger house?"

"What would you suggest, Lucy? What would have helped you?"

"Nothing lasts forever. How about that? NOTHING LASTS FOREVER."

Mark looked at her standing there, looked at her earnest expression. He saw the girl with braces from high school, the one who followed every direction on every assignment, quiz, and final exam she'd ever taken, because she had dreamed big.

"I think," he began, "that if you include an antidepressant in her milk, she might be able to handle life with that hanging over her bed. Or maybe try something that takes a slightly gentler approach?"

She looked into his eyes, hopeful. The answer to life was hanging on the tip of his tongue. She nodded, expectant.

"Stop and smell the roses," he offered.

"That's what you've got for me? Stop and smell the roses?"

"It's exactly the same message. Appreciate what you've got, Egypt. You've got me."

"Do I?"

"Nothing lasts forever, it's true. But I'm standing here. Right now. Trying to work this out."

Lucy backed away. "So are we going to date? Get married? Move in together? We don't know each other very well, after all. Besides, I don't know if I ever want any of those things again."

"I have those reservations, too. Believe me. Do we have to name what we have?"

"I think we do, yes. We have to call it something. I don't really work well without categories, frameworks."

"We could call it helping. How about that? Just helping."

"What if we painted above the baby's bed, HELP IS ON THE WAY."

"How about this?" Mark held his hands above the doorway and moved them with a flourish. "DREAM RESPONSIBLY."

"And then when she's a teen we can just change the letters to Drink Responsibly." Lucy exhaled, and said with the no-nonsense tone of a farmer, certain the blight was coming, "Well, we'd better start getting to know each other, then. We're having a baby, and I definitely need some help."

Later that afternoon, frenzied barking filled the front office at the Humane Society where Lucy stood filing paperwork and finishing up a dog adoption with a father and his son. She waited until the barking subsided and widened her eyes at the little boy.

"Whenever a dog gets adopted, he gets super excited. It's like a birthday party back there."

"Is Buster gonna get cake?"

The father put his arm around his son's shoulder.

"We don't feed cake to dogs," Lucy said, "but once he's home with you, you can bake him biscuits. We even have special recipes for dogs." Lucy handed him a sheet of ideas for dog treats. "There are recipes with peanut butter, liver, and salmon." The boy made a gagging sound and Lucy turned her attention to the father. "So when you come back later today for Buster, just show them the paperwork. I won't be here, but anyone else will be able to help you."

"You don't live here?" The little boy looked distressed at the idea of Lucy not spending the night with the dogs.

"I just help out. Don't worry, Buster will be fine until you get back." As the pair exited through the front doors, the son pulled his father along, eager to get back and pick up Buster, the dog no one thought would find a home. Scruffy, skittish, missing a front leg and a large patch of fur on his rump, he had worried the staff.

Marilyn smiled. "Just goes to show you that even ugly dogs can find a home."

Lucy gathered her purse and nodded quietly. "I'm heading out. Should I tell Sara she's on for tomorrow?"

"She knows. I just talked to her. Your niece is really wonderful with the animals. And I always know I can count on her."

Inwardly Lucy's heart did a little double-dutch. *Niece.*

"She's tough on the outside, but a marshmallow on the inside."

"You can tell her I've almost finished processing her application. She should be able to start working part-time next week. I'm glad we were able to accommodate her school schedule with evening and weekend shifts."

"Great," Lucy said in a first-I've-heard-of-it tone, and Marilyn tilted her head. Lucy scrambled to cover her inadvertent gaffe. "I was already thinking about how much I'll miss her around the house."

"We try to support any young person considering veterinary medicine as a career."

A light went on for Lucy and she said, "A vet. Yes."

She stomped the snow off her boots as Little Dog and Larry, like tiny linebackers, blocked her entrance. "Hey, guys. Where's Sara? Go find Sara." The dogs spun around and raced toward the interior of the house, scrambled back to Lucy, then disappeared again.

In stockinged feet, wiping her nose, it took her a moment to notice the lack of sound in the house. There were no empty glasses on the living room bookcase, or discarded blankets bundled on the floor. Lucy had gotten so used to Sara's presence, her habit of leaving a sketch pad next to the TV, an empty ice-cream bowl licked clean by the dogs, that the girl's absence was glaring. Lucy's old frenemy, anxiety, worked its way into her belly. She flashed on the hospital,

Charles standing over her after the car accident. The look of hopelessness on his face. She thought of the scars on Sara's arms.

"Sara?" Both dogs came running and then skidded around the corner into the baby's room. "Sara?" she said it again, quietly, not wanting an answer unless it was a good one.

Lucy frowned and noiselessly rounded the doorway into the nursery. There, on a chair, wearing one of Richard's old, gray workout T-shirts, stood Sara. Ear buds were pressed into her ears, and Lucy's iPod was just visible in her back pocket.

Against the creamy walls of the baby's room Sara had measured, plotted, and lined in pencil a credo no one could argue with. With an artist's brush and the kind of due diligence worthy of Michelangelo, she was brushing periwinkle blue paint into the penciled outlines. Glancing over her shoulder, she said aloud, "The dogs said you were home." When Lucy didn't respond, she added, "We can paint right over it if you don't like it."

"No," said Lucy, and there was reverence in her voice. "How did you know?"

"I talked to Mark. He's worse than you. Talk, talk, talk. He said you wanted NOTHING LASTS FOREVER. And he said he thought it was too negative. But I said it's only negative if you look at it negatively. If your life sucks, nothing lasting forever is a good thing."

"But you decided this was better?"

"Less confusing. Not up for interpretation."

Lucy nodded. "I hear you're going back to high school, huh?"

"It's free. I gotta do something with my life." Sara put the finishing touches on an *E*. She jumped off the chair and stood back, examining her work. "Last time I was in high school, I took a drafting class."

Lucy rested her hand on the side of her stomach, feeling a tiny swell. "Brace yourself, Sara. I'm coming in for a hug." Sara, still with her back to Lucy, didn't say a single negative thing. Lucy hugged her, and spoke out loud the words on the wall.

"PEOPLE LOVE YOU."

27

The Father, the Son,
and Aunt Nancy

On an impulse, Lucy grabbed the phone and both dog leashes. She silently collected Larry from the bedroom and hustled both Little Dog and Larry into the car, marveling at how easily dogs accepted new relationships into their lives. Little Dog climbed into the front seat, Larry into the back. Everyone knew their place. Dialing her phone, she pulled the car into the street.

At the dog park, Little Dog used her nose like a blind person uses a cane. Lucy didn't notice Mark approach until Bella barreled into her, giving Little Dog an overly personal butt sniff.

"Hey, thanks for calling."

Lucy nodded, gazed back into the expanse of the park and said, "It's a little overwhelming . . . all this . . . sparkle and shine just from a few droplets of moisture and cold."

"Yeah, it's a lot of morning glory, isn't it?"

"Like walking into a party where everyone's already having a good time and there's a lot of ground to cover before you get there."

"C'mon, let's get a cup at the keg."

"That's against your rules, isn't it?"

"It's okay if it's a pretend keg."

Little Dog stretched her leash to its limit, sniffing and snorting like a tiny, furry vacuum cleaner. "You know," Lucy said, "it's possible none of these dogs know you and I are here."

"You smell like lemons. I don't think she's interested in you."

Lucy shot a glance at him, but he didn't seem to notice how that type of comment rocked her. The undeserved kindness of it. Together they crested a berm, allowing them an expansive view of the park: a patchwork quilt of whites, silvers, and grays. The tall brown grass, leftover from the summer, poked through the snow.

Mark tugged on Little Dog's leash and said, "Why not let her go? She can't get out." Bella bowed her head, playing with the miniature Larry as if they were the same size.

"I don't think she'd come if I called. Remember the cat?"

"Suit yourself. She might like a little controlled levity."

She met his eyes, held them, and slowly let the leash run through her fingers, as Little Dog's scent-seeking nose pulled her forward. "Your eyes don't match," she said. "I never noticed that before. Did your mother have the hazel or the brown?"

He smiled. "My mother's were brown, my dad's kind of changed. We're misfits through and through."

Lucy considered conversing about meaningless things: the mayor's fascination with rosemaling paintings, the new highway the city had planned. She knew there would be none of that today. Today was a day for real words. Words with weight and meaning. Words about a future.

Little Dog traversed the trail, tail up, ears skirting the ground like a Victorian woman's dress. She paused and strolled into an alcove of evergreen trees that folded her into a prickly hug. Her wingman, Larry, was eager to follow. "When I was a girl, we went to the zoo in Syracuse, New York. They had these sweet social elephants that liked to entertain the crowds. The trainers said the elephants were happiest when they were sitting on stumps or working on handstands. After the show, they walked the elephants around and let the kids pet their hides. I guess the elephants loved that."

"That right?" Mark pushed a spiny branch away from Lucy, and she ducked onto a smaller path.

"Each elephant had her own trainer. They obviously knew each other well. I saw one of the trainers step in front of his elephant and the elephant bowed her head and covered the trainer with her ears. That's how they show love to people. That pine tree covering Little Dog made me think of it. It sort of reached down and hugged her." Lucy paused before continuing, "I know I have to call Tig. Go back to AA. But I can't do the Higher Power thing."

Mark chuckled. "If God is your copilot, he's sitting in the wrong seat."

"Yeah, if he wants to drive, I can think of at least one time I would have been happy to have him at the wheel. As far as I'm concerned, he lost his chance."

Mark trained his eyes on the horizon. "I try to stop thinking of God as one guy with plans. There's energy everywhere. Those bushes have some say in things."

Lucy glanced over, intrigued. "Yeah? What's that tree saying?"

"Cute dog. Think I'll give it a hug." Little Dog emerged from a brush pile and sniffed her way into a bright red shrub with Larry at her heels. "AA'ers don't care about what kind of higher power you choose. Could be Santa, Morgan Freeman, or Dunkin' Donuts."

"Ah, the holy trinity." Lucy smiled.

"They're just hoping people will acknowledge that addiction is not the center of the universe. It's possible other factions may be in play."

"Factions?"

"Like Mothers Against Drunk Driving. You know they've got to have crazy-ass pull in the universe."

"Is that what you think about when you're reading the Serenity Prayer? 'MADD, grant me the serenity to accept the things I cannot change'?"

Mark laughed and Lucy noticed the deep dimples in his face reminiscent of a time when he used those muscles for something other than drinking. "So you *did* give it a try. The prayer wormed its way in?"

"When I was a teenager I had a trash can. The Serenity Prayer on one side and 'Desiderata'—'You are a child of the universe'—on the other side. My aunt gave it to me. I wonder if she's psychic."

"Sounds like she's part of the trinity for you."

"The Father, the Son, and Aunt Nancy."

Silence skated between them like a referee at a hockey game. Lucy put down the metaphorical stick she usually held to keep people at a distance and Mark seemed to drop his shoulders an inch.

Out of sight, Little Dog yelped once loudly, and then released a long, fearful howl. Lucy froze as Mark took off for the underbrush, like an Olympic sprinter. Little Dog howled again and then let out a series of loud yelps. Lucy called, "Little Dog!"

Mark charged into the bush. Lucy tried to follow but a long dead branch snagged her coat. She snatched at her sleeve trying to free herself. Mark was struggling against the interior brush and Lucy could see his progress; the bush was a frenzy of limbs and dead leaves shaking in violation.

"Do you see her? Where is she?" Lucy called as she yanked her coat free and circled around the bush.

"I found her! I got her!" Mark said and the bushes calmed. "She's okay. She'd gotten her leash wound around a stump. She's not hurt from what I can see. She was just scared."

Emerging from the woods, Lucy took the shaking Little Dog from Mark's arms and sank to the ground. She buried her face in the dog's fur and whispered, "We got you now. You're okay." Then, to her surprise, she started to cry. Mark dropped his hand to her head and Lucy found herself leaning against his leg. Little Dog allowed a moment for the overwrought pregnant roommate who was holding her, but soon struggled, hoping for more free-range sniffing.

Lucy struggled to stand. "I'm a mess." Mark pulled a cotton hankie from his jeans pocket and handed it to Lucy.

"You smoked weed in high school and now you carry hankies?"

He shrugged. "People grow up."

Despite Little Dog's efforts to get free, Lucy clung to her as she and Mark called for Larry and Bella and walked out of the park to their respective cars.

Lucy said, "You know, I can't really do anything without a lot of drama lately, which is odd. Until recently, my life was the antithesis of drama."

"That's what I like about the dog park. The dogs do all the dramatic things so the humans can relax."

"I haven't relaxed since med school. Why don't you take Larry and head to my house? I think Sara would like to see you without me around. And I need to check in with someone."

28

Let Go, Let Dog

On the couch in Tig's office, Lucy unzipped her coat and rested her head against the wall. Tig handed Lucy a bottle of water and took a seat. "It's good to see you. You look really good."

"The smell of this hospital doesn't make me happy anymore." She closed her eyes. "The minute I walk in the front door, my anxiety goes up and I think of the night of the accident. I only just noticed that." Tig nodded. Lucy said, "I used to think I felt nervous here because I was excited to go to work . . ." Her voice trailed off.

"And now?"

"Now, I think it's because I associate this place with losing everything. With missing Richard. I just didn't want to see it." Lucy rubbed her eyes. "I haven't gone to twenty meetings. Of course you know that."

"We'd like you to go to meetings. Twenty isn't a magic number, but I have to show Stanley something."

"Show him I've returned the supplies I took." Lucy pointed to the several tidy boxes that occupied one whole corner of Tig's office.

"I had no idea how much there was."

Lucy glanced at the pile of boxes. "I've been living with them for a while. I guess from your perspective it does look massive." She began to feel the shame take hold, and dropped her head. She touched the thumb on her left hand, painted black by Sara the night before.

They'd taken occasionally to watching TV together. With laserlike focus, Sara had painted each of her own nails with black lacquer, swiping and blowing until the tips shone. "Why always black?" Lucy had asked. "I mean, I know it's Goth, but is it also a kind of credo?"

Sara blew across the fingers of her left hand. "I've lived in some dirty places. Black doesn't show the dirt."

"I did it again, didn't I? Showed my ignorance of your life."

"You were just making conversation. I don't expect you to understand."

Lucy nodded. "I guess I was thinking a credo might be helpful. I have to go see my therapist tomorrow at the hospital where I worked with Richard. So I have to face that place and be told I'm not doing enough to get my job back. The whole thing makes me feel . . ."

Sara lifted her eyes away from Lucy's nails. "What? Makes you feel what?"

"Weak."

Sara untangled herself from Little Dog and Larry and moved to Lucy's side. She took Lucy's hand and painted her thumbnail black. "When you're there," she advised solemnly, "you gotta remember who you are."

Lucy, instantly overwhelmed with emotion, croaked out, "A poor little rich girl?"

Sara leveled her gaze and said, "A good person."

Now, sitting in Tig's office, Lucy took a deep breath, straightened her shoulders, and said, "You know, compared to the pharmaceutical company giveaways, daily hospital waste, and patient mismanagement, this amount of stuff is nothing. It's not even a drop in the bucket."

Tig nodded. "I guess that's true, Lucy."

"Don't get me wrong. I know it was theft. I've had a lot of time to think about my behavior, and I don't mean just my recent behavior."

"And?"

"I need a grief counselor, not AA. I need a grief counselor and friends. In my life, I've spent a lot of time being alone. I was never part of any sport teams, and medical school was solitary and competitive. Once I found Richard, I thought I had everything I needed. Then he was gone." Lucy lifted her hands like a sad magician. "Poof," she said. "I stole because I needed something. Something concrete that wouldn't die. Hospital supplies may not be a solution to loss, but they are helpful when faced with a situation where death is a possible outcome. Keep supplies close by and at least you have a fighting chance."

She shrugged. "I'm a problem solver, but it turns out you can't solve death." Her gaze wandered around the room, landed on a tissue box, a stuffed bear, the windowsill, and beyond, into the winter gray outside. "I wonder if other doctors know this."

Tig let the silence drift between them. After a long moment she said, "Nope. Death isn't the problem, but it has to be acknowledged. If you understand that you have limited time, you won't want to waste a moment watching reality television, fighting about a parking space, or stealing suture kits."

Lucy met Tig's eyes and stood up. "Yes," she said. "I've decided that I'm never stepping foot in this hospital again. It reminds me of everything I lost: my partner, and my time to an institution that didn't value me. Stanley had a lot of choices and instead of being creative, he shoved me into a box and out the door."

Tig didn't move. The heater clicked on and a whoosh of warm air swirled into the room. "Some people aren't who they seem to be on the surface, and I don't want to work for a place that would risk losing me because they didn't take the time to understand me."

Tig nodded.

"The truth is, with life insurance and what we saved, I

could retire today." She took a step toward the door. "But I'm going to work again. I'm going back to what I'm excellent at, and that is helping women feel intact."

Tig smiled a broad, knowing smile. "Let me know when you resign. I'd like to have a little talk with Dr. Menken. I'm excited to see the child you produce, Luscious Peterman. I'll bet you could name her Marvelous, and she'd hold her head up high."

Lucy pulled her hat down over her curls and snapped her coat up tight. The car idled in the lot next to the dog park, its tail pipe sending exhaust into the mouthwateringly blue winter sky. It was the kind of day that was too cold for snow, or hail, or anything other than crystal-clear thinking.

"Why are we going to the dog park today, Sara? It's freezing."

"Ask Claire. She's mental about getting Candy socialized. She all but came and picked us up."

They opened the doors against the wind that whipped ice off the roof of the car and onto the dogs. Unfazed, Little Dog trotted forward. Larry, less sure, high-stepped across the parking lot, dressed in his Christmas present from Lucy: a red fleece sweater and booties.

"This is crazy. I hate this cold. Let's meet Claire, let the dogs poop, and get out of here," said Lucy.

With their heads down against the wind, the two women trudged across the frozen landscape. The solid ground held pockets of ice wherever water had pooled when the temperature changed.

Standing in a small alcove of trees, Claire smoothed her one-piece pink snowsuit and called over the wind, "Well, I wondered if you were gonna let this cold win out over a kick-ass day at the park."

Lucy and Sara picked their way through the tiny ice-scape. "I would have stayed in the car, believe me."

"Oh, hon, I saw you in there and for once in my life I let the universe do the talking. I said to myself, let that girl alone, Claire, she'll come out in her own sweet time."

"Nah, she would have stayed," said Sara. "I made her get out."

Candy snuffled up to Little Dog, welcoming her hind end in a way no human would ever agree to outside of a stripper bar.

With their dogs in tow, the three women walked down the gravel path toward the wire gate that kept the park contained. As they rounded the corner, Claire said, "Now don't be mad, but I have a surprise for you all."

Around one of the clusters of trees Lucy saw a small grouping of people surrounded by dogs of all sizes, circling a man in a wheelchair. Lucy hesitated, and Claire urged her on. "They are just people who care about you. That is all."

Sara said, "I didn't know anything about this. Claire? Seriously?"

"It's nothing but a coffee klatch without the coffee. This is not a meeting of any sort other than a meeting of friends."

"Lucy and Sara." Ron nodded and in his formal way said, "Very nice to see you again." His dreadlocks stuck out from under a multicolored wool cap. Claire lifted a mittened hand to a skinny woman with striations in her jaw and neck that looked many years and many drinks in the making. "This is Olive. She's newish—not to us, but to you two." Then she smiled and said, "Sara, check out Kimmy."

Kimmy stepped forward with a wry smile. She pulled a piece of something out of her fanny pack and fed it to a mop of a dog she held in her arms. "They didn't know it was addict day at the park, did they, Claire?"

Ron narrowed his eyes and said, "Claire?"

Lucy felt a flush crawling up her neck under the intense scrutiny of the group.

"All right, everybody," Claire said. "You all know I have trouble with boundaries. What's the big surprise?"

Ron pushed the lever on his wheelchair forward and faced Lucy and Sara. "Ladies, although it's certainly very nice to see you, I can see you were lured here under false pretenses."

"Hey," Claire said. "Lighten up, Ron." Then she turned to Lucy. "I said this isn't a meeting and I meant it. This is a social event with dogs. Nobody is going to talk about addiction, dependence, or anything other than the best dog food or chew toy. I promise." She gestured to the group. "We're nice people, you're a nice person, we have dogs. Okay? Tig isn't here on purpose, but she said she's coming and bringing Millie next time, for sure."

Lucy said to the group, "I'm just not sure that AA is right for me."

"She doesn't even drink," Sara said. Claire and Ron exchanged looks.

Kimmy said, "Nope, can't talk about that. It's all dogs from here on out." She hugged her tiny dog bundle close.

Claire held up two fingers. "Scout's honor! We don't want to know anything other than where to get discount rawhides and what you can do to discourage barking."

Lucy smiled. She looked at Sara and then at Olive.

Olive said, "I don't drink, either." Shrugging, she added, "Weed."

"Olive's fine," Claire said. "She brought the donuts! Hand 'em over. She's got both cats and dogs. See how inclusive we are!" She took the white bakery box from Ron, and the wind whipped the lid open. She offered a donut to Lucy.

"Let's get the dog introductions out of the way for Olive and start moving. "Ron's got the shepherd, Coltrane, over there in the brush. Watch yourself with him; he'll hump anything alive or dead."

Ron laughed. "It's true. I don't know what gets into him."

"It's your fault," Claire said, pointing at his wheelchair. "Those who can't do, teach." Claire continued, "Miss Crab-Ass over there has the miniature pinscher named Larry." Sara touched his back and the dog sprang around her feet. "After my stepdad," she said.

They waited for clarification, but when none came, Claire continued. "Olive has the cocker spaniel named Joe."

Olive scratched her face. "Joe Cocker, get it? 'You are so beautiful'?"

Lucy smiled at her sitting there with her luxurious dog, guessing there would be an extra donut in the box that never touched Olive's lips.

"She *is* beautiful," Lucy agreed, and they all took a minute to admire the dog's sweetheart of a face and glossy black fur.

Claire pointed to Kimmy's shih tzu. "That's KiKi. You gonna let that dog use her legs today or is it the princess chair for her?"

"Claire always gives me trouble about carrying KiKi but she's just not a joiner. Plus," Kimmy said, stroking her white coat, "I just bathed and blew her dry."

"Suit yourself, Kimmy. Don't come crying to me when she can't make friends at obedience school."

Kimmy held her dog closer and said, "KiKi is never going to school. She's perfectly behaved."

Ron began a wide turn with his chair. "C'mon, you hens, let's get a move on. I'm cold and I've gotta get something done today."

As the group moved forward, its members convened in little staggered gatherings. Sara joined Ron while Claire paired off with Olive. Lucy could hear her voice on the wind, "Sweetie, no matter what ails ya, this place has got a kind of healing magic. You'll see."

Kimmy took up the rear with Lucy. The dogs ran randomly around their owners' legs, barking in canine solidarity.

"I feel terrible about this. You must feel a little manipulated," said Kimmy, stroking her dog.

Lucy raised an eyebrow. "I gotta say, I'm like KiKi; I don't like groups."

"Claire just doesn't understand that. She's always cross-pollinating her collections."

A bundle of dogs raced by them in a flurry of tails and fur, barking and neck biting. Lucy pulled Little Dog out of the way just as the pack switched direction and plowed into Kimmy. "Gotta be on your toes here. Those dogs will take you out."

Lucy kicked some mulch out of the way and said, "So is this really just dogs and chat? No therapy? No talk of God and drinking?"

"I'm not going to say we don't talk about things that are important to us. But nobody recites the Twelve Steps. We're going to meet here regularly every day around 8 A.M. to hang out and chat."

Kimmy continued, "We still meet at the Serenity Center for AA, with Tig in attendance, but we decided that there is nothing like a dog park to make oddballs feel like they fit in somewhere. Dog people love other dog people—gun lovers, peacekeepers, and alkies alike. It's the place we can all convene with a mutual love of everything canine."

"Funny that it takes dogs to bring the masses together," Lucy said. "Wouldn't it be nice if there was a people park where humans got together to hang out?"

"There is a place like that. It's called the mall." Then, as innocent as can be, she said, "So what do you hear from Mark?"

Lucy approached Sidney's house and was surprised to see all the lights on. Frost hung in the air, and Little Dog pushed herself between Lucy's legs. When Sidney answered the door, she ushered Lucy inside and said, "I'm so glad you called. Come in. How are you?" Chubby Lumpkins jumped up on Lucy's leg and turned to sniff Little Dog in one fluid movement. "These two should be in Cirque du Soleil," Sidney laughed. Then she hugged Lucy. "How are you?"

"I'm better. But look at you! You look amazing." Sidney's hair shown gold in the amber light of the vestibule. Her skin was flushed and she wore jeans and a white button-down shirt and a honey-colored dishtowel was tucked around her middle. "You're cooking? It smells good."

"I can't take the credit. It's the lasagna that Stewart gave me. He's coming over for dinner. He's bringing the salad."

She was barefoot and moved soundlessly back into the kitchen, motioning Lucy to follow her. "I just put the garlic bread in and I actually made Rice Krispie treats earlier today. I found a recipe for a low-fat version that gives the word *sticky* a new meaning."

"Does he know you have trouble with food?"

"Oh yes. I told him right away. He knew from the start.

He doesn't miss much." Sidney wiped the counter with a paper towel and said, "I'm going to do my best tonight, but there are no guarantees I'll eat very much. He said, *No flurries*. Doesn't he crack you up?"

Lucy smiled. "I didn't know it at the time, but he was really good to me. He knew I had a problem, too. If I'd have given him a chance, he might have talked with me about it. Instead, I made the same mistake that I blame others for. I assumed, and then I marginalized."

Sidney touched Lucy's shoulder. "Well, who isn't guilty of those two sins?"

"Are you two . . . together? Like a couple?"

"No. Not together-together. We're friends. I've got too much to work out for a romance of any kind. And Stewart, he never even broaches the topic. There's no expectation between us, and that seems just right."

Lucy said, "It's overdue, I know, but I wanted to stop by and thank you for calling Mark that day with the Tic Tacs."

Sidney breathed deeply. "I made an executive decision. I'm glad it was ultimately okay with you. I just know, if it were me, a complicated friend might be easier than a complicated family member. So have you two made any decisions?"

Lucy shook her head. The doorbell rang and the dogs tumbled over each other to get to the door. When Sidney opened, it, Stewart stepped into the foyer holding a salad bowl, a pepper grinder, and a bottle of wine. Sidney leaned in and gave him a little chaste kiss on the cheek and handed Lucy the wine bottle.

Stewart said, "We used to give wine to my mother to stimulate her appetite. I thought, you know, maybe . . ." Then he spotted Lucy. "Oh, Dr. Peterman, it's so good to see you. I'm sorry about that mess at the store. I couldn't do a thing."

"Actually, Stewart, it's taken me a while to admit that I have a problem."

Stewart thought about this and studied Lucy's face. Finally he nodded, then looked down at the dogs still awaiting recognition at his feet. "Now, I've met Chubby. Who's this other little gal?"

"Her name is Little Dog. She was a stray sent from the universe to help me with my problems. And she's been more effective than any amount of schooling or counseling."

He looked through his glasses at the flurry of wagging fur. "Ah, yes," he said. "Let go, let dog."

A laugh bubbled up somewhere in the middle of Lucy's chest. "So much better!" she cried delightedly.

"Better?" said Stewart, confused.

"Better than 'Let go, let God.'"

Straightening his glasses he said, "Isn't that what I said?"

29

Misfits, Fertility, and Dogs

If Lucy closed her eyes in her backyard and inhaled, she couldn't tell if it was spring, fall, or summer, even though it was August. The weather was in that sweet spot: seventy-five degrees and sunny, with a bright blue sky and well-being seemingly alive in the clouds. She lay on her back and a whisper of a cloud floated across the sun.

A hysterical gurgle of a giggle broke the air and Charles called out, "C'mere, you little weasel, I'm gonna eat your feet."

"Nooooo, Uncle Chuckie. No feet!" Laughing, the boy ran wildly toward Lucy.

Lucy pushed herself to a seated position. "You're going to eat his feet? Come here, sweetie, I'll protect you. Mommy won't let weird Uncle Chuckie eat anything!"

"Nuffing!" The boy giggled and Lucy said, "No feet for Chuckie."

When he connected with Lucy, it was with the full force of a two-year-old boy who hadn't mastered his brakes.

"Oof. Oh, honey, be careful of Mommy's belly. The baby needs to sleep and with you knocking into it, it's sloshing all around in there."

"Sowee, Mama."

Phong rushed the threesome with a wet cloth. "Brady, let me get your hands and face." Using Lucy's belly as a springboard the boy jetted off, with Phong following him.

"Phong thinks baby wipes are the best invention since the airplane. We have stockpiles at home. He swears they clean mini blinds better than anything."

"Do you have everything for the party?" Lucy asked.

"Yep. Cake and juice boxes. Balloons and hot dogs. It's a bummer they didn't get your entire addition finished before Brady's birthday, then we could have the party here."

"Yeah, but it's more fitting there. We're scattering her ashes today, and Candy can be there. She didn't want a wake, funeral, or memorial. Brady's birthday is the perfect time for it."

"Well, I think it's morbid," said Phong, running past.

"No. It's right. Claire wanted only happiness for everyone and everything. We're going to scatter her ashes when we sing 'Happy Birthday.'" Lucy huffed to a standing position. "Mark is already there, setting up a table and streamers, then he's coming back to get us. Don't forget to pick Sara up at school."

Charles nodded, steadying his sister with a careful hand on her arm. "The addition looks huge."

Lucy shaded her eyes, admiring the skylights in the vaulted roof, the shingled siding that matched the old Victorian cedar.

"We'll need the space. Did I tell you Sara is staying here while she takes classes at the university? And there's all of Mark's man stuff. Of course, there's way too much of that, if you ask me."

Brady ran by, fell, scrambled to his feet and yelled, "Phong can't get me." Phong lay on his back panting, waving the baby wipe like a flag of truce.

"He's going to need a nap," said Charles, loud enough for Phong to hear. "And I'm not talking about Brady." More quietly to Lucy, he said, "I think it's good we decided not to adopt. Now that we know MS was causing his fatigue, he feels freer to rest when he's tired. It's perfect. We come here for our kid fix and then go home."

"You taking care of yourself, too, Charlie?" Lucy looked closely at her brother. "Don't forget, you count, too."

He squeezed her arm. "I do like a project, but Phong takes care of me more than the other way around."

Lucy closed her eyes. "I'm more tired with this pregnancy."

"You're working this time around, *and* you have a two-year-old. I'm not surprised. Are your clinic partners coming to the party?"

"No. It's just for us weirdos."

"A whole group of people who specialize in only boobs, are in my opinion, prime candidates for this party."

She winked at her brother. "We're bringing sexy back."

"I'm so glad you're in private practice now. I hated that Stanley Menken, even before he was a dick to you."

"I kind of miss teaching medical students, but being on call only once every month is such a relief."

Phong trotted by, carrying Brady like an old carpet. The boy's head and feet bobbed on Phong's shoulder. "Are you naming the new baby after Richard?"

"Not if it's a girl."

Phong put Brady down and said, "Brady, go get Uncle Phong some vodka."

"Vodka!" shouted Brady and ran into his playhouse, slamming the door.

Panting, Phong walked over to Lucy and Charles. "Lucy, I've gotta ask. How's Mark doing with this?"

"I didn't spring it on him. I've been talking about it since day one."

Lucy touched her belly, felt the bump that was either her new baby's head or its bottom, and gave it a little pat. "Richard was an only child, without a single male cousin on either side. Without this bump here, there would be none of Richard Lubers's DNA left in the world. He was so smart and good; the world needs more of his kind. It's the best kind of recycling in the world." She laughed. "This completely takes care of my ozone-guilt."

Ann Garvin

"Mark's one secure guy," said Phong, shaking his head. "I don't know how I'd feel in the same situation."

"Sure you do, Phong. You were going to adopt. That's really the same thing. Mark knows it's not a competition. Sara has none of our DNA and we love her."

Charles put his arm around Phong, "Haven't you heard? It takes a village to make Lucy happy."

"Little Dog, get ready for some doggie fun."

Brady said, "Be fun, Wittow Dog."

Mark took a hard right and Little Dog counter-balanced, gripping with her toenails and panting, always excited, always game. The asphalt drive circled, leading them into a clearing and a gravel parking lot. There was an old Buick, a shiny Toyota, and a cheeky Volkswagen Beetle parked near a gated entrance. Summer had taken charge of the afternoon and the sun lit the leaves with a mouthwatering green that seemed to pump the air with endorphins.

Lucy's thoughts drifted to a similar drive into the park, almost a year and a half ago, when Sidney strapped the seat belt around herself with Chubby Lumpkins in her lap. Claire was still alive then, and Lucy had wanted Sidney to meet her.

"Are you sure it's okay if I come to this meeting?" Sidney had said, fidgeting with Little Dog's collar.

"It's not a meeting. It's just a friendly gathering of dog lovers who first met at AA. I asked if I could bring someone. People come and go all the time. It's the nature of the group."

"I don't do well with new people, Luce. I'm just getting used to Stewart."

"Honestly, if they weren't such friendly oddballs, I wouldn't go myself."

Out of the car, Little Dog had pulled at the leash, searching for the perfect scent. Lucy and Sidney spotted a group of people loitering near the park entrance, surrounded by the tall prairie grasses and the goldenrod of late fall. Ron in his wheelchair traded barbs with Claire in her lipstick-red pants and hazard-cone-orange windbreaker. Kimmy stood nearby, carrying KiKi, while the other dogs circled, tumbled, and bowed to each other.

Claire called out as they approached.

"This is my friend Sidney," Lucy said. "I told her it was okay to come."

"Well I wish you had told me. We like to have donuts for newcomers. You sure look like you could stand a donut or two." Claire smiled, touching Sidney's beautiful hair.

Sidney stared at the woman in front of her: bald, round, and colorful. Claire said, "Wanna touch my head? First round of chemo and boom! Bald! They told me it would happen gradually but I don't do anything small. Even when I try to live less large, my genes mutate like wildfire." Then she turned her attention to Lucy. "And you! You didn't return my calls, and it was all I could do to not show up at your house and haul you back here. But Ron kept saying"—and she said this in her whiniest of tones—"*it's inappropriate.*"

Ron said, "It *is* inappropriate. We're not the AA cops. We're not the dog-park police. We're just people who are minding our own business and giving support *when asked.*"

"I kept saying to him, 'Life's short, don't wait to be asked.'" Kimmy said, "I don't see Sara."

"She's working at the Humane Society," Claire said. She turned to Olive. "We worry because she used to go AWOL when things got stressful. She'd come and go. Friends' houses, homeless shelters. She has a shitty family somewhere down south. She hadn't been on solid ground since she learned I was sick."

"Yeah," Kimmy broke in. "When Claire got sick the first time, Sara disappeared for two weeks."

"Not this time though. She's living with Lucy. She looks great."

Lucy watched Little Dog: tail up, nose down, completely engrossed in the scents of hundreds of stories like this one. She flushed. "We're working on making it legal."

Ron pushed the stylus on his wheelchair and it lurched forward. "I had my reservations about you all. I wanted to make T-shirts that read, GOT CODEPENDENCE? Kimmy, for God's sake put that dog on its own legs."

"Oh, Ron," Claire said. She rolled her eyes. "Ron's decided to speak his mind even if he's got nothing nice to say."

Ron rotated his chair a half-moon toward Sidney. He eyed her and said, "You can't put the oxygen mask on another person if you're passed out in the aisle, blocking the exit, starving to death."

Sidney stiffened and Lucy whispered in her ear, "Ignore him. He's all fire and fury lately because he finally got custody of his grandchild by being less passive and more proactive. Now he just goes for it everywhere he can."

Ron lurched away from the group and said over his shoulder, "If you gaggle of geese wanna help, you gotta fix your own broken selves. C'mon. Let's get started; we have a lot of work to do."

"Ron," Claire said, "you call me a goose again and I'll tip you on your ass, I swear it." Then she bent to scratch under Candy's chin. "You are lovely, aren't you? You're my lovely. Yes, you are."

Suddenly, as if realizing that this gushing display revealed more heart than sass, she stood. "Gotta split," she said. "I'm not payin' any bills out here. See y'all." She turned and was out of the gate. And that was it.

Claire died a month later.

Today, Lucy hugged the urn of Claire's ashes close, saw the entire group dodging dogs and chatting. Mark unclipped Brady from his car seat and hoisted him onto his shoulders. "Dogs made this all possible, you know," she said to him. "You, me, all of this."

"Dogs and Claire," Mark said, and stooped to kiss Lucy on the forehead.

"Then you added your little spin to the whole project and the next thing you know my life is all misfits, lucky fertility breaks, and dogs. I was just fortunate that the men in my life had amazing swimmers, hot or frozen."

Mark smiled. Over the past two years he had become accustomed to Lucy's need to analyze, to put words and situations into a metaphorical file cabinet. He unclipped Little Dog and watched her parade away with confidence—nose down, tail up.

Lucy watched. "It was Emily Dickinson, wasn't it? Who wrote 'Hope is a thing with feathers'? But in my case, in both our cases, actually, hope is a thing with a tail."

The Dog Year

DISCUSSION QUESTIONS

1. What is the significance of Lucy's kleptomania in the story? After suffering a crippling loss, she does not turn to alcohol or drugs, but to the thrill of stealing. Why do you think the author chose to write about a character whose husband and child were taken from her, but who then takes things that aren't hers?

2. How do Mark's and Lucy's adolescent selves affect—or even misinform—their illusions of their adult selves? Are we all still versions of the class clown, the overachiever, or the wallflower?

3. What kind of impact does Sara have on Lucy's life plans? How might Mark and Lucy's "happy ending" have differed if Sara were not a part of their unconventional family?

4. Even though Lucy does not have a "problem" with drinking, a drunken night leads to self-reflection and attendance at

Alcoholics Anonymous meetings. Why do you think the author chose to have Lucy unravel in this manner?

5. What is the significance of Stewart's inability to get aphorisms right? What might his accidental edits to common phrases say about his character?

6. The author chooses to set all of the major losses in the novel—the car accident that results in the loss of Lucy's husband, Richard, and her unborn baby, as well as Claire's death from cancer—offstage. Why do you think the author made this choice? How is the aftermath of the deaths more important than the deaths themselves?

7. The AA group is ultimately united at the dog park, and they share not only their various addictions, but also their love of dogs. How are dogs able to be agents of unity and healing in a way that people are not?

8. Lucy's real name is "Luscious," but she is embarrassed to admit it, let alone be called by it. How is her resistance to this name reflected in her character and her attitude toward her own attractiveness and sexuality?

9. At the opening of chapter seven, the narrator comments that, "Getting in to see a particular physician at a health-care clinic is like trying to train a cat to come: It will only come to you on its own time." What had to "come to Lucy on its own time," and what was she able to actively seek out and embrace?

10. The theme of human frailty is ever-present in the book,

manifesting itself through incidents of cancer, alcoholism, disordered eating, and MS. As a doctor, Lucy should in theory be the ultimate combatant of these diseases. How does Lucy's job as a physician make her stronger and more prepared in the face of human frailty? How might it blind or handicap her?

11. What is the significance of Lucy's visit to Sidney's home? How does her deeper understanding of Sidney's situation change her perspective and her course of action?

12. Were you surprised to learn that Lucy would carry Richard's child? How might this change the dynamic in Mark and Lucy's family, for better or worse?

13. Charles and Phong are reliable constants in Lucy's otherwise unstable life. Where do you see fissures in their generally stable relationship? How might Charles and Phong also be struggling with difficulties of their own? Do we see Lucy offer them the same kind of support they offer her? If so, how?

14. Where do we see Lucy change her life course after the accident, admit frailty, and let others into her life?